Baddha

Baddha

ELSON QUICK

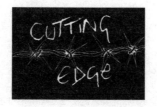

A Cutting Edge Press Paperback

Published in 2012 by Cutting Edge Press

www.CuttingEdgePress.co.uk

Printed and bound by CPI Group (UK) Ltd, Croydon, CR0 4YY

PB ISBN: 978-1-908122-34-6
E-PUB ISBN: 978-1-908122-36-0

For Lisa Moylett

BITE THE BIG ONE, PRETTY BOY

It wasn't just the dead cat, but it helped.

I'd thought it was a stuffed toy, left at the foot of the gates. I'm in southern Thailand, just off the bus, rotating my shoulders, looking at the temple gates. Thai temple architecture can be beautiful, or it can be a parody of beautiful. This was the parody version; cracked concrete gateway, peeling paint, signage propped up wherever. The usual smoking cluster of food carts, the usual litter.

But it doesn't feel usual. It doesn't feel right. For one thing, I expect a retreat to be up in the woods somewhere, as in *retreated*? Not on a highway, trucks grinding their gears, shit and stink and noise all over the place. I heft my bag over my shoulder. I'm *absolutely* not a backpacker, this is a black ripstop kit bag, and I'm wearing a black synthetic Tiger Woods shirt and gray micro-fiber pants, stuff I can wash and dry in minutes, lasts forever and cooler than cotton. I can see people off through the gates, walking in the grounds of this holy place, dressed in white, and I've come as Darth Vader.

I negotiate the foodcarts, ducking the pointy spokes on the parasols, the smoke stinging my eyes, and I see this stuffed toy at the foot of one of the gateposts. At least it looks stuffed. Overstuffed. Legs sticking out straight.

This does *not* feel right.

By now I'm close enough to see the flies around it, this cat corpse, the color of gutter ice and bloated with gas, the flies blurring the eye sockets. People walking by, off the bus like me, taking no notice, kids playing. How long has this horror been here? Why hasn't anyone bagged it up, or kicked it off to one side or something? This is one of the major holy sites in southern Thailand, and I'm greeted by a cat corpse about to explode under the pressure of its own gases.

I hate the place already. This is a mistake. The ugly concrete swirls of the gateway, the refried cooking oil and exhaust, the dead cat. But I'm here to learn, right? To better myself. So I walk through the gates and up the path to what I'm guessing is the office. The grounds are wooded, scruffy, with concrete paths obstructed by coarse statuary with a kind of Hindu garden gnome feel, and the ever-present signage, probably sayings of the Buddha. It's a theme park, full of references to what it represents, so you know what it is because you're being told. The faithful – all Thai, I notice – wander the paths respectfully in small groups, eyes down, and I try to reconcile what I'm seeing with the sylvan serenity of the guidebook photographs.

I make my way to the office, a low concrete building with some fancy woodwork nailed to it, where there's a display of gifts, amulets and Buddhist tracts and the like, but nobody behind the desk. I can hear the trucks fart and snarl on the main road, and my own breathing.

Which is why I'm here. To learn to breathe.

Because a monk in Burma said it would be good for me. Exactly where in Burma I couldn't say. We'd flagged a cab down in the city, my friend Frog and me, paid the driver for the day, and told him to take us out of the city – *down there! turn right! left! that looks good!* – until we've left the hallucinogenic seething decay of Rangoon way behind, and we're in the semi-jungle where maps are truly useless. The junta doesn't like people knowing how to get about, so maps are all sketches at best, deliberately misleading at worst. Street maps of Rangoon show blank unannotated blocks where the government installations are, should you be interested in attacking them, even though the mad soldiers have mostly decamped up to their mad secret mountain hideaway at Naypyidaw, on the advice of their mad astrologers. You can see exactly what's going on up there on Google Earth, the vast construction works of their mad new capital, the blunt-ended mad roads terminating at mad underground bunkers, the whole mad thing captured on mad-cam. But they censor all the maps, in case you can't get Google Earth. They censor the internet, too, but every wired back room in the city has kids smarter than they are, leaping over firewalls like foxes in the night.

So anyway. This taxi. In common with most Rangoon cabs, it'd be refused by wrecking yards back in the west. In Burma, it's somebody's job, and also his house. There's no interior trim, it's all been stripped out, the doors are bare metal, held shut by wire loops, windows stuck half-open, seats split and taped, springs surgically removed. The instrumentation on the dash – well, it is not. But our driver is a saint. This is something we just recognise, a beautiful calm that comes off him like a cool breeze in the oven-hot car. And he's delighted, Nu Win, to get an all-day fee up-front. He stops for gas where there's a branch in a bottle at the side of the road, the Burmese improvement on Texaco neon. Someone materialises from the bushes with a can and a piece of plastic he twists into a cone for a funnel. Frog and me on bamboo recliners at the side of the road while the tank gets filled, can by can. We see stalled trucks with their hoods up, people leaning inside, reaching back for wrenches with black-greased hands. You run a car or a truck in Burma, you learn to fix it yourself, jury-rig something that'll last until it snaps. And then you do it again.

Gassed-up, we drive on, to be stopped by a soldier at what looks like a checkpoint, with a rusty barrier and a tilting guardhouse with smoke curling from a tin-can chimney. I get my passport from my pocket, and Frog produces a photocopy of his, and we pass them over, me wishing I'd photocopied mine too. The soldier, hatless, skinny, a battered bolt-action carbine slung from his shoulder, retreats into the guardhouse. Frog surreptitiously ejects the memory card from his camera, slots in a blank. As far as I know, the card contains nothing but unflinching documentary research into hookers performing their professional duties, but it's a suitably dramatic gesture. The soldier comes back with another soldier, in his undershirt, smoking a skinny twist of a cigarette. They stare at us like we're aquarium fish, squinting through the cigarette smoke at our passport photographs. They exchange some words with Nu Win, give us our papers back. There's even a flicker of a smile. No problem.

Nu Win says he told them we were teachers from a Christian school. This was lucky, as we'd written "teacher" in our visa applications, as "investigative journalist" and "sex tourist" would have reduced our chances of getting into this country to zero. But there's still something disquieting about being able to pass for a teacher, and worse, a Christian.

The road is a track now, red dirt ruts. We're out on the edge of nowhere, maybe even over the border into nowhere itself, which would explain the checkpoint. *It's okay, they're going nowhere.* I doubt there's been white people out this way for a while, or city cabs. We see a gold-painted *stupa* poking above the trees, and ask Nu Win to stop at the track that leads down to the temple. There are countless thousands of temples in Burma, many looted of their gold and treasures by the junta, monks taken at gunpoint and forced to work in government amphetamine and heroin factories. But hey – that's enough bleeding-heart white hand-wringing. Back to the First Person apolitical polemic. I, me, mine, right?

Nu Win stops the taxi in the middle of the track (it's not wide enough to have sides) and we get out. It feels cooler outside that tin oven, even though the flags on their slender bamboo poles hang motionless. A monk appears, wearing the rust-red Burmese robes. He says, *would you like to see the snake?*

We're a little surprised, not so much by his English (spoken more than you'd think, and with a touching pride – there's a greater chance of it being understood in the Burmese jungle than the average French town, *par exemple*) as the question. *Sure*, we say, and follow him down the track, past incurious buffaloes, hides gleaming blue-black, prehistoric fossil-horns rocking as they chew the foliage. The track widens into a scruffy field around the stupa, pecked by ink-splatter hens. There's a peak-roofed temple hall and some small huts on stilts where the monks live, and a timber barn that looks like it would fall over if one of the hens leaned against it. Our monk shows us into this and points up. We crane our heads back.

As my eyes get used to the dark, I see the snake, coiled along a roof beam. I point up, pointlessly. I can't see either end, just this fat tube of endless snake belly looping across the full width of the building. *Shit*, I say, then apologise.

He comes here to sleep. We leave the door open.

We stand there, trying not to wake him up with our heartbeats. I'm holding my breath, my body is all tensed up. Primal, jungle fear. The monk says the Abbot would like to see us, and we follow him out across the yard, blinding white and hot underfoot, like we had an appointment. Frog grunts that meeting an Abbot is *pas normal*. He's been to Burma once before, so he's the total authority on what is *normal* in the Burmese jungle. He's a travel writer, ten years younger than me, full of the confidence and charm that are the blessings of an upper-class French upbringing. Only upper-class Frogs have *upbringings*. It makes them confident and charming, and sometimes a bit fucking annoying. Like he's always *le chef*, always the one who makes decisions, always in front of me, telling me what to do. Okay, I do it. I'm there with him, not the other way round. I'm here to learn.

We nod at some monks hanging out their laundry, the long red robes like banners against the green foliage, and go up the steps to the temple hall, spacious, calm, shabby. We kick off our shoes at the door, me thinking, these over-designed North Face clown strollers costing a year's salary for an average Burmese.

Inside we're immediately directed to pay respects to the Buddha figure on the left wall, so we both kneel (like women – neither of us limber enough for the lotus) and contemplate the gilded Buddha figure, surrounded by the usual bewildering array of miscellaneous religious paraphernalia, flowers, framed photographs of scary monks, and a life-size shiny painted statue of a sitting monk, looking incongruously hip in real Elvis sunglasses. We've done this ritual before, at the Shwedagon and other temples. You're just quiet and respectful of the place for a while. I don't pray to Buddha, petition him for good luck, a wife, a job, a winning lottery ticket, whatever. Prayer isn't for me, and it's not for Buddha, by his request. So I quiet my monkey mind with a simple circus trick you can try at home. Use the eyes to take in the entire field of vision, without focusing at the center. Not going all mad-eyed or acting foolish, just being aware of everything within the perimeter of vision – right up to its blurred limit – without that bulls-eye target thing happening, the focus that gets the mind reacting like the opinionated bore it is. Flatten that habitual cone of focus into a field of vision. The ancient adepts had a secret word for this mystic technique: *gazing*. You're in this bubble, listening to things floating through, and it lasts as long as you don't follow any of them individually, which you have to, eventually. You can get lost for a while, and then you lose it, and the eye, that tyrant of the head, bullies your mind into thinking about some crap or other, Elvis sunglasses, whatever.

The monk leads us across the hall to where the Abbot sits on his Abbot chair, and we bow and kneel, and I'm taking him in, this smiling little old guy with the big horn-rimmed spectacles, a bandaid over one hinge, one grubbily bandaged foot up on a cushioned stool, and he's folding a newspaper into his lap, the sports pages, there's a picture of Wayne Rooney, a British Premier League soccer player, across the fold. Out here, everyone knows *Wen Looney* and *Da-Wid Bekkum*, enormously revered men. Nu Win sits off to one side. He'll translate, as the Abbot has no English (and *bien sur*, no French, a continuously amusing source of irritation in South East Asia for Frog, who still believes in Indo-Chine, the Golden Era of French cultural benevolence). Frog sits nearer the Abbot than me, and I can tell the Abbot's taken with this handsome, bright and smiling visitor. The Abbot, through Nu Win, asks him a lot of questions. Asians generally want to know how old you are, about your family, how many brothers and sisters, how old they are, that kind of thing. So Frog twinkles winningly, answering the Abbot's lengthy questionnaire. My legs are getting stiff, and I'm a little jealous of, and/or annoyed by, the attention my friend's getting, but I'm used to it. It's the same in whorehouses.

So the Abbot, eventually, turns to me, asks my name, a question about my family, and then says, *what was in your mind when you were in front of the Buddha?* I'm surprised, don't really have an answer, but say something that sounds pretentious to me as I say it, about being a *writer*, too many words, and trying to stop the words for a while, empty my head.

But something strange is happening, like I'm catching up with something I was too slow to see just a fraction of a second ago, or the shockwaves of a depth charge have just reached me. I don't know what's happened, what's *happening*, but I do know the Abbot's question is happening it. Suddenly, it doesn't seem like a question any more, more like a bottle-opener flipping off the top of my head. This seems banal and meaningless and fake typed out in front of me now, but I know I'll never describe it better (or worse), so it'll have to stand.

The Abbot is telling me he has a little meditation that will help me empty my head, and he touches the tip of his nose like he's smelling a pinch of spice. *Breathe in, think of the breath here, at the nose, where it comes in . . . out, at the end of the nose, put your mind here . . .*

Our audience is over, and we're led out, me wiping my eyes, probably watering from the light. Nu Win stays on a couple of minutes, catches up with us at the car. I'm blowing out my cheeks with heavy sighs for no apparent reason, running my hand back through my hair, Frog asking if I'm okay, the goodhearted guy that he is. *Yeah*, I say. Oh yes.

In the cab, Nu Win looks at me – *the Abbot says you have a good mind*. Wow! Also, I'm preening myself that the Abbot asked me the cosmic stuff, and used Frog for the census-taking. I am the Prom Queen. I nudge Frog in the ribs. *He didn't say* you *had a good mind, merde-for-brains, he said* me. *Moi. Bite the big one, pretty boy!* Frog does a face-palm.

Nu Win folds into an effortless lotus position in his driver's seat, shows us how he meditates, the breathing, *inside, outside . . . inside, outside.*

And the sudden impact of his words – *inside, outside* – hits me like the undertow of the tide that lifted me back in the Abbot's hall. I'd heard them, under radically different circumstances, breathed in my ear only a couple of days before . . .

THE UNPUNCHED MONK

Anyway, that's how I come, by and by, to be staring emptily at a display of photocopied Buddhist tracts and some dusty plastic flowers at a meditation retreat in southern Thailand, a year or so later. That *inside, outside* thing. I'd called ahead, to see if there was a place for me to stay, and the woman I spoke to was very casual, very Thai. *Yes, reservation no have, yes, no problem, up to you.* I'd left my name, anyway, for her to mis-spell illegibly on a Seven-11 checkout ticket and put by the fan so it blows out the door.

I've failed to finish a book on the breathing meditation this place apparently specialises in. I am having no luck with a bunch of stuff, so it's not like the meditating *fail* is thrown into sharp relief by glittering success in other areas of my life. But the practice seems simple enough, concentrating on breathing, and although I doubt the theory involves much more than that, it has to be better taught by a master, or someone who looks like a master (and a lot of monks look like they know what they're doing), in the company of like-minded souls treading the path less trodden.

But the appalling augury of the dead cat at the gate, which I'd foolishly ignored, is followed by the appearance of a monk from whom all signs of life have been removed. He may, in fact, have been there when I came in, hanging from a coathanger. He's like a crumple of ectoplasm in a Victorian seance photograph. A grubby muslin spectre, with eye sockets spookily recreating the effect of the dead cat's flies. It's not just that he looks as if the life-force has been drained from him by some hideous aetheric liposuction performed by Madame Blavatsky, there's a heavy-liddedness to the way he's eyeing me, an unmistakeable whiff of insolence that would get him punched in a bar. But this is a holy place and he's a fucking monk, so punching him in the face would be inappropriate. He's saying nothing, so I introduce myself, tell him I called ahead . . . and I dry up. I'm beginning to wonder if I've conjured this silent phantasm from the grimoire of my own worst fears when he opens a book on the desk and indicates – mystically wordlessly – that I should sign it. He wants my name, permanent address, occupation, and passport number. I glance through the previous entries – all *farang*, foreigners, I notice – write my real name, and improvise the rest, which I consider my own damn business, thank you. The monk continues to look at me in his unblinking, unsmiling, *almost not* insolent way for a while and then glides off, giving the faintest indication he can manage that I follow him. We walk up the side of the building into the woods, and I notice the tilt to his hips, the exhausted wrists, the signatures of the *katoey*, a male morphing to female. People become monks for all reasons, and it is to Buddhism's shame that a small minority take the robes because it offers them an opportunity to learn about Buddha's teachings.

We stop at a crossroads, and I'm looking at the sign marked *non-Thai*, wondering why apartheid should be enforced at a holy retreat, when my monk dematerialises, his job done. I pass a shithouse, a corrugated steel shack. I know it's a shithouse because of the smell and the flies, and because someone has kindly left the door open. It's a hole in the ground, with a plastic bucket of water and a dipper. There's a building ahead, which I guess is the non-Thai dormitory, because there's a white-dressed white person sitting on the step. He's got his hair in gray-blond rasta braids, in the Rough Planet at-one-with-all-cultures style that black guys really respect (pardon my mirth).

So many signs, and I'm ignoring them all.

It's just getting dark. There's no such thing as a drawn-out twilight in this part of the world, night falls early and quick. The dormitory is dim, the unglazed windows shuttered, probably to keep the mosquitoes from escaping into the woods. These guys look like they eat mosquitoes. There's a raised platform down each side where the faithful have unrolled their sleeping mats and bags and whatever. There's maybe ten men who couldn't wince up a smile for an orphan's lottery win, dressed mostly in white, daintily occupying themselves with preparing for the night's sleep, folding clothes, locating toothbrushes, anything but acknowledging each other's presence. I get the impression they're all old hands at this, know the ropes. Nobody looks at me, says hello. There's enough space – I can see empty places at the far end – but I haven't brought anything I can sleep on or in. I'd expected a bed – hard, spiritually correct, maybe just a mat and a pillow. But something. Personal territory has been precisely demarcated with possessions, and someone has strung up a laundry line wall curtained with off-white Y-Fronts. A bearded person shuffles toward me, his eyes raised heavenwards, tightly clutching a roll of toilet paper in the hollow of his chest. *Toilet paper*. Ri-ight. That's something else to mentally add to my spiritual retreat shopping list. I move aside for him, smiling a greeting. Maybe if we become Buddha-buddies he'll slip me a couple of sheets. But my cheeriness is not only at odds with the ambience of deprivation and isolation, it's apparently un-noticed, and he passes me by. Why trek out here, *to be part of a community*, if you're going to play the hermit card?

It's nothing to do with me; it's the old spiritual seniority trip that trips up every preening bangle-wearing bead-rattler when he meets another like-minded mosquito-eater. One of the more powerful ways of promoting your own spiritual advancement is through a serene detachment, an enigmatic smile on your lips, a distant look in your eyes. The more silent you are, the more you know. It's no good pulling this kind of stunt while you're alone on a mountaintop, chewing roots in a cave, who's to be impressed? What this is, is the spiritual equivalent of a cage fight. They lock 'em up together to slug it out, and the serenest wins. And with that clenched toilet roll, the accumulation of ill omen has reached critical mass. I say, in a voice that sounds surprisingly loud, *the beatings will continue until morale improves*, and leave.

Back out on the road, it's night, and the foodcarts have gone, and I'm hungry and I want a beer. But mostly I'm pissed off with Buddhists and Buddhism. All of them and all of it. I can see no connection between the words I read – Buddha's words – and the behavior of the people who claim to think about them. And I've done some looking. I've really tried. But this gulf between his words and his followers is unignorable, huge, glaring.

Buddha said, *don't worship me, don't make me offerings*. And yet, all across the East, great gold-painted statues of Buddha are erected for his followers to kneel at while they make offerings. I'm not saying this is bad. Any ritual that helps people cope with life, helps them to be good, cannot be a bad thing. But it specifically and unambiguously goes against what Buddha said. Why does no-one notice this? Or if they do, why does nobody say anything?

He said, "I don't teach the truth, or a method for knowing the truth, because the truth can't be taught, or broken down into a method." And yet, all over the world, people study Buddhist scriptural teachings, memorising, learning commentaries and practices that have frothed up in Buddha's wake, applying methods and techniques that he never taught. Again, I'm not saying that chanting mantras in the lotus position is bad. Any method that temporarily calms an overheated brain cannot be a bad thing. But Buddha was at pains not to specify any such method or ritual. The closest he got to prescribing a physical regime was to use breathing to be attentive to what's happening in the moment.

The meditation retreat was just another place where people behaved in a way they believed would be beneficial for their souls, and as Buddha denied the existence of the soul, the whole deal seemed off the mark, and its grubby misery the absolute opposite of the happy loving kindness that Buddha wishes for us.

Neither worship nor meditation is working for me, but I'm just one of the ordinary slobs for whom religion means, if it means anything, being herded into place and told what to think. My parents were atheists who didn't make a big deal of it. If I'd wanted to go to church they wouldn't have stopped me, but my experiences with the happy Christian fellowship had left me, well, creeped out. Very creeped out. The only good Christians are the ones who never say a word about their goddamn faith, don't hang around churches, don't give a fuck if you know or not. And you don't know. But every time a Christian proclaims his faith, encourages me to invite Jesus into my life, I feel sick. Jesus always seems to be speaking to someone else, banging on about sin and guilt and how belief in him will bring salvation. Buddha doesn't make a big noise about sin, calling it error, which is a much more civilised and helpful way of dealing with the problem.

I'd started to read Buddha in my early teens, in that brief historical epoch when human consciousness seemed to be opening like a cosmic flower for young white middle-class boys across the universe. I warmed to his breezy denial of responsibility when it came to my own thoughts, beliefs, and actions. He never claims to die for my sins, to be the son of God, or to be on a mission to save my soul from eternal damnation. He doesn't even ask for faith or belief – very specifically, he says that these absolute fundamentals of organised religion are not only un-necessary to know the truth, but even get in the way of it. At this point, I'm going to back away from this for a moment while you re-read that sentence, because you need to.

Faith and belief get in the way of knowing the truth. There, I went to the considerable trouble of typing it out again because I have no faith in you, you shallow, unthinking fuck. I was right, yes? We have to work harder if we're going to make this thing work, and by we, I mean you.

Buddha is elitist – not in a social sense, he's no snob – he knows he'll be wasting his time shooting his mouth off to everyone. He only speaks to people who are already open to some extent, never trying to persuade or convince or argue. You don't hear anything in it, fine. During his life, hundreds of thousands come to hear him speak, maybe millions. This is quite a sizeable élite, and it can't all be down to the lack of something funner to do. There was obviously something very special about the guy, it couldn't have been *just* the words. The words he spoke are still available to us, but the flame that ignited them has gone, and unless we work hard at it, his words will remain just ashes.

And Buddhism is raking through the ashes. Very pleasantly, politely, nicely, calmly, harmlessly ... raking through the ashes.

"I NEVER FELT SO ALIVE!"

At a teahouse in Rangoon, I talk to Frog a little about what happened back at the monastery, but my words are clumsy great broken stumbling blocks, when they should be hummingbirds. I can't describe to *myself* what happened, and also I'm attempting to describe my *memory* of that event, and my memory is a second-generation cassette recording, compressed to hell, so the whole process is a lo-fi headache. But he can see my eyes, knows *something* happened, the very fact that I'm having so much trouble talking about it. I'm pretty laconic most of the time, words come easy to me, and not being able to be glib about something is a new and troubling experience. But I can at least tell him about Nu Win's words, *inside, outside*, how they exactly echoed Nui's words in Bangkok only three days previously.

And now I have to talk dirty, so if you're the sensitive, bookish type you may want to back away right now, avoiding eye contact. Please. Let's say goodbye while you still like me just a little. Go read about Buddha someplace else. There are plenty of comforting windchimey American Lifestyle Buddhist blogs on the internet where you can exchange tofu recipes and kitten pictures and your own deeply sensitive *haikus*. This is not that.

Nui is gorgeous. Delicate face, eyes like clear lotus pools, long dark hair, dazzling Thai smile, willowy as a cricket bat factory. That's not all. She speaks excellent English, and she's a treat to be with, polite, witty, and fun. That's not all. She's a Bangkok hooker. But that's not all, either. She has small, graceful hands and feet. Put a pin in that. Frog had taken her one night, and, in the spirit of Christian charity, pimped her out to me the next. He's afraid of the second fuck, which is the marriage fuck. He is to commitment what the Dutch are to extravagance. So I'm fucking Nui in my hotel room, and she's moaning something I have to concentrate on to make out. I'm not really up for concentration right now, the sweat is pouring off my face, making my eyes sting, and my legs are kicking into pre-orgasm spasm – you know when they hook up those electric CPR things to near-death patients in hospital shows on TV? When they flip the switch – *clear*! – that's what I'm like when I come. But she's repeating *inside, outside*, and our eyes meet and there's, well, a moment. In the eyes. In happy copulation, if you know your William Blake. You'll have to take my word for it (presumably) that this is not a phrase you hear often from Bangkok hookers. So to have heard it twice, in such different contexts, gives the phrase a wall-of-sound resonance I can't ignore. Something is telling me something. There's also the synchronicity of *Nu-i* and *Nu-Win,* the names are effectively homophonous. And if I didn't imagine that word, it sounds as if I did.

And it's in this conversation with Frog that I first come up against the difficulties of talking about Buddha. Buddhists talking together, there's always an unspoken competitive subtext of who's further along the path (although they're adept at hiding this behind a pose of smiling empathy). You can't tell a Buddhist a damn thing. Unless you're a Celebrity Monk addressing a herd of gravy-eyed guru-groupies hanging on your every word. Talk about Buddha to a non-Buddhist, and his eyes glaze over, look over your shoulder, at the clock. This is mainly to do with preconceptions. Most Westerners are familiar with the trappings of Buddhism, the Buddhist clichés, and this tired, superficial familiarity tells them there's nothing else they need to know. They've seen the trailer, they don't want the movie. Also, they inevitably conflate Buddha with Buddhism (it's okay – I had to look up *conflate*). Which is an easy and convenient and lazy thing to do, and people love easy and convenient and lazy things to do. To get at what Buddha was getting at, you have to forget whatever you know about Buddhism, whether that's just a smartass movie line or the entire Pali canon off by heart. *Buddha did not become Buddha because he was a Buddhist.* In fact, he found all the Buddhist meditative and yogic practices inadequate, and left them behind once he'd done them. They made him content and peaceful, and that is as far as they went. If he'd found any of them relevant or useful to what he experienced, he wouldn't be hiding it, keeping it to himself, there'd be a step-by-step list you could follow so you could be Buddha too. The less you think you know about Buddhism, the bigger the advantage you have when it comes to understanding what he says.

And then the hard bit starts.

This is not about you.

Suddenly, what Buddha says loses its charm for a lot of people who like to think that the whole point of Buddhism is to better their souls while treading the mystic path to personal enlightenment. That's what those empty-eyed wraiths were doing back at the retreat; working away at their souls like miners chipping the rockface, hoping for the glint of gold. That's what American Lifestyle Buddhists (ALBs) are doing when they chant on the deck overlooking the ocean at sunset, with the windchimes a'tink-erlin', a pert little Chardonnay cooling in the icebucket and a pert little intern cooling in the pool. It's all about *them*, their very unique and special individuality, and their beautifully personal progression on the path.

In the East, Buddhism is a religion, although claims are made for it to be a philosophy. If it walks like a duck, quacks like a duck, it's probably a duck. Buddhism has a hierarchical priesthood, temples, images of its god, and believers come to pray, to make offerings, to petition their god for favors, and to thank him for answering their prayers. A fairytale version of his life (with crowd-pleasing miracles and a colorful supporting cast of gods) is taught to schoolchildren, and there's an established liturgical calendar. *It's a duck.*

I've never met a monk yet who went into the priesthood with the intention of nurturing his soul, or exploring his inner self or any of the asinine reasons Westerners give. While monks are just men in monk's clothes, they are at least not setting themselves up as being spiritually superior, or even interesting. For many of them, understanding Buddha is pretty low on the list, after escape from a shitty life, food, shelter, companionship, and an education. Being a monk for a while can add to your social prestige and help your career. For sons of rich families it's an accepted step up onto the corporate or military ladder. And sometimes it's a business like any other, and monks can get very rich selling amulets and blessings, or letting out temple land to traders. And sometimes boys become monks because they like boys.

So in the East, pragmatism. In the West, an adoring obsession with the Self. The Middle Way, which Buddha points down, is the hardest way after all. Neither the hair shirt nor the silk. He doesn't say you have to be a monk, or go off into the woods. He doesn't say you can't be rich, which is a major attraction for ALBs who like to justify the four homes, the Botox and the Humvee because they're not real. They're *illusory*, see.

So I've become a Buddha-bore. I can see the faltering, clichéd exposition of my *what happened* is starting to wear on Frog. I don't care. We're in the airport bar at Dubai or Abu Dhabi or somewhere, the airport that smells of feet, on the way home, and I feel sick and crazy. Home is exactly where I don't want to be. In fact, *you can't go home again*. Why can't you go home again? Because it's not home any more. Frog takes a picture of me thinking about Nui, and I look wrecked, a condemned man. My first trip out East, in my early fifties, has blown all the fuses I have left, mental and physical.

Back "home", in the gray, I carry my Soundbite Buddha with me always, flick its furry pages, and some of it is beginning to flip the bottle cap, I can feel the fizz of it. And I'm in the internet café most nights, speaking to Nui. She's in the internet shop near her apartment; I recognise the high-back orange chairs. I've witnessed enough of these hooker/hooked internet conversations back in Bangkok to know the form, and I don't want to follow it. She says she'll wait for me *darling*, and I say bullshit, *darling*, which it is. Hookers say this crap to their darlings to keep the money coming in. I'd Western Union-ed her some cash, which I know will fill her dainty purse to overflowing with amphetamines. I don't care. But I can't afford to do it again, and I tell her that's it, that's all I have, it's gone. Amazingly, we're still talking, still interest each other. She tells me about her customers. They're all besuited business types, introduced through her agency. She gets wined and dined at the most expensive places in town and then limo'd back to five-star hotel rooms where these decent and possibly Christian men, out to fly the corporate flag, hide the family photograph in the bedside drawer and fuck her in the ass, moaning terrible things into the night.

When I stop calling her, it's not out of jealousy, I don't feel I own her, she's a whore. What I *feel* like is, wires have been barbed into my gut, pulling me back. It hurts, but in a good way. I decide next time we talk, it's going to be in the same room, and soon. I can't sit still, can't concentrate. I have that wide-eyed, desperate exultation of the serial-killer

– *I never felt so alive!* And I know that I'm a stranger in my own home town. I talk to my friends about my (ah ...) vacation, and they're either pruriently curious, or dismissive, especially when I edge into Buddha territory, which I want to do all the time. They want the sleaze, so I show them photographs of bombshell Nui (male junk tactfully tucked) and they're drooling like a Tex Avery wolf. They look at her and then at me, asking what this gorgeous creature is doing with a balding, skinny, and frankly unattractive – *hey, no offence* – middle-aged man. It's purely financial, I say, a fee for services rendered. Some are derisive, saying it's pretty pathetic – *how old is she? Twenty*? And *they* don't have to *pay* for sex, thanks. And some are really ... *wow*! They're thinking, *yeah*. But they all *would*, I know, all these regular straight not-having-to-pay-for-sex types. All it takes is a look from those eyes, and a little away-from-home what-the-hell.

But I'm clueless as to what's going on in my personal life, in spite of my Buddha insights. I've been skating on very thin ice for some time, with monsters waiting in the dark waters for me to fall through; phosphorescent, scaly, ice-cold nightmares. I'm making vague plans for the future while the ice has been cracking, and I haven't heard a damn thing. And before I know it my decision to move out East has been made for me. In a few brutal days, in separate incidents, I lose my mother, my home, my dog, and just about everything I was attached to.

My life is blown to bits.

It's Rahu.

WAYNE LOONEY AND THE PHANTOM TOYOTA

I know it's Rahu because a little later I'm sitting in Terry's back room in Bangkok, having the first reading of my life. Terry's a part-time astrologer and full-time obnoxious asshole. I'd always considered astrology bullshit, right up there with the legal, real estate and banking businesses in terms of thieving ass-sucking charlatanry, but it's clear I've been doing it a mis-service. The evidence is right there in front of me. My chart is up on the monitor of his computer, and he's shaking his head, wide-eyed, his hand over his mouth, like he just cannot believe what he's seeing.

Oh shit, he says eventually. *Oh shit*. And he does this kind of disbelieving laugh, looking at me. *I'm amazed you're still here*, he says. I haven't told him anything about my life, other than I'm a writer, and my date and time of birth. He taps the screen with his finger. *Really, this is as bad as it gets*, he says. He explains how Rahu, which I dimly understand is a phase or ecliptic of the moon with the effect of a planet in astrology, is now a catastrophic malign influence in my life. In Hindu mythology, Rahu is a terrible severed head, screaming obscenities, riding in a chariot pulled by flaming dragons. And it's his job to fuck me up. He's got me by the hair and is thrashing me around, spitting red-hot bile in my face.

Terry reaches for a book, flicks through it, running his finger down the page.

"An outcast, an irreligious person, in a foreign country."

That's me.

It's one of the attributes of Rahu. There's this saying, as above, so below?

I heard of that.

It's all about correspondences, patterns. Nothing's unconnected.

This explains everything.

And then Terry tells me – in startlingly intimate detail – about my life, my marriages, my income, my work, all the stuff he couldn't possibly know, private information about who I am and what I've been through. *You receive a large amount of money, connected with work, for doing no work.* That'll be the movie option for my first novel. *You will be thrown out of your own house at a fairly late age.* Wow. *Your first marriage was characterised by frigidity, the second by impotence.* Double wow. Not by staring into a crystal ball, but tapping through a computer program. And it's all absolutely, precisely, totally, correct, up there on the screen, he doesn't put a mystic spin on it or interpret anything, he lets me read it. I'm stunned. He passes me a joint and I take a peck at it out of politeness, I've always been an LSD guy myself. We go through the future a little, and it's looking good, eventually (I'm going to be famous at 62!) so he tells me to hang in there, and I take the elevator down to the street. The night air is soft, scented, with that delicious sub-tropical weight slowing things down.

Bang.

An explosion shatters everything. Right up ahead, close enough to feel the punch of heat in the air, the sharp taste in the teeth. I can't see *what* blows up, all I see is the white-orange flash, and hear the explosion. It's not a deep, earth-shaking boom, more like an extremely loud firecracker, with a silence after it, no Hollywood alarms or screaming hubcaps spinning off, just the soft Bangkok night closing in again. And the numb buzz in the ears and the after-image of the flare flashing as I blink.

I look up at the stars. *Missed.*

I learn later that it's a political statement, an opposition group is blamed, but I know it's Rahu, screaming his head off.

Terry has given me a jewel he had made in return for a little writing I did for him, to bring me luck and protection. It's actually a seed, a Nepalese *Rudraksha*. This one has eight natural divisions, which allies it to Ganesh, the Hindu Elephant God, and it has an enlarged division, a bulge known in itself as a Ganesh, like the elephant's trunk. It's a rare thing. The gold mount contains a green jewel, a chrome tourmaline. Rahu's color, apparently. It's a beautiful, strange object, and I wear it on a plastic cord around my neck, because I can't afford a gold chain. I don't know if I believe in its power or not – well, I don't believe in it. But I wear it, because it may work without my belief or understanding, like a CD player.

I'm fingering it, this curious thing, as I walk toward the lights up the road, away from the dead cat, which I'm thinking about.

Remember the dead cat? It's still there. Death is much more a part of life out in the East. It's not a taboo subject, hidden away. It's always there, in your face. Short lives, violent deaths, so *live for today* isn't bumper-sticker philosophy, an excuse for frat-house behavior, it's the way of Buddhist life, it's all you can do. The dead cat was there because it died. People weren't offended or disgusted by it, as I was, they didn't give it any thought at all. And I'd already given it way too much.

The lights turn out to be decorating a restaurant. Thais love fairy lights, string them up all over. Fluorescent tubes, too. They hang those from trees, so you know you can get a meal, sing some karaoke, get mentally unsound on Thai whiskey. In a cruel genetic twist, Thais have been given the undying love of song and vocal cords made from packing twine. I can hear some pipe-stretching now, a banshee wail over the thud of a sound system. The poorest palm-leaf shack in Asia has a blackpainted speaker cab on the porch the size of a telephone booth. I once saw a hammock strung between two beat-up cabs, the guy sleeping off the rice whiskey as the speakers thumped out the beats.

The restaurant is the usual collection of tin tables under a palm-leaf roof, steaming kitchen in front, half on the street, and a raised stage under a vinyl Chang beer banner. On each table is a plastic tub with a toilet roll in it, to clean your fingers and mouth, and a plastic rack of sauces and toothpicks. Faded pictures of the Royal Family and British

Premier League soccer players are taped to the walls, and I recognise the eyeless scowl of Buddhist monk poster-boy Wayne Looney. There's a party of seven at some pushed-together tables, and the girl up on stage clutching the microphone, eyes closed, this hideous ululation coming from her lovely throat, she's possessed by Cthulhu, the Blind Idiot God. I don't know the song (Thai pop songs all sound the same to me), but she's not hitting a single note the karaoke machine is feeding her, she's all over the place, and it's not funny, it's horrible. Her friends are chatting together, the men sharing a bottle of Black Label poured over tumblers of iced soda water. It's like the dead cat, nobody seems to be aware of the demons struggling to escape the girl's frail body.

I'm tired and hungry and pissed off and I seem further away to whatever it was I was close to in Burma, now a year back. It's not just the dead cat, or the live caterwaul, it's me. I'm making the same mistake the poor slobs at the temple were making, coming to a place because I thought the place would help me find myself, or, failing that, someone who looked like me. The physical yearning I felt back in the gray-faced, grim old occident has not been replaced by a feeling of satisfaction or completion.

I am flailing.

I sit down, turn the fan away, order a bottle of Leo and study the laminated menu. I see I can have *cow meet feeds to cook spicy* or, perhaps the delicious house speciality, *pig in whore dust*. I raise my glass to the party table, get smiles back, take a gulp of ice-cold beer. They won't be getting any of *this* back at the dorm, the whey-faced soul-stroking toilet-roll-hoarders. The girl with the mic starts singing Country Roads, which is practically the Thai national anthem, which they pronounce Cunty Load. Suddenly the sheer stupid wonderfulness of Thailand gets to me, the girl is singing in tune, the night is warm, the beer is cold, and my waitress has a smile that won't quit. The moral: travel light. Don't pack any dead cats.

And it's this moment that Old Guy chooses to interrupt my life.

He's wearing riceworker blues, a straw coolie hat, but he doesn't look Thai, the face is longer.

He says, "Excuse me, sir?"

Hello.

"Do you remember me?"

I don't think so. I always forget faces. Faces and names. Faces and names and numbers. There's something else, but those are the ones I remember.

"May I sit with you?"

Sure, I say. He signals the waitress for a beer, but she doesn't see him for some reason, so I call to her to bring another bottle, and I have to ask for another glass when she comes because she's forgotten. Even then she doesn't pour the guy's beer for him, and I guess it's a class thing. He may be an old laborer, but she doesn't have a clue about him, his education. His English, that surprising use of *may.*

The first thing he asks me is where I'm from, and I start to tell him, but he cuts in with, "No, I mean just now."

The temple up the road?

"You're interested in Buddha."

I'm interested in what he says.

He drinks, carefully, holding the glass carefully, and sets it back on the table, carefully. Like it's the first or the last time he gets to do this.

Where are you from?

"I was born in Burma, but I come from somewhere else." He's enjoying this. There's a playful quality to him. He reaches slowly across the table and points at my forehead, stopping just short of touching it. "That's why the waitress didn't see me."

I look at him. There's no meat on him at all, and it's impossible to guess his age, but what I can see of his hair is white. He's wiry, used to manual labor. His skin covers him like paper, with no padding. His eyes are sunk, his lips thin and wide, and his cheekbones show. One of his incisors is missing, and the rest of his teeth look ripe for falling, ivory yellow and separated. If you were very small and had a tiny little mallet you could climb in there and play the Burmese national anthem, very quietly, on his teeth. A cataract clouds his left eye, and white hairs curl from his ears. His hands are long and shiny with callouses, and his fingernails bitten short, except for one pinkie nail, which is as long as a ladyboy's. His coolie hat isn't made from straw or bamboo or whatever, but woven strips of plastic. I can see the badly-healed hollow scar on his elbow where he fell off a *moto-sai*.

"You're looking for someone to help you with this Buddha business, yes?"

I don't know. I don't.

"You're not going to find him, ever. That's why I'm here, for the material in your book which is beyond you. No offence"

He's crazy. *What book?*

"The one you're writing."

I tell him the book I'm writing – well, my laptop is in Bangkok, so I'm on hiatus – is a thriller, so I thank him for his application but regretfully inform him there's no part in it for him this time, but I'll bear him in mind should a suitable position arise in a future novel, and I wish him success with other authors.

He says, "No, the book you're writing *now*. This instant. A long way from here."

It's like he's waiting for me to give him the green light – what for, I have no idea.

Do we have to do this now?

"Now is always the only time for it."

Make it short. I'm working on the waitress.

He takes a sip of his beer, gathering his thoughts for a moment before he speaks.

"You can start from anywhere, but starting with the self is good. Unless you understand what Buddha means by the self you'll have trouble with the other aspects."

I nod. Sounds reasonable. Boring, but reasonable.

"We split ourselves up into components, separating and listing what we are made of. The first division we make is mind and body. Everything physical here, and over there, everything else. Okay so far?"

I stifle a yawn with my fist.

"But we still can't locate the *self*, so we keep on dividing. The body we split up into bones, organs, nerves, hair, nail, whatever, the list goes on forever. The mind, well, we create categories like consciousness, personality, intellect, emotion, perception, and fanciful notions like ego and id, intuition, ESP, whatever. We never tire of these sub-divisions, we slice ourselves up finer and finer, into subsections of subsections, and we get further away from knowing what the *self* is all the time. You can never isolate the self in this way, because *it is the self that is doing the dividing*. Each of these subdivisions, these slices of self, is not, in itself, the *self*, the *I*."

I have to give myself a little shake, blink. *Subdivisions. Gotcha.*

"Would you like another drink?"

He's managed to finish his, quite a trick. I *nong-nong* the waitress, waving two fingers.

"So, the next step is to acknowledge that you are a combination of elements which *in themselves* are not *you*."

I'm prepared to do that.

"So where are you? Where is the self, the *I*?"

This is a fairly common way for angsty, existential adolescents to waste time in their bedrooms when they should be masturbating. I still don't know the answer. But I have to give Old Guy credit, he's really working for his drink. He goes on.

"You've seen that Monty Python film, the Holy Grail? The Black Knight gets his arm cut off, blood's jetting out, but he goes on fighting. It's still the Black Knight, he's still *himself*. He gets his limbs hacked off, one by one, but it's still *him*. Eventually, it's just his head on the ground, shouting and swearing. *Come back, coward! Come back and fight!*"

So, what . . . you're saying that the self is – in the head?

He looks momentarily puzzled. "No. I just mentioned it

because it's a very funny film. I enjoyed *Mr Bean's Holiday, too.*"

I couldn't imagine anyone enjoying Mr Bean's Holiday.

"No fooling you, is there? So anyway, Buddha used the story of the cart, which we'll update to a car, say a Toyota pickup, although the analogy works just as well with a Hyundai. You and, oh, I don't know" – he leans back, looking around the room for a volunteer. He points to a Manchester United soccer poster – "you and Wayne Looney are standing next to this Toyota, because Mr Looney has just bought it and wants to show it off to you, his best friend. So you play stupid and say, *where is the car, Wayne? I can't see it.* He pats the bonnet with his hand. *Here she is!*"

I cut in with *hood*, but he takes no notice.

"*But*, you say, a mischievous twinkle in your eye, *that's the bonnet! Can you touch the car?* Wayne, increasingly anxious, crawls around the Toyota, touching the exhaust pipe, the headlights, the steering wheel, repeatedly asking you *is this the car*? And you're saying, *nope*, and *uh-uh*, wagging your finger and smiling indulgently. But Wayne is determined to get to the bottom of this, and starts tearing the car to pieces – he's also a trained mechanic with a Snap-On toolcart and a diamond disc cutter. He triumphantly presents you with each disassembled component, saying *this is the car, yes*? And you have to sigh and tell him *no, that's the windscreen, Mr Looney*, or whatever it is. And then he starts breaking down the components into *their* component parts, and eventually he's sitting on this enormous mountain of bits and pieces, there's nothing left he can take apart. *You mean*, he says, *I bought a car made of stuff that's not my car?*"

Old Guy spreads his arms to express Mr Looney's consternation. I mirror the gesture, saying, *Dude, where's my car?*

"Mr Looney has to accept that his Toyota is a temporary coming-together of elements that, in combination, express the car idea. It's just a temporary conjunction, like you might recognise an animal shape in a constellation of stars. Or like *you*."

He reaches slowly across the table again to touch my chest with a bony and very non-imaginary forefinger. "You are centered nowhere in this intricate and extremely temporary assembly – no one bit holds the essence of you, or represents you any better than any other bit. There is no jewel in the crown. No king in the castle."

I see the waitress smiling at me and lifting another bottle of beer. I like her a lot. I like her low-cut jeans and the tramp stamp in the small of her back, a pair of blue-black wings.

Old Guy gets my attention back. "How old are you?"

Fifty, fifty-four. No, fifty-three. Fifty-four.

"Your body, right now, is about ten years old. Red blood cells go through a four month renewal cycle. Every cell in the body is in the process of being exchanged. Ninety-eight percent of the seven billion billion billion atoms in your body are replaced yearly, without you knowing a damn thing about it. If this isn't scary enough, most of "your" cells aren't even human. For every human cell in your body, there's ten that belong to *bacteria*. There's over five hundred species of microscopic beasties crawling through you as I speak. This isn't philosophy, or opinion, it's scientific fact, which you Westerners seem to put a lot of faith in."

Excuse my bluntness, but – your point?

He puts his hand on my arm, a surprisingly hard grip I don't think I could shake. It's like a bench vise.

"The point," he says, "is the *starting* point. If you insist on slicing yourself up like a cake into ever thinner and thinner slices, arguing about the existence of a soul or whatever, you'll never understand what Buddha is on about, you'll never eat the cake. *Simplify*. The self is *I*. You shouldn't even give it your name, which is just another label. *I* is the simplest mark you can make. A line in the dust. A fingertrail of blood on a cave wall. Its similarity to number 1 is not coincidental, but we'll get into numbers later."

Oh, goody. Numbers are my best subject. After names and faces.

That seems to be it. He lets go my arm, sits back, picking his nose with his long pinkie nail in that alarmingly blatant Asian way.

Finished? I say.

He flicks the booger away. "If you're interested in Buddha, be a Buddhist. If you're interested in what he said . . . you're on your own."

And he disappears.

Well, he goes to the toilet, but it's effectively disappearing. He re-appears, wiping his hands on his pants. His voice, for the first time, is urgent, insistent, as tight as his grip, and he leans forward from the waist a little, fixing me with his one good eye. "This is not about *you*," he says. And he's out of here, leaving me with six empty bottles of beer and the distinct feeling I need another.

PIGSFOOT AND TOMATO PIE

As the empty bottles line up on my table, and the waitress becomes more and more beautiful, I'm thinking about what Old Guy tells me about looking for a teacher I'm never going to find. I once met a guru in the flesh. At college, a member of our acid-eating knitting club comes back from a stay at an *ashram*, which is like a hippie pad, the incense and the posters of Krishna and the girls with no bras and the dogs drinking out of the toilet, only nobody does drugs, which seems to miss the point of the exercise, you ask me. But Beard's eyes are alight with divine inspiration. He's hooked up with some Children of the Divine Light, he's totally fizzing with this stuff they've been telling him about their leader, a twelve-year old Indian boy called Maharaj Ji. *Guru* Maharaj Ji. He teaches techniques that turn the senses inwards; you taste the divine nectar, hear the divine note, see the divine light. When it comes to the senses of touch and smell, Beard's a little hazy on what happens, and so are we. He refuses a hit from a joint, says he's going to London next week because Guru Maharaj Ji is dropping by the headquarters of the Children of the Divine Light. I say I'll go with him, and he says, *uh-uh, I'll be with, you know, the ashram guys* (there's an Indian word for *ashram guy* I've forgotten, for some reason). But I can go on my own if I want. Which is my first little shudder of creepiness, like there's this cosy spiritual brotherhood I'm excluded from *already*.

The headquarters turns out to be a house in the London suburbs, Wimbledon or somewhere, a very ordinary and bourgeois 1930s house in a nicely kept and respectable street. Followers of the guru are spilling into the streets by the time I get there, and a few concerned neighbors gather in their gardens to *tut-tut* about it in that very English way they *tut-tutted* when Hitler's bombs dropped on their heads in the Blitz.

The sense of anticipation is sending everyone into a tizzy. The house has been garlanded with gold cloth, and hundreds of bunches of flowers are stuffed everywhere. I'm ignored by everybody, although I think I must look pretty much like them, the shoulder-length ratty hair, the denim, the dope pouch. Except that I'm not skipping around singing *I tasted the nectar!* and breaking down with great sobs of ecstasy to be supported by caring ashram guys. I mean, I'm pleased for them, but I feel as out of this as I did the time a Sunday School teacher forced me to sing about Jesus on the beach when I was a kid. There's a big part of me that wants to be part of *this*, though. I really want to get into these techniques, but mainly I really want to get into the pale-skinned willowy girls dancing barefoot in the front garden. Later, I learn these secret meditation techniques from an ex-Child. The kneeling acolyte is ceremonially poked in his closed eyes, and the resultant kaleidoscopic disturbance of the optic nerve proclaimed as a revelation of the Divine Light. The Divine Note is just that tiny humming you get in the ears when you're in a quiet place (people suffering from tinnitus don't know how blessed they are, evidently), and the Divine Nectar involves curling your tongue back to suck your tonsils or something. I'm still unclear about the other senses. Everybody is. But standing in a suburban London garden, surrounded by people who are all happier than me, I know none of this, and I want in. In *her*, mostly. The red-head with the finger cymbals.

A lot of these people are wearing baggy white cotton (which I've now learned is a warning signal), and some of them have flowers in their hair. I can't imagine Beard with either, but I don't see him anywhere. A girl actually faints with excitement, and I catch a glimpse of soft, bra-less cleavage as they carry her upstairs. Someone announces that the Master will be among us very shortly. I squeeze into the front room, edging around the bay window and the far wall. There's a stage with an armchair covered in gold cloth, and news-conference-style microphones set up, and enough flowers to apologise to half the wives of Wimbledon. Everybody's taking their positions, sitting crosslegged in rank and file. I make myself a place near the stage. I've come all the way to Wimbledon to see this guy, I don't want to be in the hall peering through the coats. I'm not managing to catch anybody's eye, though, for a friendly chat. Some Children are chanting, their eyes closed. They're so close to the divine light I can smell their nostril hair singeing.

A retinue of bearded and beturbanned Mystic Elders appears, wearing heavy silk Indian clothes and gold jewellery. I feel like fainting myself. One of them leans in to the mic, smiling beatifically. Tap tap.

Guru Maharaj Ji will be with you soon. He's playing with his electric car race game, slot cars.

At this, the crowd goes gooey with love – so human! Still a boy in so many ways! Girls clap their hands together under their tilted faces, men whistle *phew* soundlessly, shaking their locks in astonishment at the Master's cosmic sense of play. Slot cars! Oh, *wow!*

When the Guru at last makes his entrance, I feel swept up in this nauseous wave of adoration in the room. It's like we've all started lactating spontaneously. It's *scary*. There are gasps, disbelieving laughs at the miraculous bodily manifestation of his divine form, right here in this room! The tears flow as the portly little chap makes himself comfy on his golden throne. He's got his black schoolboy hair slicked across his portly little head, with an Oliver Hardy cowlick waxed to his portly little forehead, and he's wearing a golden silk coat-thing stretched across his portly little belly, and a gold watch the size of a carriage clock, and an Aladdin's cave of rings on his pudgy little fingers. He looks like what he is – a spoiled little Indian kid.

I can't remember a damn thing he says. Even while he's saying it. But I do remember a few days later a guy throws a pie in his face, and some Children of the Divine Light beat on him so hard his own children will walk with a limp. Which makes me grateful I don't have a pie in my lap when I am within easy throwing distance. A nice steaming hot and undercooked pigsfoot and tomato pie.

WHITE GUY SHIT

Frog, suddenly remembering something, opens his wallet and passes me half a business card. We're sitting – squatting, actually, on tiny plastic elves' chairs – in a tea house in Rangoon, day one of our trip out here, watching the rain turn the street into a fast-flowing blackwater river. We've completed a week's intensive combat whoring in Bangkok, and have come to Burma for a change of pace, and to freak ourselves out.

Don't take it while I'm around, he says. *I don't want the responsibility.*

The card is from the Embassy of the Islam something-or-other – it's been torn off.

The Islamic Republic of Iran in London, he says. *It's the first bit of card I found.*

I thank him and slip it into my own wallet. It had occurred to me to take it at the great golden Shwedagon temple on the hill, but it'll have to wait. It's waited eight years in Frog's desk, so another few days shouldn't affect its sell-by date.

I'm pleased that he remembered. I'm less grateful when, much later, he mails me the other half in a stupid little envelope with the cheapest stamp he can find and it gets lost on the way from London to Vientiane, in Laos, where I'm staying at the time.

The last time I'd taken LSD was back when I was learning to abuse drugs at college, in the late sixties. It wasn't exactly on the curriculum, but we were keen students and cut less important classes (that is, any of them) in order to study the clinical effects of LSD on teen consciousness. This is one of the few truly great and good things I have done in this life. Here's Buddha on taking LSD: *There is a wonderful doorway to a dazzling intensity of sights and sounds, color and beauty . . . the infinite structures of the world are as clear as a starry night sky* . . . See? The guy is completely wired. And while it's obvious he's as familiar with LSD as he is with the electron microscope, he knows whereof he speaks, as anyone who's been through that Wonderful Doorway will tell you. I wouldn't go so far as to recommend LSD to everyone, but well . . . yes, I would.

You cannot know LSD from reading about it – this is not knowledge, it's information. Similarly, you cannot know what Buddha's on about by reading about it, on this page or any other. You can silt up your brain pan with every word in the Pali canon (and some do) and still know Jack Shit about what Buddha wants you to know. If you take LSD, you *know* something about Buddha, a little bit, enough to know he knows way more than you. For him, it was just one of many Wonderful Doorways he went through without any help from Dr. Hoffman or anybody.

Baddha

That passage in my Soundbite Buddha book, as note-perfect a description of an LSD trip as you'll find, made me want to take acid again. So I asked Frog to bring his stash with him. In Bangkok, we're way too distracted by our field research into Women's Issues to think about it, but here in rainy season Rangoon, it turns up as promised. It's not really Frog's drug of choice, anyway. He prefers the party drugs that hotwire the optic nerve to the genitals. He likes to get cosy with crack whores, finds their company amenable. His dream of domesticity is to come home to slippers, a crack pipe, and a blazing *katoey* in the hearth. The only drugs I do with whores are Vodkaredbull, which is a vitamin-rich health drink, and occasionally a blue pill which gives me a hard-on I have to feed through a mangle two days later to deflate. But there's none of that larky indulgence in Burma, at least not this time. We're pretty serious, and upset by what we see, which is basically a lovely and cultured and elegant and great-hearted people being crushed into the mud *by their own fucking government*, the worst guys in all the world.

But this is not that. *I, me, mine.*

We're sipping sweet milky tea from dented aluminum mugs, sitting on this doll-house furniture they use, deafened by the biblical torrents of rain, watching army trucks sending up roostertails of grimy water you could surf on. Nobody in the street looks at the soldiers, this is something we've noted, but the soldiers look at us. They don't return greetings, we give up after the first try. The citizens wade knee-deep, holding up dainty parasols against the downpour. The row of colonial shop-houses opposite momentarily ignites in sunlight ripping through the stormclouds, streaky yellow and green and green-blue dazzle and shimmer, hard on the eye.

And I'm thinking about Nui. And when I think of her, I don't think of the dirty stuff, I think of her eyes. These aren't among the most prized attributes for a hooker, maybe, but in a person they're pretty important. I've already described them as being like "clear lotus pools" which is as poetic as I'm prepared to wax on the subject. They're – oh, *nuts*. You describe them.

She wasn't my first whore. My first whore was two whores, taken while I was still jetlagged. Before the trip, I tell Frog, in my primly ignorant way, that I'm not going to consort with prostitutes, he can if he wants, but it's not for me, oh *noes*, I'm *married*.

How very wrong I am.

Three hours off the plane and I find out what happened to all the fun left in the world – they keep it in Bangkok. I'm fucking two gorgeous girls wildly up for it, me, and each other, and my marriage of seven grim, effortful years is as vivid in my mind as the Agnew administration. And I can't go home again. So I enter into the swing of things with the same dedication I applied to my groundbreaking clinical research into hallucinogenic pharmaceuticals. There's hardly a waking moment when I'm not actively draining down into some country girl's bank account.

So, tea house, Rangoon. They serve you a pot of tea free, while you wait for your tea. The tea you pay for is very milky and disgustingly sweet and I prefer the scented water in the pot, and consider I'm paying for that. You can buy take-away tea in the street, in a clear plastic bag with a straw, and you can hang it on your pecker while you're not drinking, and then just throw the bag away anywhere. I have a theory about the ever-present and ugly litter out here. Before they got into plastic, they packed everything in natural materials, palm leaves, banana leaves, coconut shells, I don't know, organic stuff. So when they threw it away it decomposed and everything was fine. Old habits die hard. The stormwater in the street, at least, sees all the crap and is doing something about it, carrying a bobbing tide of plastic waste down to the river.

When the rain stops, we'll go across the river, Frog says. And an hour or so later, under an epic blue sky with great golden clouds piling across it, we slip and slide down the muddy bank of the Rangoon River close to the fish market. There aren't any tourist boats here (there aren't enough tourists to fill one in all of Rangoon), and I'm thinking maybe Frog will stride forcefully across by sheer power of will, when he leaps down onto the blunt prow of one of the many stone-colored timber longboats moored along the bank. The guy in back of the boat looks up, surprised to see us. Frog stands with his chest out, grinning, and pointing to the opposite bank. *You take us!* he says. This is the kind of attitude that endears the French to the whole world, I think, warily getting down into the boat. Frog takes a few crumpled dollar bills from the clip in his zippered pants pocket and gives them to the now smiling boatman, who beckons his boy on board from a couple of boats away.

The Rangoon River is wide and busy, and not fed by Swiss mountain springs. It looks like it needs a good rinse. So I'm shocked to see people leaning over the sides of boats, scooping it into their mouths. In addition to the longboats like the one we commandeered, with diesel pickup engines bolted to the back, there are small ferryboats crossing the river, a few fishing boats. No big shipping activity, nothing military that I can see, all local. The city doesn't cross the river to the opposite bank, it's jungle over there, with nothing rising above it except mountains of cloud. Frog points to a collection of shacks on stilts, a break in the trees at the river's edge, and our boatman swings the long screw shaft so we head toward it. We wave and smile at people on other boats, nothing too stupid or touristy, just a hello, and some wave and smile back, but most give us the blank yet curious stare we get all over Rangoon. Burma isn't called the Land of Smiles, and for a reason – they have a junta. If you had a junta, you wouldn't feel too LOL about life either.

We get closer to the jungle, and I see smoke rising from the cluster of palmleaf shacks on bamboo stilts at the river's edge, and kids playing on the banks, swinging into the water from the trees, laughing. Our boatman edges up to the mudslide that serves as a jetty, with a narrow planked walkway laid up it. Everyone has turned to look at us. *A lot of these people won't have seen a white man before*, Frog says.

You're kidding, I say. *This isn't the Amazon.*

No kidding. In fact, especially the kids, who don't go across the river. There's no TV here, no books, no newspapers, no way they can see what white people look like.

I'm amazed, but not as amazed as some of the faces I'm looking at. Our boatman ties up to a bamboo pole, and we

climb the walkway, which tilts underfoot, making the mud
bubble, and only luck keeps me from making a spectacular
pratfall into it. Business seems to have ground to a halt, kids
carrying plastic jerrycans of river water set them down to
watch the white guys teeter up the gangplank. Walking up
into the village, we're surrounded by a crowd of kids,
talkative and excited now, although one toddler starts bawling
at the sight of us. *When I was in South America*, Frog says,
*kids followed me into the jungle to watch me have a shit. They
thought it would be white. Bloody nuisance, actually.*

We walk around the houses, which are just shacks made
of bamboo and palm leaves. Up here, they're not on stilts,
the river doesn't rise this far. We smile and nod at everyone,
and everyone smiles back once they've gotten over the shock
of seeing visitors from another planet walking like men
among them. There are clay ovens full of white-hot charcoal,
with mystery meat sizzling on blackened grills, and women
squat with mortar and pestle, grinding up spices. It's
pungent. Bumpy, sick-colored dogs snarl and cringe. We get
a brilliant smile from a girl in a window, then her hand goes
to her mouth in shyness and she ducks back into the
shadows. A man appears holding a fighting cock under his
arm. He's wearing the *longhi*, the plaid wraparound skirt
cloth that all the men here wear, and he welcomes us to his
village, in hesitant but perfect English. While Frog sprays
him with charm mist, I feel my arm touched, and a man
peers at me from under the brim of his coolie hat. He starts
to speak, but Frog pulls me into the conversation with the
village elder, and by the time I can look for coolie hat, he's
gone.

We take a few photographs, give out ballpoint pens, and back in the boat I remember the man. Actually, what I remember is, his coolie hat. I tell Frog about him.

He said something.

In English? What?

I don't recall. Something like, not yet, you don't need me yet. Something like that.

Frog makes a tiny, polite sound that's nearly a chuckle. *You imagined him.*

I think he's worried about me. I already told him I've seen the Buddha in Nui's eyes.

A NEIGHBOR DROPS BY

My second trip out east, after Rahu's cataclysmic behind-the-scenes destruction of my life, and I'm on my own. My cunning plan to finesse myself out here gently, in stages, has been violently thwarted. There is way too much thwart in my life. I'd like to get a good night's sleep, but that's thwarted by the sobbing and writhing I don't have time for in the day. Other than that, life is good. I wear a short-sleeve shirt all the time, I'm writing my novel, which is getting rave reviews from me, and I'm reading my Buddha Soundbite book as a weird kind of comfort. Weird because Buddha doesn't really give a shit about me. Or, rather, what I think "me" is.

When I stumble off the plane I hook up (ha!) with Nui, and we go to her apartment, where I'll stay until I find a place of my own. It's a typical working girl's room in the Bangkok boondocks, in an apartment block full of katoeys throwing shoes and screaming at each other in the hallways.

They get food from the all-night foodcart in the street, amphetamines from their cousin at the night market, and milk their back-home farang customers from the internet shop next door. Nui's room is just big enough for a bed, a small dressing-table, and a closet. No "air", so the usual plastic fan in a tangle of wiring blowing way too hard. This is a pretty deluxe room, so there's a real glass window onto a balcony broad enough to stand sideways on, where you can take in the panoramic view of the wall of the next apartment building, about five feet away. Next to the balcony, and the same size, is a cubicle with a flush toilet and a showerhead, close enough to perform the two operations at once. And you could brush your teeth at the same time, because your chin's in the basin when you sit on the toilet. She's decorated the room nicely, dark colors, reds and golds, artificial flowers, a silk coverlet on the bed, soft lamp in the corner made of a varnished root or branch, and a little Buddha shrine on top of the closet. I see she's framed a small drawing and a letter I sent her. I'm touched but wary. I'm not there to marry her. I've been brutally honest about my diminishing funds. I can't afford to keep her, or her habit, even if I wanted to.

We take some food to her neighbour upstairs, who's so depressed she can't move from her bed, won't eat. I try to talk to her, but she's only just good for drooling out the side of her mouth right now. Nui shows me her photo album, and I see a picture of this girl on the arm of the handsome collegiate guy, a big US male, who took her on holiday. She looks cheerleader gorgeous, slim, smiling, happy, young. I look at her on the stinking mess of a bed, make-up trodden all over the floor, and it's tough not to do her crying for her. She's overweight, her hair is ratty and discolored, her face is a battlefield, and she's barely conscious. Nui leaves the food, some hot rice noodles in a styrofoam tray, on the floor next to the bed.

The first night I stay there I sleep on my own. Nui has a gig from the agency, fucking a BMW sales executive she knows from last year. She makes some observations about her German clientele that reinforce my prejudices. I lie alone in her bed for a while feeling like, well, an idiot. A sleepless idiot. I pull on my clothes and get a cab to Soi Sii, which is like Whorestock. The only way you're not going to get laid here is if you're somewhere else. I take a beer at the rail of Big Dogs, and wait for closing time at the Nana Entertainment Plaza, which is when a boiling flood of sexworkers spills from the clubs, comely maidens hoping to share a shy glance with that handsome prince of their dreams resting his gut on the rail. The heady air of romance is enhanced by clouds of acrid smoke billowing from food carts burning unrecognisable livestock parts, insects, and other hazmat. I bump into a jolly country lass and we fuck in a short-time hotel, making barnyard noises and laughing until we cry. This is probably the biggest taboo area of Bangkok prostitution. More often than not, it's *no big deal*, just stupid, simple, forgettable fun for both halves of the beast with two backs. Unless you're German, with a suitcase full of rubber funnels.

The second night at Nui's is my last. We're sitting on the bed talking, and from the corner of my eye I'm aware of something dropping past the window, Nui screams, a terrible hoarse cry that frosts my neck hairs, and leaps for the balcony. It's her neighbor down there in the alley, snapped over a wall, the back of her head like a wet geranium. Suddenly, the apartment building is one horrified shriek of katoeys, and the cops will turn up in their own sweet time, so I duck out of there, my bag over my shoulder. I leave a couple of thousand baht on Nui's dresser for drugs. She tells customers she sends her money back home, but I know some of it goes up in smoke, inhaling ya-baa pills burning on a ten baht coin. Amphetamines are diet pills for katoeys, an antidote to the hormones they're taking, which go straight to the hips and thighs. Some do crack, too, but Nui really does send her crack money home, where it's spent by her lesbian sister who's a sales trainer for 7-Eleven specialising in tasty beverages. Trying to figure out the micro-economics of Thai prostitution is as rewarding as trying to inflate a bicycle tire by the power of thought.

Suicide is common among katoeys, it's like their MBA. Nui tried it a few years back, drinking bleach, pretty much the same story as her friend. Broken promises, broken hearts, and the bleak desperation of knowing you can never have what you want – at least not from the lying scumbag businessman with the platinum card and the soccer mom wife picking up the kids in the SUV *at the exact same moment* he's being rimmed by a swivel-eyed crack whore half the world away. Some katoeys win the dream, to be sure, a lucky few get the man and the money and the operation and the *love*, but most just get older, if they live that long, move back home to mind the store and the sister's baby.

It's suffering, all over, and it's exhausting me. Suffering

is what starts Buddha thinking, before he's Buddha, when he's a prince called Siddhartha Gautama, a nice name he should have kept, you ask me. People have issues with that *Buddha* thing. Anyway, Siddhartha sees sickness and death, and, being a smart kid, understands he will grow sick and die, too. Even kings and princes fall apart. So he makes a mad assumption: if everything in the world, and the world itself, is in the process of growing and dying (coming to be, ceasing to be) – and you can't pick a fight with the guy over that – there has to be something that *isn't*. If everything is born, or created, as it evidently is, there has to be something unborn, uncreated. Something that is beyond time, beyond change, and beyond the suffering that comes with dying. So he sets out to find out what it is. He supposes this thing is out there, or in here, and he sets out to find it, without having a clue as to what it is, but a pretty clear idea of what it is not. Which is, everything else.

This is already too far out for most people to want to think about. Buddha's lost about ninety-nine percent of his demographic right there, people are staying away in droves, flipping TV channels, pecking out LOL on YouTube, fucking their best friend's wife, building models of the Chrysler Building out of matchsticks, hang-gliding over active volcanoes, freebasing weedkiller, twisting themselves into yogic pretzels . . . anything at all in this whole wide world but working on this goddamn Buddha crap. Even if they admit there may be something in it, life is too busy, there's just too much to do. There's the job and the kids and the food and the school and . . . Buddha is fine if you've got the time. If you're a hermit or a monk or Richard Gere or the

Dalai Fucking Lama, you can sit on your thumb, cosy up to the ineffable void all the glad afternoon, but excuse me, I have to get this bucket of eels to market, I have to take a meeting, a dump, a hike . . .

Making *suffering* Buddha's big unique selling point, claiming that he's going to end your suffering, is wrong and a lie and a waste of time. Anyway, Catholics have pretty much co-opted the suffering franchise, so if you're into the whole self-important self-obsessed woe-is-me-lord I-have-sinned suffering thing, buy into Catholicism. They got blood and nails and whips enough for everybody over there. Pain and suffering and torture and sin and punishment – this isn't religion, it's pornography.

I get a room in an apartment hotel on the Petchburi Road, a great looming, echoing Tower of Babel, that's either being refurbished or demolished, it's hard to say. This is to be my Lair of Solitude, where I will shake away the sleepless nights and sit on the ledge on the roof, looking at the smoking six-lane highway thirty floors below.

Bring it on, Rahu, you big fucking blowhard, bring it on.

ANNOYING OLD ASSHOLE
WILL WORK FOR FOOD

Dog Djini is lying across my bare foot, making it hot, and I can hear birdsong, a tuk-tuk puttering down to the river, the soft bass thump from the electronics store next door, women speaking Lao in the sunny street. Old Guy is leaning over my shoulder as I type this. His eyesight isn't too great, so he's leaning in to peer at the screen of my laptop.

We sell all kinds of stuff in this shop-house. Buckets, bangles, rat-traps and razors and Rubik's Cubes, vanishing cream and probably something else beginning with v. It's kind of a continuous surprise to me that I'm here, selling Chinese rat-traps on the banks of the Mekhong. I was set for a life of literary ease, sifting idly through offers from major motion picture companies, polishing a briar pipe with the oil from my nose while Peaches, my intern, shakes me a Daiquiri with such enthusiasm her towel falls from her still-wet body. That or flying a desk for an advertising agency with a major san-pro account. Anything but doing what I'm doing and where I'm doing it.

And business is bad all over Thailand right now; the only people making a buck are the government workers. In any Thai town you'll see new SUV pickups, new houses going up, all on credit for government workers (who wear a military-style uniform for authority). The rural poor are barely scraping by. Our shop sells mainly to market traders, the very basis of Thai consumer society, and they're finding it tough to make back the gas money at rural markets, so they aren't buying much wholesale from us. In the couple of years we've been here, business has declined to a trickle, for all the shopkeepers and market traders, not just us. The Thai in the street doesn't have the baht in his pocket any more. But like I say, the government workers are doing very well for themselves, and it's inspiring for the rest of us to see them driving their piano-black Hiluxes through the magnificent gates of their lovely air-conditioned homes after a hard four-hour day in the office securing themselves another bank loan. As an immigrant with no resident's status or work permit, there's nothing I can say or do about this anyway.

I'm fighting a riptide of underachievement just to tread water, and there's still six years of hard labor before I become (according to my astrologer) famous, but day-to-day life isn't a hardship. And there's Old Guy. He sees something in me, or imagines he does, and he works away at me, even when I'm working, like now. He taps the screen with his finger. *Don't do that,* I say, *it leaves a mark on the screen*.

"You need me here, at this point. You're going to do your Buddha bore thing."

Baddha

He sits back in the metal frame folding chair we bought off a street salesman for him to sit in. It's falling apart already, but Old Guy doesn't weigh much. Although I notice he has put on weight since he came to live with us. His coolie hat rests on a box of Chinese rat-traps next to him, you can see the stubble of white hair on his bony scalp, and his riceworker blues are faded but clean.

"Come on," he says. "What are you paying me for?"

Do I have to be here while you do it? I need to take a dump.

"I'll imagine you sitting cross-legged at my feet, gazing up in awe."

The sarcastic fuck. *Whatever works.* I roll sleeping Djini from my foot and put my laptop in Old Guy's lap, strangely not on top of his lap, but in it. *Don't touch the screen. Don't launch any other programs or apps, don't open any other files, don't go on the internet. Don't quit out of anything.*

"Are you gone yet?"

Be right back. I hear him crack his knuckles as I walk away.

"Suffering is not unique to anyone. It's not your suffering, you don't own it. The circumstances that cause it may seem uniquely personal to you, and because you identify the suffering with the cause, you think it's your own personal suffering, and different to other sufferings. Buddha says *consciousness is a general condition, do not own it.*

Consciousness is the sea we all swim in, not your personal pool.

You can define consciousness as all mental activity, anything that causes a spark in that low-watt brain of yours. Thinking, concentrating, imagining, feeling emotions, creating, calculating, dreaming, suffering. That's what consciousness is, there's nothing cosmic or mystical about it. Everybody does it. And as much as you'd like to think that your own mental activity is special and unique to you, it's not. It's a shared thing. Your happiness is exactly the same as everybody else's happiness. There's only one love, one hate, one worry, one contentment, for everybody.

It's like when you go for a swim in the sea, there's a cold patch you swim in and out of, a warm patch, a rough patch, a smooth patch. There are other swimmers all around you, all experencing exactly the same changes that you are. This isn't a cosmic thing, a far-out blissed-out thing, it's very mundane and ordinary. It's the exact opposite of personal and individual, it's communal. Consciousness is the sea we all swim in, not your personal pool. You don't own it, nor any part of it."

That's it? I say, leaning over his shoulder. *This is all you wrote? Thirty-five minutes? For this?*

He shrugs. "Thirty-five minutes for a bowel movement? Anyway, I spent some time reading back over what you've written about me. I don't think I come across as likeable as I am in real life. All this . . . nose-picking."

It's not about you, remember? I take my laptop from him, tilting it in the light. *Look at this, your greasy fingerprints all over. Can't you type without pawing the screen for chrissakes? It's retarded. Like mouthing the words as you read.*

"I do that. I mouth."

I sit down at the desk I bought for my Literary Endeavors that has been co-opted (more usefully) for shop use, and read through his Unique Insights.

You put experencing for experiencing, missed the i.

"Buddha tells us there is no *I*."

I stare at him, thinking, *smartass.*

"I heard that."

Suffering is suffering, I say. *That's why we call it suffering, duh-uh, not a million different things for every time it happens. We all know what suffering is. Some more than others. And if you get rid of the cause of suffering, you get rid of the suffering, there's no need to get all mystical about it. Give a starving man a meal, he stops suffering from starvation. Duh. Duh. Duh.*

"Brilliant. And totally missing my point. You think that by tossing him a cheeseburger this universal quality of suffering will diminish? Or disappear? Drowning men blaming the water. It's not only the quality of mercy that is not strained and droppeth as the gentle rain from heaven, though. Happiness, doubt, erotic arousal -"

Whoah!

"*Irritation* . . . no aspect of consciousness is yours to own, or yours alone to experience."

Groovy, I say.

"Your *I* is not the unique, separated entity you think it is, operating in a kind of cocoon, growing and creating original material that is uniquely you, and your own personal property. Everything you do, all your mental and physical activity, is a shared thing. Nothing special about it. Everything you are, down to atomic level, is shared. You are shared."

Maybe this is just me, but the cosmicness of your words is mitigated somewhat by the fact you're picking your nose.

He wipes it off somewhere under the chair. I'm never going to fold that sucker up.

"You *understand* what I say about the self," he continues in a very patient voice, "but you're still formulating your opinion, like it's been presented for your consideration, in the hope of winning your incredibly valuable and rarely-bestowed seal of approval. In your opinion, what I tell you is my *opinion*. Opinions are weeds. They're not *like* weeds. Opinions *are* weeds. They grow without you planting them, and they grow over everything. Most people are lazy gardeners, especially Americans. They reduce everything to opinion, and their's is as good as anyone else's. A nation of arrogant, stupid weed-gardeners."

I believe some Americans do rate weed highly.

"*Belief* is just a particularly deep-rooted opinion. Everyone thinks their belief is really precious and *justified*, but that's all it is, an out-of-control weed that covers everything and stops the good stuff from growing. But it's not just opinions and belief that trip you up, *understanding* does its bit to fool you, too. You're an educated man, you understand what I say to you, but as soon as you understand it, you feel you've bettered it, and you file it away on the dusty shelf in the back room."

You're so smart, I say. *How come you're not rich?*

"I could describe the sensation of eating an apple and you'd understand, but you wouldn't be eating the apple. Knowing about apples has nothing to do with the experience of eating one."

Apples! They're my favorite metaphorical device. I set aside the Sudoku puzzle I've been doing during his lecture. *Know what? You have some nerve to tell me I'm a Buddha bore. I mean, do you ever listen to yourself? All you need is an Indian accent and some flowers round your neck.*

Djini barks, paddling her front paws in welcome. My wife is back from the market with grilled chicken wrapped in banana leaf, and spicy sauce and sticky rice. And – a bag of apples.

Old Guy chuckles, a little bit smugly I think.

THE SEX TOURIST HAS ISSUES
WITH WHITE WOMEN AND BACKPACKERS

Siem Reap Old Town is party town. Plus, you can buy a visa from any travel agent. It's not like Thailand, where they think it's really smart to make it a pain in the ass for ex-pats to live there. Cambodia sucks your bucks like a one-eyed whore. I've just bought a year's business visa over the counter, because I'm here on business, apparently. I've rented an entire house with a cracked cement yard and a hammock for a third the price of a guesthouse room, and I don't have to share it with backpackers, either, although the town is infested with them.

They're all over South East Asia, like a rash, haggling mercilessly with shoe-less market traders because they think they're being ripped off. Rough Planeteers – you know, *white tourists* – have turned the third world into a resort, developing the internet cafés and smoothie bars and surf stores and Irish Pubs and chill-out zones that the locals have been deprived of for way too long. Siem Reap is like the flagship of this global corporation – *Planet Khmer*, built on a landfill of old Rough Planet guides. The streets are clogged with groups of young white women doing that slumped, round-backed slo-mo shuffle in the hot sun. They wear bare-arm spaghetti-strap tops that show a lot of wobbly, sunburned cleavage and a white-chocolate bulge of flesh above the waistband of their low-slung pants, and each of them carries a bottle of water. They're on Mars, they could die of thirst.

Asian women don't dress like they're on the beach, they dress modestly, but white women don't seem to want to follow their fine example and cover up. They're on *holiday*, and want to be *comfortable*, and *tan*. So they dress like male sex tourists in Bangkok, in beach clothes. Male Rough Planeteers tend to go for long shorts with more pockets than a pool hall, even the pockets have pockets, and stagger under coffin-sized backpacks, bristling with straps and netting and clips and zippers and even more pockets, that have me wondering what the fuck they carry in there – sides of beef? A refrigerator? My own luggage is barely bigger than an overnight bag, and I don't dress in beach clothes, not even in Bangkok.

Then there's the sub-group of backpackers who like to think of themselves as *travellers*, or – oooh! – *nomads*. They're easily recognised by their White Rasta dreadlocks and sneering expressions. The White Rasta comes in virtually indistinguishable male and female forms, equally skinny (*gotta* be skinny) and grubby-looking, and dressed in clothes any Asian peasant would happy to drop in the trash. White

Rastas affect these threadbare fisherman pants and sagging army tee shirts to bond with the poor peoples of the earth, to not flaunt their Western wealth. The poor peoples of the earth, meanwhile, who are nothing if not realists, say *Why dress like that if you can afford not to? Why not get a haircut when you can afford one? We're, like, WTF?* White Rastas come over here laden not only with their hairstyles and tribal face piercing but with guilt and shame for Western wealth and extravagance. I've never yet met an Asian who sneered at a good pair of shoes or a gold watch or an ironed shirt. The poor over here respect wealth, because they don't have it. They're not offended by its display. They don't resent you for it, they're even – incredible as it may seem – happy for you. The first time I heard the phrase *good for you!* in Thailand, I weighted it with sarcasm, as in, *yeah, good for you, you selfish fuck,* like we'd use it in the West. But they don't use the phrase in that twisted way, they really mean it. You're doing well, and probably because you were good in a previous lifetime. Good actions reap good fortune – so when they see your rewards, they think you've made a lot of merit, and *good for you.*

So Asian puzzlement with the mud-loving eco-friendly White Rastas – who come over on ozone-frying airplanes with credit cards and visas, like all the other tourists, and have well-built family homes they can nomad back to when the funds get low – is genuine and profound. It's also worth mentioning that these guys spend the least of any tourist. They never tip, always haggle, because they don't want to upset the fragile economic micro-climate with a sudden influx of their wealth. You know, give a guy enough to feed his family today, and he'll want two meals tomorrow, and that's not *sustainable*. These vain, hypocritical, privileged, smug, and *stupid-looking* sons-of-bitches porter their roughly-coiled tresses across the earth, ticking off cool destinations in their battered Rough Planet books, *in the fatuous belief they're outside the planet-destroying tourist industry*, before jetting home for a pulse shower and that internship at Microsoft. And hey, how cool is that?

Siem Reap is also flypaper for another type of tourist – the Non-Governmental Organisation volunteer. In Siem Reap, a lot of these are women – white, middle-class women – exporting their white, middle-class women's *issues* to Khmer women. I'm sitting upstairs in the Blue Pumpkin, a bakery restaurant with generously deep and comfortable white seats along two walls, like beds, and subtly stylish, very European décor. I come here to sleep because it's cooler and more comfortable than sleeping in my house, and the waitresses are sweethearts and don't wake me up. But today I'm roused from my precious slumbers by a group of these NGO volunteers starting a meeting at a table in front of me, the big table with the bundles of dried grasses. They've all ordered sinful cakes, exchanging hopeless *there-goes-the-diet* eye-rolls, and they all seem to have dressed from the same Caring Women's Earth Planet mailorder catalog. Loose clothes in subtle earth tones and natural fibers, cotton and hemp and Khmer silk, with their hair up in bands or cut sensibly short for the climate. They wear those shoes that look like bath toys, or earth-conscious leather sandals, or cute little Nike pumps with those short "I don't wear socks" socks. If they're wearing make-up, it's not on their faces.

Some of them open laptops. An arty-looking and authoritative woman with red-framed glasses on a chain (who I've seen at the Foreign Correspondents Club, the other favored venue for airconditioned caring outreach sessions) passes some papers around, and they all make sure everybody has a copy, smiling and chatting and taking big-eyed guilty forkfuls of chocolate cake. It's the *most* fun.

The boss tinks her iced coffee glass with her cake fork and they all fall silent. I hear her say, *Welcome, especially to our new faces*, and a big, creamy, oestrogen-rich simper passes round the table. *As you all know, the WWWI mission here in Siem Reap is to* make a difference *for Khmer women.* . .

That fucking horrible phrase, *making a difference*, makes me raise my voice to match my hackles. *Yeah. Where are the Khmer women?*

Heads turn, and the boss eyes me over her red-framed glasses. *Excuse me?*

There are no Khmer women at your table. They're all breaking their backs in the fields or getting punched in the face by their drunken husbands. But I'm sure if they knew you were here eating cakes it'd be a big fucking relief.

I stand up, a little unsteadily, buffeted by the waves of hostility. I smile thinly as I walk past the table. *Ladies . . .*

I can hear their outraged voices as I go downstairs to pay my check. Well, I would have done, had I made this devastating speech, but it's something I've only just typed. I *think* all this stuff at the time, but it's not composed, it's just pissed off. At the time, I keep my thoughts to myself because, although they're morally and factually *right*, they'd help nothing and nobody voiced out loud. The WWWI (which stands for White Women With Issues – I forget the actual acronym of this particular association) would have seen this redfaced old sex tourist in a creased Hawaiian shirt, *obviously the worse for drink, I mean, really, as if our poor Khmer sisters don't have enough problems without types like that coming over, it's disgusting*, and become even more entrenched in their *issues*. Issues come off white women like chlorine off a public swimming pool.

I'd seen other representatives of this fine organisation in Bangkok go-go bars, actually weeping, crying real tears for the poor girls enslaved by the sex industry and forced to parade their nakedness in front of the scum of the earth. The dancers, up there out of their own free will and getting paid good money for dancing and fucking (which is what they do on their day off anyway), regard their distressed white sisters with something close to contempt. A white woman never has a good time in a go-go bar, even if she goes in for one, in the adventurous spirit of sampling Bangkok's naughty nightlife. *Never again!* she spits as she sweeps out (already composing the impassioned and informed email she'll send to the girls back home on the subject), her reluctant male partner dragged in her wake like a sodden sack of waste. One of the saddest sights in the city is the Male Partner, so very *not* looking at all the girls he could have had if he'd thrown his wife off the plane. I struggle to come up with an analogy for this, but *it's like taking your wife to Bangkok* is already the analogy for something else too horrible to think about. Bangkok is Boy's Town, and the WWWI would like to carpet-bomb the

Sukhumvit Road simply because of that. It's one of the last places on earth where a guy can surprise himself with how much fun he can stand before he blacks out, and as such constitutes a valuable fieldwork laboratory for outreach sociologists specialising in Men's Issues, such as myself.

It's also the reason I leave. I've had enough of bellying up to the bar with types I don't like the look of (who look something like me), drinking beers I don't enjoy, and taking a girl because I can, rather than because I want to. If you're in Bangkok, you can't *not* go out at night. You sit in your room on your own, you might as well be living with your parents, or your wife, wishing you were somewhere else. Like Bangkok. And once you're out, you can't *not* have a drink. It flies in the face of reason to be out and not have a drink – it's sheer recklessness. And you can't have just one. And after you've sampled one or two tasty beverages, it seems downright obnoxious *not* to respond charitably to the kind attentions of the exotic beauty writhing in your lap, after all the trouble she's taken stripping down to her lipstick. I mean, what you going to do? Take your hard-on home and beat it to death with your Rough Planet book?

But although the thrill has gone, the expense hasn't, so I must be. I make a policy decision, to keep Bangkok as the R and R destination, and get back to the Buddha business, which I've been neglecting. Well, not neglecting entirely. I carry my Soundbite Buddha in my pocket always, open it at random, there's always something inspiring, eventually revelatory. For a tough guy who knows that there is no Santa Claus on the evening train, Buddha can be surprisingly comforting. I even dip into the book in go-go bars, to distract myself from the sex-worker convention going on around me. But I know whatever I'm looking for – what flipped the bottle cap in Burma – isn't going to be found here, in Boy's Town. I've looked. I've *really* looked. The Tower of Babel on the Petchburi Road has been my home for, I don't know, months. I've bought a refrigerator the size of a television and a television the size of a refrigerator, and a bowl and a spoon for my breakfast cereal. In spite of my rigorous anti-religion stance, every morning I perform the pointless and superstitious ritual of opening my grubby MacBook (keyboard warping in the heat) and troweling more wordage on my novel. I haven't done much sleeping here, but I haven't done much diving from the roof, either. Rahu's shit-storm is still whirling about me, I'm still a mess, but I'm still alive, and somewhere out there – away from the harsh grate and grind of the city – a scented breeze has to be blowing.

So that's why I'm here, a do-gooding NGO volunteer, standing in the scented breeze of the air-con at the counter of the Blue Pumpkin. While I'm waiting for my change, I notice the torn corner of Frog's hallucinogenic business card poking out of my wallet, and check the clock on the wall. I can get to Angkor Wat in thirty minutes, it'd hit in an hour or so, peak around, ooh, two or three pm, smooth out nicely around dusk. The checkout girl – cardiac arrestingly cute, in black t-shirt and jeans and her hair pinned up in a square of orange cloth, showing the lovely nape of her neck – looks at me strangely as I put the card into my mouth and start to chew.

THE DANCE OF THE AMPUTEES

I choose Siem Reap because it's close to the Angkor Wat temple complex I want to visit, and because I have an unlikely contact, Julius Krist, a born-again Jesus freak I've insulted on the internet who works for an NGO here, the Luckless Cambodian Sons Of Bitches Association. I'm not the type to defuse landmines or dig septic tanks or do anything that involves getting my thumb out my ass, but Krist (maybe he comes to me in a dream) suggests I visit and work on their web site, which is a mess. And hey, words is my business. I'm also hoping that immersing myself in other people's problems will loosen the sick and destructive hold my own have on me.

The LCSOBA headquarters is a little way off Airport Road, which is as ugly a strip of development as you'll find outside L.A. Mall-sized hotels heave up out of the red soil, catering mainly to Koreans and the Asian tourist industry. They're heavy on the red and gold plastic signage and Disneyland "oriental" architectural brutality, and the blocks are interspersed with "respectable" massage and karaoke joints, set back from the road. The entire strip is enclosed with "ironic" quote marks, but nobody sees them. Which is kind of ironic. The tour buses are nearly as big as the hotels, great three-storied karaoke palaces with ruched curtains and violet halogen lighting in the engine compartment and shrieking paintjobs designed by schoolboys. I've given my tuk-tuk driver a print-out of directions from the web site, in loopy Cambodian script. He has to confer with four other drivers for ten minutes to understand them, and even then we make a wrong turn. He makes another left off the main road and we're soon on a pink dirt track, sending up plumes of soft dust, like theatrical make-up. We bounce past palmleaf shacks, litter, some more litter. I'm guessing this is another of Marco Polo's wrong turns when we lurch through the gateposts of a big house in a scrappy-looking yard.

The LCSOBA is one of many NGOs fighting for funding in Siem Reap. The money comes from individual contributions, corporate sponsorship, sales of handicrafts or whatever, and highly-prized UN handouts. It's a big, big industry with well-paid desk jobs, but you wouldn't know it from looking at the LCSOBA headquarters.

The house looks like a failed businessman's idea of a family home, with Palace of Versailles-type gates (the gates are always the first to be built, as a bold statement of wealth), and an ugly bulge of a balcony with glans-purple ceramic "Greek-style" columns and stainless steel railing. But like countless other such optimistic ventures in South East Asia, the money ran out and so did the businessman, leaving

Xanadu unfinished. Ground level construction has hardly begun, leaving a completed upper floor resting on concrete pillars. In the yard some rickety school desks are shunted together under the trees, with plastic beer banners strung up for shade, and a lot of litter and busted bicycles and whatever spreads into the house, pecked through by skinny, disgusted-looking hens. In the shade of the house, there's a busted-up couch and armchairs where a broad timber staircase curves up to the second floor.

The place looks deserted. But strangely, and it's something to do with the silence, the suddenly-noticed stillness of the place, a feeling of calm washes over me, a familiar feeling, like the embrace of an old friend.

I feel the sun on my shoulders, working its way into my stiff bones. The air hums with color, that spiced-up spectrum you only get in the east. I close my eyes, feel the slow tide of my breath lift me up, let me go, lift me up, let me go. I can smell the dust, the red dust. Breathe in, breathe out . . .

"I'm over here."

I open my eyes. In the shade beneath the house I make out a figure stretched out along the couch. I raise my hand to screen the glare of the house, the streaked white-painted cement. It's an old guy, his coolie hat on the floor next to him. He stirs as I get nearer, swings his skinny legs around and sits, rubbing his stubbly jaw with a big bony hand. Fingers like roots, polished knuckles.

Hello? I say.

I can see his eye gleam in the shade, and he gives me a big gap-toothed smile.

"We meet again."

I'm surprised as much by his perfect English as what he says. I drop my bag, outraging a chicken, and sit down gently in one of the armchairs, like it's made of glass. *I'm sorry – we've met?*

"You don't remember? A karaoke bar in southern Thailand. You'd just come from the temple retreat. Where they teach breathing meditation."

I'm really trying to place him. I remember the meditation place, the dead cat, and I remember the waitress at the bar down the road, up in her room, watching a cement-gray lizard as big as my forearm climb the wall behind her head as I fuck her. It's hard to see through that to anything else, but I dimly remember an old guy coming to sit at my table, and yes, it could be this old guy, but they all look alike to me. I shake my head.

I'm sorry, I don't recall . . . that was, what, a year back? What brings you here?

"You do."

It occurs to me he may be here to act as translator. Krist told me he doesn't speak Khmer. That must be it.

I cough. My throat is dry. *Right!* I look around me. *Where is everybody?*

"They're in town, there's a show. They do Apsara dancing."

They're dancers? I thought they were . . .

"Cripples? Yes. They dance with what they have, like anybody else."

I can't think of anything to say. But he can. Only a few words into his speech, and I remember who he is.

"Buddha is a word that means *awake*."

I can visualise him talking about soccer players ...
Toyotas? His voice is quiet, precise, like he enjoys the sound
of it. An old voice, like dry leaves.

"It's also used as a name, but it's like calling someone *Awake* in English. It's what he was called after waking
up."

And while I'm doing this remembering, I'm not really
listening to what he says. It doesn't sink in. I'm too busy
wondering at him, the stubble of white hair on his head,
the missing tooth, the cataract over one eye. His plastic
coolie hat and riceworker clothes.

"First he realised he was sleeping, then he found out how
to wake up, then he woke up. This is really simple. It is also
the hardest thing in the world."

It's freaking me out. He's not the translator. He hasn't
even followed me here – he was here ahead of me.

"You don't listen to a word I say, do you?"

*Sure I do. It's just, ah, not a good time for this, uh, Buddha
stuff right now.*

"There's never another time for this, *uh, Buddha stuff.*
There's nothing more important." He picks up his hat and
fixes it on his head, his long hands spreading on the plastic
weave, and I see the ugly scooped-out scar on his elbow as
his sleeve rides up. "It's also all there is. Everything else is
a distraction. Craziness."

He looks past me toward the road, and I hear my name
called, and this gangly-looking type lopes up the driveway,
with a kind of apologetic slope to his shoulders, a big grin
on his face. I recognise him from the web site, only he has
less hair than his photograph. I step out into the sun, and

we shake hands. And while we're talking, I'm thinking, I'm not going to look back, because if the old guy is still there, he's crazy, and if he's gone, I am.

Later, his words come back to me (and he does too). It's an important thing, this Buddha-name, because if we think of him as *Awake*, and not Buddha, all the boring, tired Buddhist crap falls away, and we're left with something fresh, without baggage, the way we should approach him. One day a long time ago, someone meets Buddha, and is impressed by the calm and beauty of the guy, and very politely asks if he's a god. Buddha says, "No, I'm not a god". Are you an angel, then? "No, I'm not an angel." A spirit? "No, not a spirit." Then what are you? "I'm Awake."

That's his name. And this *awake* aspect is the most important thing about Buddha, the quality that makes him what he is. He's no longer Siddhartha Gautama (Bill Smith), he is transformed. And understanding this change, getting some kind of grasp on what happened, defeats most people. But there's a simpler, easier way of doing Buddha-business. Don't concern yourself with what he is, and the difference between him and Siddhartha Gautama and us. Don't try to think about what being *awake* means. What concerns you right now is your own state of sleeping. If Buddha is awake, it follows that the rest of us are asleep. There's obviously some kind of word-play we have to do at this stage, because we know we fall asleep at night and wake up in the morning. We are awake already, yes?

When you wake up in the morning, there's no doubt in your mind that you're awake, and your state of mind is utterly different to the dream-state of sleep. You're not confused or unsure if you're still asleep and dreaming, you *know* you're awake, and the difference is obvious. It's like a totally different world. You can move around, do things, experience the world around you, interact with others.

What Buddha experiences is so different to our normal state of wakefulness, it makes ordinary day-to-day consciousness seem like sleep in comparison. There's no doubt or confusion in his mind, he *knows* what's happened, he *knows* he's woken up from a deep sleep, and he can remember his old waking state like we remember our dreams.

How would you describe your own *awake* to a sleeping man? How would you tell him he's asleep? This is the problem Buddha has. He wakes up, and he finds himself in a world of sleepwalkers. But some of these sleepwalkers are dimly conscious that they're dreaming, and it's these guys he wants to speak to. He doesn't have the power to wake them up – he's not a god (nor even the son of God) or a saint or a miracle-worker, and he's not here to save our souls or any other imagined sub-division of the self.

He's *Awake*, and his voice is a whisper in your sleeping ear. If it's too difficult to hear, well, you dance with what you have.

LAST NIGHT IN THE STARS
FOR THE VOODOO PRINCESS

I don't see Nui for some weeks after her friend's swallow dive onto a broken glass-topped wall. I call her, she calls me. Everybody's linked the suicide to the destruction of the apartment block's spirit house, which used to stand on the corner before a drunken tuk-tuk driver drove into it and dragged the wreckage down the street, a clear sign that something bad was going to happen. A collection has paid for a new spirit house, duly blessed by a monk, but the tenants are moving out anyway, and Nui is one of the first, because the girl's ghost is sure to haunt the hallways. Thai belief in ghosts is unshakeable. They play major roles in TV soap operas, and appear as anti-smoking warnings on cigarette packets. I'm disinclined to scoff. Ghosts make as much sense as weather forecasts or the stock market. So Nui's staying with some of her family, and she's not a hooker anymore. I ask her where she'll get her money from, and she says not to worry, she won't need as much if she's not a hooker anyway, with that beautiful Thai logic. I say, let's meet, one more time for the old times. She says, it won't be cheap, and I say, you never were.

She wears a short oyster-colored linen jacket with a wide neckline and a broad diagonal collar, black cigarette pants, patent pumps, purse to match. Jewellery restricted to small pearl earrings and a tiny gold watch. This is a long way from how most Bangkok hookers dress, but Nui's clients haven't been off the street, either.

I've done my best, in my one good shirt I had cleaned and ironed, and good black jeans, and I remembered to shave my ears. When I do this, or reap the rich harvest in my nostrils, it is a mystery to me why the hair on my scalp suddenly decides to move south. Maybe because it's retired, and the climate's kinder down there. Anyway, I am grateful to the gray old-timers that cantankerously refuse to quit the old homestead. Not quite enough of them to club together for a combover, but I like to think they add a saintly nimbus to my noggin. Not that any hooker gives a shit about your hair, anyway, or any of the other things you think are so vital to your manhood and so impressive to the fairer sex. They've seen better than you, and will again. You're just another guy with a bone and a bank account – they're not smiling because they *like* you. Far from inflating male vanity, whoring can be a humbling experience, like visiting a cathedral. Better men than you have entered before you, and you're not likely to be remembered for long no matter how good you are.

This cocktail bar is up in the sky, on the roof of a five-star hotel close to the river. It's another world to the one I'm used to, but it's still a whorehouse. Girls sit at the bar, their legs crossed, waiting for Corporate Man to charm them off their heels. It turns out that I dressed exactly right. Here, Corporate Man relaxes in an open-neck white shirt and jeans, kicks back after a hard day doing whatever it is he does that requires a business trip to Bangkok. *Night life! I wish! If I know Bill, it'll be non-stop meetings, meetings, meetings. I'll be glad to get home for a break!* I've heard so many conversations like that, the weary sales exec Skyping home from the hotel lobby, making sure his exotic assistant (checking her makeup with the camera on her phone) is out of shot. Meanwhile, *Bill* is getting his cock sucked in the shower.

The barman nods to Nui, smiles, slides napkins in front of us, a two-handed semicircular motion. Nui has what she usually has, apparently, which is pink, unpronounceable, with a lotus flower in it, and I have a Daiquiri, which he knows how to make, without throwing in any garden produce, and the glass has a frosted salt rim. Everything is perfect. The bar is open to the stars, and we find a seat on the cushions next to the rail, look out over the dragon's-eye glitter of Bangkok. There's a jazz trio playing on a raised stage, some way up from the bar, right on a high corner of the building, like they're in the sky, and a rooftop restaurant on a lower level, with candlelit tables. It's like we're floating, and there's an atmosphere of calm and delight. No loud conversation or laughter, no need for that. We're skimming up here, it's the mile-high club.

As breathtaking as the place is, it's just a setting for Nui's brilliance. I get a lot of pleasure watching the heads turn, the sneaky glances she gets from men with partners, and the stares from their girlfriends, who flick sidelong looks to make sure their boyfriends aren't looking too. It's her business to look perfect. Her clients don't want a shrieking great trannie with her tits in the soup, painted up like a carnival float. Well, Frog does, but he won't find one here.

You know this place, I say.

She smiles. *Oh yes. And I have never, ever, had to pay for my own drink. I sit at the bar, ten minutes, I have company.*

Do they know? I mean . . .

If they pay enough, they get to find out. Then it's up to them.

Ever get any disappointed customers?

She shakes her head and laughs, her hand going to her mouth. Thais consider it bad manners to show you the inside of their mouth. *I give them a few hints before we get to their room.*

I look away. The view is stunning everywhere, but nothing compared to her eyes. Look into those for any length of time, you start to feel funny. Your compass spins.

One of the many questions my ex-wives would like to put to me from the audience is, *what can you and a prostitute half your age possibly find to talk about?* I'm guessing that question is fairly low down their list, but it's relevant here, and so I'll take it. First, Nui is thirty-one, and not a girl in more senses than one. Second, she can talk about pretty much anything, reads the Trib, watches CNN, keeps up with all the major sporting competitions, golf, soccer, formula one motorsport, boxing. Plus she watches movies, reads magazines, and even listens to the BBC World Service. She's more wired to the world than I am, and can chat about any of it as much as you want. I admit she's an exception, and most hookers only know enough English to do their job, which is five words and some numbers, but the point is you don't pay them for conversation. I'm tired of conversation, anyway. It's over-rated. It's fine in your smart-ass twenties when you know everything and can impress your oh-so-clever friends, but as you grow older you should talk less, think more. You should have done enough to think about.

I certainly listen more with Nui, because she has some interesting stuff to say about none of the above. She's an old school animist Buddhist, whose beliefs and practices predate the man we know as Buddha by millennia. Offerings and augury, spells and potions – all the magic that Buddha has no time for and speaks against. She's spooky. She does a card trick, where she guesses the card you're holding. I once ask her how she knows which card I choose, and she looks puzzled for a second and says, *I choose it,* as if it's obvious. What am I, stupid?

Call me a giddy old fool, but there's magic in the air tonight. We both know it's her swansong. She's quitting while she still can, at the top of her game. We get drunk on one drink, our heads spinning. She puts the lotus flower behind her ear.

We walk out into Bangkok, through a dark maze of narrow back streets to a Chinese temple, crimson and gilt, blurred in incense smoke. There's some paintings of Buddha's life, with all the gods and miracles. One picture shows a beautiful woman, a princess, an Apsara dancer. Nui asks me how many people are in the picture. *One*. I've disappointed her. I look again. A tiny Buddha is carried in a white flame above the princess's head. *Two*.

We kneel at an oracle, a rack of papers. There's about a hundred numbered sticks, like big chopsticks, in a lacquered cylinder. You rattle the cylinder until a stick works free and falls out, and you check the paper that corresponds to your number. Nui goes first. Number two. She replaces the stick, passes the cylinder to me. I shake it. Eventually, a single stick works its way out and clatters to the floor. I pick it up, squint at the number inked on the end. *Two*. She gives me a sidelong glance. *How many people are in the picture?*

Out in the street, Bangkok whirls around her holy head. I ask her if she wants to come back with me, and she closes her long eyes.

And all the lights in Bangkok go out.

SHOWER GEL, TOOTHPASTE

I find Old Guy in his hammock by the river. The shop isn't busy, and there's no box-flattening or portering for him to do, so if he's not occupied with something he likes to take a look at the river, mostly through his eyelids. The Mekhong here is broad and tricky with sandbanks and hidden shallows, so there's no shipping, no big traffic at all, just the stone-gray longboats, the lone fisherman crouched on the prow, checking his lines hand over hand, somehow in perfect control of his twenty-foot craft in the current. And there's the occasional covered ferry over to Laos, busy on market day. Old Guy strung himself a hammock the day he arrived, between the concrete pillars under the riverfront walk. You have to hop the rail to get down there, but he's surprisingly nimble.

I take a couple of cold bottles of Beer Leo, pop them with a bottle-opener I bought from a guy in a Burmese bar. It's a beautiful piece of design, the most perfect object I own.

A piece of wood about the size of a knife handle, with a bolt through one end. You hook the bolthead under the cap, press down gently, and the cap lifts off. It's such a simple piece of equipment and it works so beautifully, yet nobody I show it to can work out what it's for. The guy in the bar wanted to give me a new one, but I wanted his, worn smooth, scarred, the bolt rusted to black.

I lean back against a pillar, feeling the cool air drift from the void under the walkway. The Mekhong is hammered copper today, under a silk blue sky, and the Lao People's Democratic Republic looks jungley and low on the far bank. A few clicks further, you're in Viet Nam. Old Guy sips his beer, as always, like it's the first and last time, savors it. Then, his throat lubricated, he gets into gear.

"Understanding what Buddha means by *self*, as a temporary combination of elements, none of which contains the self, and *consciousness*, as communal property, isn't too hard, if you can forget your opinions on the subject for a while. Buddha doesn't care for your opinions, and nor do I, but more importantly, nor should you. This leaves nearly every American out of the equation," (I don't rise to the bait) "because they're incapable of thinking without forming an opinion, and mostly that opinion is expressed as *sucks/rocks*. Although *stuff* can be *cool*, too. The sucks/rocks stuff is cool, because it sums up the West's dualistic, linear thinking."

Uh-oh, I say. *Big Words advisory.*

"Dualistic thinking involves positioning opposites at each end of a line. Sucks at one end, rocks at the other, degrees of suckiness and rockiness in between. Good, bad. Hot, cold. One-hundred-per-cent extremes at each end."

Inside, outside.

"And ne'er the twain shall meet. The tiller is not mixed with the bowsprit. Eastern thinking isn't straight line thinking, it's cyclical. Understand this small word, cyclical, and you're well on your way to getting a good hold on what Buddha was all about. It's important."

Important, unimportant.

"You want to hear what Buddha says about non-duality?"

I get the feeling you're going to tell me anyway.

"Light and shade, long and short, black and white can only be experienced in relation to each other. Light is not independent of shade, nor black of white. There are no opposites, only relationships."

So?

"So, Little Grasshopper, what you think of as an opposite, an extreme at the end of the line, is only a point on a cycle, and the cycle turns, that's the point of it. There is no black without white, they are both changing moments on a single black/white cycle. There is no breathing in, no breathing out, only breathing. They are the *exact same thing* viewed at different times during the cycle, the one always changing into the other. Your consciousness is like a series of snapshots. You see these cycles in cross-section, simplified. You live in flat world. Snap! Good. Snap! Hot. Snap! Heavy. These qualities are not fixed, and have no independent reality of their own. You only think of them as fixed and real because of your restricted point of view."

Male, female.

"Right. In the West, you have a big problem with the male/female cycle. You struggle to nail down the absolutes, the one-hundred-per-cent alpha male, the total female, neither of whom exists, except as an ideal. You've noticed we're not so worried about that out here. To call sexuality a gray area is to deprive it of its color, its broad and vivid spectrum. Nobody's worried about where they are on the masculine/feminine cycle. It's a matter of complete indifference, and there is no moral aspect attached to it. You're as masculine/feminine as your position on the cycle, like everyone else. No one position is better or more correct or more justified or more rewarded or reviled than any other."

He takes a hit of the cold beer, and seems to have lost his thread. *Cycles,* I prompt.

"The wheel is seen a lot in Buddhist imagery, and it's normally dressed up in liturgical symbolism, the number of spokes symbolising the eightfold path or whatever. It's usually understood as the cycle of birth and re-birth, which is popularly misunderstood as reincarnation, a deep-rooted weed that's very hard to pull up. Buddha is explicit in denying reincarnation as it is popularly conceived, but he knew when to back off. Arguing for or against reincarnation is unnecessary, like worrying about the existence of a soul. It's a waste of time, off the point. The wheel means the turning cycle," he moves his beer can in a circle, as a visual aid for the hard of hearing, "and that's it, that's everything you need to know. Simple, but limitlessly profound. Everything is a cycle. Your body as a whole has its own life-cycle, but its individual components have their own cycles within that larger cycle. The liver renews itself every eighteen months or so, the skeleton is entirely replaced every decade. Everything in the world is a cycle, turning at its own pace, and is both part of a larger system of cycles and comprised of smaller ones. Our planet is one cycle, as is the sun, the solar system, this can of beer, and the belch I feel gestating in my belly. Wheels within wheels, and all interlinked, interdependent."

He tucks his chin in, belches through his clenched teeth.

"This isn't the province of mystics or physicists, it's apparent to anyone who's watched the sun come up and thought about it a bit. Are you taking *notes*?"

I look up from the pocket notebook I'm writing in. *Don't flatter yourself. It's a shopping list.*

"You're taking notes!"

I am not. Look – I wave the book at him, *shower gel, toothpaste.*

"You just added those at the end. You're writing a book about me."

It's not about you.

"So you've started it." Smirk.

I haven't been writing for over a year. My novel got rave reviews from publishers who didn't want to publish it (*I couldn't put it down*, and *too well-written for the genre* among my favorites), and I'm, like, WTF?! I'd had so much faith in it, and it was nearly all I had to keep my days strung together, and it's disappeared into nothing at all. Two years' work. Fuck, fuck, fuck. But Old Guy keeps giving me this Buddha crap, which I don't ask for but won't go away, and so I'm trying to get it into some kind of order. Which is a problem, because there is no systematic way into it, no order to set it down. Buddha doesn't teach a system, with ordered steps of increasing difficulty. "I don't teach the truth, because the truth can't be taught, only experienced. I don't teach a system for knowing the truth, because the truth cannot be broken up and ordered into a system." The more I think about this guy, the more I like him. No promises, no demands, no claims, no bullshit. But we like systems, and learning without one is . . . well, you can't get there from here.

The only way you can get into this is any old way at all. It doesn't matter. There may seem to be many different aspects (self, consciousness, cycles, whatever) but they're all only slightly different views of the same thing, there's no step-by-step order to them. Buddha pitches the same ball over and over, changing the spin on it each time, in the hope that you'll catch it one way if not the other. But there's no way you're going to pick up useful *information* about the process, either in what Buddha says or anywhere else. Knowledge, information, and learning are useful, but you have to see their limits. If truth could be taught, it could be learned, and it would become knowledge and information (all those dead files on the dusty shelf in the back room), but truth is not to be known or held that way.

Buddha uses the analogy of a boat you use to get to the other side of the river – when you've landed over there, you don't carry the boat with you. Leaving the boat behind – this beautiful, expensive, impressive craft – is tough. You worked hard for that boat, you like to be Captain, standing at the prow so everyone can see the braid on your cap. You do need to do the learning information bit, but there'll come a time when you need to leave it behind. Unless you're happy being saluted in mid-stream, of course, you big fat pompous jerk.

He flaps his hand. "Book. Book."

I pass it to him. What the fuck. Who cares. He reads aloud in a fake Indian guru accent. "Our planet is its own cycle, as is the sun, the solar system. Wheels within wheels. Shower gel. Toothpaste." He laughs so hard he coughs.

Oh, shut up.

"You left out the bit about the beer and the belch."

It's important?

"Only as important as the solar system, or the shower gel, so no, not very. The ham sandwich you had for lunch is no less remarkable or miraculous than an exploding galaxy a billion light years away, just more familiar. And it's this familiarity – our supposed knowledge and understanding of the world – that prevents us from seeing it. We are familiar with nothing except our own ideas. We spend each day walking around in a cloak of our own ideas. Pencil, pencil."

He puckers his face up in concentration, biting his lower lip with his gappy teeth, the skin on his face creasing like paper as he works. When he's done, his face relaxes, and he appraises his work with satisfaction, head tilted, before passing it back.

"As an old hippy," he says, "You'll be familiar with this."

It's that black and white yin-yang circle symbol, but it's not very round, and he's gone over the lines coloring in the black half. As if reading my mind, he says, "You may think it's badly drawn, but it's perfect, couldn't be done better. This is the exact same thing as the Buddhist wheel, that fancy spoked device. It's the turning cycle. Night, day, everything. The trouble with this symbol is that it's so familiar you see it as a decoration, an emblem with vaguely

Eastern mystical associations. There are more complicated versions, sometimes you see a dot in the center of each half, or Chinese letters or whatever, but this version is nearly the best. It's better without the black-white teardrops, and best without the enclosing circle. The important thing is the idea behind it, the turning, the changing, not the way it's drawn. The changing *is* the turning. Here -"

He reaches out of the hammock, gesturing for the book. He rips out the page and tosses it into the darkness behind him. "There is absolutely no point in looking at it, ever again. It's just a distraction."

And with that he puts his hat over his face and folds his fingers across his chest. I sit for a while, looking at the river, turning the Burmese bottle-opener in my hands for the pleasure of it, and trying not to see metaphors in every damn thing that presents itself.

HIGH FIVE FROM THE MAN
WITH THE STEALTH BOMBER HEAD

Frog-free in Burma. First time around, I trailed in his wake, walked in his shadow, so I feel weirdly exposed the moment I step off the plane, like people are looking at me. Which they generally are in Burma, at any tourist, because they don't get that many, on account of having the filthiest government outside Africa. I already learned not to look at soldiers, so I ignore them on my way across the hot concrete to the new terminal, which is a beautiful piece of contemporary architecture, airy and clean and weirdly calm, on account of the lack of advertising or commerce, as well as the lack of passengers. It's a perfect airport, as simple as they used to be, before mall mentality ruined everything. They'd have the commerce and the advertising in a flash, though, if somebody offered. The junta is anybody's whore, spreads its cheeks for any corporate or national dollar. So maybe by the time you read this, there's a Starbucks and a KFC to cheer the place up.

I'm here to find the monastery where the bottle-cap flipped. And the only way I can find it is to find our driver, Nu Win. I have a print-out of a photograph I took of him at the wheel of his cab (that beautiful smile), and you can see the cab number painted on the door, and I even have a phone number he gave me, which would be great if he still had a cab or a phone. But at least I have his name, which narrows my search down to a few thousand Nu Wins in the Greater Rangoon area.

How hard can it be?

I check in at a hotel I saw the previous visit. It's a shabby place down a side street, but small enough to not have to pay a kickback to the junta, as do all the large hotels and any business that attracts the tourist dollar. And they are dollars, too. Try to pay for a rail ticket or a museum ticket or anything state-run, and they won't take their own currency. The junta may be evil, but it's not stupid (put a pin in that – it actually is stupid), and knows its own currency isn't worth wiping its fat ass on. And as there are no ATMs, you need pockets full of dollar bills, nothing larger, because nothing costs much more than a buck here and your change will be in their waste matter, the kyat. It's bafflingly illegal to take kyat out of the country; if it's worthless here it'll be worth even less anywhere else.

The Rough Planet stance on Burma is an *oooooh-dear-don't-really-know-if-you-should-go* anguish, because tourism swells the coffers of the junta. Spend your money on the street, and it doesn't. Change your money on the black market, where you get three times as much for your native currency as you do from the prison-like state bank, and your money goes straight to the people who need it – the people. The big reason backpackers and *nomads* tend to stay away is they're scared, and nothing to do with personal politics. There are no Rough Planet comfort zones here, no smoothie bars showing back-to-back episodes of Friends where you can top up your iPod with Buddha Bar chill-out mixes. You actually find yourself in a real country, not a tourist destination.

So I'm the only white man in the Happy Favourite Hotel. I can't quite get a handle on the other guests, when we pass in the lobby or on the narrow stairs. Burmese businessmen, maybe. Highwaisted black pants, goldframe aviator glasses, plastic briefcases, but everything scuffed and worn. My room has a door slightly stronger than a bead curtain, and a gray bed that slopes with the floor. There's a shower room that looks like a water-boarding facility, with an emergency toilet in case I can't find a place to shit in the street. The days when I could afford (and was stupid enough) to pay the junta for a lakeside view over the Shwedagon Temple and sushi and cocktail piano stylings are long gone. It's too late at night to visit the taxi square where Frog and I found Nu Win, so I decide to saunter out for a tasty beverage. Maybe I'll meet a girl and we'll fall in love. I hide my passport, taping it under a drawer, and my dollar bills, which I put in the waste bin under the plastic liner. Anyone turning the room over will find them, but I don't want to carry it all with me and there's no safe at the desk. Also, the Burmese have never given me any indication they're a nation of thieves. Crime victims, yes.

In the backstreets of downtown Rangoon, the nightlife

is muted, sporadic, and I don't see any working girls on the streets, which are underlit and treacherous with broken paviors, open drains, tilting concrete slabs, and rats. Rats are the most disrespectful animals, they don't give a fuck, they'll walk over your foot or just sit in your way if they've nothing better to do. I sit at a bar which is like an open storefront, and make my contribution to the junta through a bottle of the excellent state beer, which comes out of a plastic cooler bin full of icewater.

Burmese people are more taciturn than Thais, and rarely pro-actively get glad at you, but they do return a smile with real warmth, not the Thai-lite smile. A skinny young man wearing a too-big safari jacket comes to my table (pre-cast concrete, like the bench seats) and asks if he can sit with me, and we go through the usual. I tell him I'm looking for a friend I made last time, show him the photograph of Nu Win. The chances of him knowing my driver are virtually zero, so it's just something to talk about. But he shows the picture around the bar, there's maybe six or seven drinkers back there, he comes back with real apologies, his face working like it's all his fault my trip to Burma is a total failure. I take back the laser-printed photograph, which is already showing wear, I wish I'd had a gloss print made.

As if to make up for his failure to find Nu Win, my new friend suddenly asks if I want a girl (you know, like, *instead*?) I'm not sure I do, I'm tired and depressed, but I say *well, okay,* and Safari looks delighted at being able to help me. I pay for our beers, and as we walk away he puts his arm through mine, which is disconcerting. It's how male friends walk in Burma, and a beautiful and innocent thing to see, but it's awkward for me, the gesture has too much romance about it, and I'm old enough to be his father. I go with it for a while, then disengage myself on the pretext of taking another look at the picture of Nu Win, and carefully avoid a re-linking. I think I may have hurt his feelings a little, but hey. Then he says he wants me to meet his mother, his home is just around the corner. I don't ask him *why*, it seems impolite, but I get the feeling he wants to show off his new friend from the western world. I try to make some excuse, *maybe some other time*, but he insists, *really, my home is here! Next street!*

His mother is nowhere near as delighted to meet me. The house is lit only from the street, watery neon filtering through the slatted shutters. The room is cluttered, furniture draped with rugs, thick with dust, the boards bend with my weight. I can't make her out at all, just that she's wearing the traditional *longhi*, with a headscarf wrapped around. The room smells of illness, a thick, dirty scent. She mutters something, turning away, and this seems to offend Safari boy. I touch his arm, say, *come on, let's go,* but he still has something to say to his mother, and follows her into the next room. She raises her voice.

There are times when you feel you don't belong somewhere, your presence is a mistake, and this is one of them. I sneak back down the slanting stair to the street, walk quickly away, making turn after turn in the dark, feeling all wrong, feeling lost. This isn't normally a problem, I've learned that not knowing where I am can be a great and liberating thing, it's only a matter of time before I find a familiar corner. But tonight, getting lost is part of the homeless, hopeless flailing, a desperate thing. My memories of the previous visit are all golden, hazy, beautiful, open, and this time around everything is shut in and dark. I know I won't find Nu Win, I won't find the Snake Pagoda, it won't happen again. I got a glimpse and in some ways it has fucked me up, not made me wiser or more content.

When life sucks, we think that's how life *is*. Life is shit and then you die. When it rocks, this is how life *should* be! This is *living!* And when sucks changes to rocks, we get a feeling of personal justification, as if we're owed this good stuff, we've paid our dues. And when the good times change to bad, we feel like our good fortune has been stolen from us, like it was our own personal property.

When you're down and out, that's how *you* are, not how it is. And when you're down and out, you can't step aside and see the state you're in, because you identify completely with the suffering, you *are* the suffering. When you're on a roll, of course, seeing your good fortune and good mood as a passing thing is the last thing you want to do. Step off the wave just so you can see it? What are you, nuts?

Getting a distance from the good and the bad as they happen, not owning the feelings, being aware of them coming and going, isn't easy. Nothing Buddha says is easy. You want easy, make a confession to a priest. Go to church. Pray. Chant a mantra. Watch TV. Put this down and check your Facebook page, LOL.

The black streets I walk aren't *me* any more than the sunlit temple hall, but I don't know that. That's the kind of comforting stuff you can know when times are okay-ish. Right now, on this broken street corner, under a dirty lamp haloed by flies, I do not have a clue. I don't want to go back to my room, I don't want a girl, I don't want a drink. I don't know what I want. I have no fucking idea what I'm doing here.

I hear a whistle, a white guy in a big black SUV parked down the street, grinning and waving. I check over my shoulder, the street is empty, just me and the flies, and why would he beckon to flies? So I walk over. He looks like a cyborg, a death robot engineered from titanium and weapons-grade polymers. His head has the angled planes of a Stealth bomber, and his hair looks like a sanded-down wire brush. He's giving me a big grin, teeth like bullets.

Hey!

He raises his palm for a high five, which I give him. In slightly less than three of your earth minutes he will show me the Steyr A2 assault rifle he keeps under the seat, but right now I think I have another new friend. I grin back.

Do I have to meet your mother?

A VIOLIN TO HAMMER A NAIL

The acid hits earlier than expected, as I'm paying for my ticket at the entrance to the Angkor Wat complex. Your tuk-tuk driver drops you off outside the row of toll booths, you walk through, buy a ticket with your photograph on it, and rejoin your driver who takes you for the tour. I'm having a real problem handling the dollar bills. They slide away, stick to my fingers. Elusive feathery things, made of elves' knickers. This is the acid saying *hello*. In the end I hand the roll to the girl at the counter, with a *too much for me* grin, and she peels off a couple of bills and gives the rest back. Fine.

I've done the tour before, and this time I know where I want to go, the Bayon temple, a mad monument to the god-king Jayavarman VII, whose face emerges everywhere from the mountainous stone, repeated endlessly like in a hall of mirrors. There's some debate if it's him or top Buddhist Avalokitesvara, but as we know from other statues it looks like Jayavarman, and we have no clue as to what Avalokiteshvara looks like . . . it's a duck. It's possibly the most extravagant shrine to *self* in the world. *This is me, I can see everywhere, and I will live forever*. Over two hundred representations of his face, many of them tall as a man. Architecture as self-portrait, and *Khmer* architecture, borrowing nothing from the Greeks or Romans, built to different measures, different dimensions, different visions.

I had confused feelings on my first visit to the Angkor Wat complex. Awe at the incredible beauty and vast scale of the temples, the skill of the men who built them, and the appalling power of the men who caused them to be built. And disgust at the crass greed of the tourist industry which has reduced these amazing, humbling structures to photo souvenir backdrops. Busloads of fun-hungry clowns (mostly Asians – my touristophobia isn't occicentric) perform comic antics and clamber over the stones, posing in laughing groups, making rabbit ears behind some fat head. Their numbers are as vast as the architecture, their behavior shameful and harmful, but at a hefty twenty bucks per fat head, they drop around fourteen million bucks a year into the combat shorts of the "people's government", so the situation isn't likely to change anytime soon.

I'm not above being called a tourist myself, or being accused of shameful and harmful behavior, but I do know how to behave at a place like this. I dress soberly, don't climb on the stones, pull funny faces, litter, or raise my voice, and I eat a lot of acid. Exactly how much is rapidly becoming clear to me as I leave my tuk-tuk driver and head for the towers of Bayon. Look at a cement wall on acid, you'll see jewelled richness and beauty beyond imagining. Look at somewhere already covered with detail and strangeness, and . . .

The temple is seething. The towers writhe with iridescence, lizard-roots snaking from lightning-bolt fractures. The stones shift and turn, crystalline facets reflecting emerald tendrils twisting and sparking with kaleidoscopic jewels that effloresce into polychrome flowers. And everywhere, Jayavarman's face, ecstasy and laughter and serenity passing like leaf shade on a sunlit wall. The activity on the towers – organic, vital, erotic, *outrageously* erotic – sends ripples up into the blue sky, waves that cross and re-cross in shimmering prismatic nets. It's blissful up there, but it's the thing happening down below with the tourists I'm surprised by. They're *tickling* Jayavarman. He's having a fine time, doesn't mind at all, a bull gorilla playing with tiny baby gorillas. The stones inflate with Jayavarman's breath – the temple built to crush his people into submission has become a bouncy castle for his children. He's having the last laugh, and it's a long one.

Next time I look, the temple is brand new. They just finished it today. It's blinding porcelain white, semi-translucent, and yellow and red, and gold as brilliant as the sun. It's breathtaking, the sheer immaculate joyous splendor of it passes through me in waves, wave upon wave . . .

Impossible to say how long these changes take. I sit on a fallen stone, feeling it soften under my hands. I look down, it's crocodile skin, it's breathing. I stand and walk away, because I know I'm about to tip into it, head-over-heels, and I want to see the jungle before I tumble down the rabbit hole.

Baddha

You don't have to walk far at Angkor Wat to get away from the tourists. There are no fences, you can hack into the jungle at any point, although I wouldn't recommend it, there may be landmines and serpents or, worse, NGO volunteers. It's a little cooler in there, although this isn't full-blown Tarzan jungle, this is like overgrown forest, dry and dusty underfoot, with giant silver-trunked trees bending up. Even wearing the crash-hat of your normal consciousness, this place is very strange indeed. There's a broken wall in front of me, with a silk-cotton tree squatting on it, its pale, snakey roots spread out and gripping the masonry. The stones are pitted, rust red, spongey-looking, scattered like giant croutons over the jungle floor.

What I'm seeing, tasting, hearing, touching, smelling, is *life*. The forest swarms with it, and it swarms through me. The distinctions I make between the things I'm aware of – tree, stone, butterfly – are names that have lost their meaning. There are no divisions, nothing is separate, there's only life, *only everything*. I can't even say that I'm a part of it – there is no *I* to be apart, and nothing to be a part of or apart from. Everything is all the same, and it's breathing. This breath – there's no sense of in-out, inhaling and exhaling, not even in my own lungs, there's just breathing, an ecstatic cycle with no beginning and no end. The ruined wall lifts in slow, muscular waves, a shimmer of leaves, sighing stones turned by the gently inquisitive silver roots. Insects buzz and rattle as the rippling trunk bends and stretches, bark incised with intricate filigree calligraphy, changing and shifting, primal alphabets empty of meaning. I balance on the floating stones, swept by leafy currents, hold onto a tree. My hands fuse to its silken skin as the jungle warps around me, my sight a transparent sphere, illuminated . . .

Down the rabbit hole.

There is no darkness with LSD. Everything is illuminated, reflecting or burning with its own light. The rabbit hole is the DNA helix, through your neural universe. This is the molecular you, and you're inside-outside the outside-inside. The charges in your brain and nervous system take on physical form and color, organic-electric. This is what thinking looks like. But it's not you doing the thinking. This isn't about you. There is the thinking, and an awareness of the thinking. And this awareness is silent, neither projecting meaning or order onto the world nor losing itself within it. Awareness still as a rock, shining like a star in a field of stars.

By the time I emerge, I'm lost, I'm exhausted, and the sun is low. I'm not at Bayon, the stones are different here. I stare at one, hoping to see the shadowplay, the cursive writing, the breathing . . . but it's just a stone, wrapped in the shroud of the word. I see some food carts, souvenir stands, off through a line of trees, tourists moving. As I get out of the jungle a kid comes up to me with concertina'd postcards. I give him a dollar bill, which doesn't do any fun tricks as I peel it off the roll. I climb into the first tuk-tuk I see, and just as we're pulling away, Old Guy swings up opposite me.

"Going my way?"

Is there another?

By now, I'm almost getting used to his appearances. Almost. But I'm careful to talk out of the side of my mouth, not let the driver perhaps see me talking to myself. *I don't know*, is the answer. Everything about Old Guy is photo-realistic, and I'm always catching little details, this time the coarse mend in the hem of his shirt, with red cotton stitched any old way. But I cannot account for him as a real person, how he keeps turning up, or what he says. Where does he live? I don't want to ask him that, because I'm afraid he'll tap my forehead with his rooty old finger.

"LSD is cheating," he says, grabbing the rail as we bump over ruts in the road. "Breaking down the door of heaven."

Do we have to do this now?

"What other time is there? Come on, you cheated back there."

Nuts. And it doesn't break anything, and it isn't theft. You can't bring back any souvenirs. Here – I pass him the postcards. *For you.* He says "Oh!" in genuine pleasure, and spends a minute looking through them before folding them up – the concertina fold seems to delight him, he does it a couple of times. Then it's back to business, and he fixes me with his good eye.

"Some say," he wags a long finger at me, "meditation gets them high, thank you very much, without resorting to the artificial aid of drugs."

Self-righteous cowards. No matter how good you are, how hard you meditate, how loud you chant, you're not going on an acid trip. It's like waiting for a boat at the bus station. Not going to happen.

Old Guy doesn't seem too impressed. He starts to speak, then freezes, like he's forgotten what he was going to say. He reaches into his shirt pocket, peeks at a grubby slip of paper.

"Some say ... it's not ... *teal*? Oh, *real*. Not real. It's dreamland."

Oooh, I say. *I see your autocue.*

Old Guy appeals to the heavens, arms outstretched. "You've got me playing this corny devil's advocate role, when I can do so much more. You're using a violin to hammer a nail."

I've got you playing – but I cut myself off. I just got out of one jungle, don't want to go into another.

Old Guy sighs, repeats the line flatly, as if we're on the stage, and he's prompting me. "Some say it's not real. It's dreamland."

Our ignorance of reality is as monumental as the temples of Angkor Wat.

I see Old Guy mouthing along with the words during this little speech, and nodding in approval, as if I've learned the script.

"And how would you answer those who maintain it's dangerous?"

So is a pillow, if someone smothers you with it. Commonsense rules apply.

He takes the scrap of paper from his pocket, checks it, balls it up, throws it into the road. "No more questions. This is where you deliver your keynote speech to the nation. I'm not your autocue." He makes himself comfortable, wedging himself in the corner. If I had a pipe, this is where I'd be filling it with tobacco, tamping it down while I collect my thoughts.

Acid is a glimpse of somewhere where all your learning and knowledge and opinions are absolutely valueless and useless, and this is its great gift. (And this is where I'd be lighting the pipe, shaking the match, puffing great fragrant clouds). *You can get this particular view of heaven, whatever you want to call it* (airy wave of pipestem) *no other way. Buddha could, but that's why he's called Buddha and you're not. Acid takes you to the other bank of the river, that's the boat, to use his analogy. LSD is the most important and beneficial human advance since Buddha's enlightenment, and it's to nobody's credit that it's perceived as a mind-destroying recreational high for escapists and losers. And it's to everyone's shame that it's illegal. We had a chance to change the world for the better, and we fucked it up, left it to the lawyers, the bottom-feeders.*

Old Guy coughs theatrically, his tongue out, waving a hand in front of his face. "Smoke."

Fuck off.

"And I notice you use the E-word."

I frown for a second. *Enlightenment? Oops, my bad.*

It's one of my CBWs (Crap Buddhist Words). Our brain-dead "familiarity" with CBWs is the result of labelling an ill-understood idea so we can file it away with the rest of what we think we know. For some, especially ALBs, CBWs are a big part of what Buddhism is about. Using mystic and esoteric terms makes you mystic and esoteric, makes it sound as if you know something the others don't. You don't need words like *samadhi, dhamma, satori, nirvana*, or even *Buddha*, to get into what Buddha was into. They have *nothing to do with reality*, and they certainly won't reveal anything to you. Leave them to the Buddhists who like to drape themselves with religious paraphernalia. These words are nothing more than heavy amulets strung around the neck to impress. And for those who maintain that you have to learn the "original" language because there are no English equivalents, I have my own mystic Hindi word, *bakavāsa*. Bullshit. Language – *any* language – is totally inadequate when it comes to giving information or description of the truth (the Buddha experience), as Buddha himself said. Language *evokes*. Language is hypnotic, spell-weaving – a fog that obscures while convincing you that it reveals. Like my description of an acid trip. Reading that gives you a very vivid and accurate impression of what a description of an acid trip is like.

Most of us have a vague idea of what *enlightenment* means in the Buddhist sense, and it brings to mind all the clichéd cartoon baggage of meditation, sitting cross-legged, chanting, whatever. Maybe a sitar twangs exotically in the background. The word in itself carries no such baggage. Our understanding of the word *enlightenment* is like a blind man's understanding of the word *red*. He may be able to grasp it in some abstract sense, to get an idea of what the term means, an *understanding* of it, but he can't *experience* red. *Enlightenment* is the lazy label we put on what Buddha experienced, so we can form our precious opinion and move on to something more worthy of our time, like checking our MSN, LOL, or putting on a cute leotard and doing some yoga with our hair up in a fucking band.

"You should let me do this stuff for you," Old Guy says. He's sitting on the balcony, in my chair, with my laptop on his knees. "What are you paying me for?"

There's boxes downstairs need flattening.

Baddha

Old Guy passes me the laptop, a little too casually. I grab it. He stands, stiffly, rubbing his leg.

What, you going to start limping?

"Using a violin to hammer a nail. So very *you*, don't you think?"

THE STORY OF KRIST

I'm calling my born-again NGO chum Julius Krist, because it's as unbelievable a name for a born-again Christian as I can think of, and because it's more believable than his real name. He shows me his business card, *Julius Krist, Working For Jesus – Worldwide!* We're sitting in the Shitfaced Pizza restaurant, one of the two or three pizza joints in Siem Reap where they think cannabis is oregano. They also do nutritious fruit shakes with about a pound brick of hemp lightly dusted in. They don't like to see you leave your table unaided. On the way here – him walking in that doggy, apologetic lope you sometimes see tall men do, hands deep in his pants pockets – Krist talks about the LCSOBA, how they have no money, how he put the last of his into renting them a house for a year, how much he appreciates my help. He wants to do good so bad it crimps him up.

We study the menu, but his thoughts are somewhere else.

He says, *You believe in nothing, right? That's just a different type of belief.*

That's like saying not crossing the road is just a different type of crossing the road. I do not believe. In anything.

So you don't get to cross the road, then?

I let him have that one. We order the planet-sized pothead pizza and a couple of herbal health drinks.

God exists without your belief, you know. He's not dependent on it.

Yes he is. Absolutely. That's the power of belief. I don't deny the existence of belief, and I don't deny the power of it. But you can believe in whatever you damn well choose, and if your belief is strong enough it will have some kind of effect. You can believe in Satan, in UFOs, in Santa Claus, the Federal Reserve, the Land of the Free. None of these ideas would have any reality at all without belief.

Who created you? Who created the universe?

It's not a question that I need to ask, let alone answer, but we created god, and in our own image, because we are unbelievably vain and unbelievably unimaginative. We created a Creator God, and made him look like a wise old man, and we gave him a big white beard and a staff and the power to smite. And then we elected real representatives of this non-existent power to funnel our prayers up to Him, and to relay His messages back down to us. It's fucking nonsense, and it's unhealthy nonsense. No offence.

None taken.

The pizza arrives, which is a dull green-gray color on account of all the herb they threw at it. Krist tries to hold my hand while he says Grace, but I tell him to fuck off, nicely, and he says *thank you O Lord for sending my new friend to help us in your work, and, uh, forthispizzaforwhichwearetrulygrateful. Amen.*

It's not long before we start giggling, saying stupid stuff like, *I could really go for a pizza right now, let's send out.*

He tells me a little about LCSOBA, but I'm more interested in him, how he comes to be here, so he tells me his story.

I was in the septic tank clearing business. This was in Idaho. Swe-eet little deal. Drive a tanker around, suck people's shit up, they pay you, you go and spray it over some farmer's potato crop, he pays you too. Strictly speaking, you shouldn't do this, it's technically illegal I think, human waste as fertilizer, but anyway. I was working with my brother-in-law, he kind of came with his sister when I married her, moved in with us. He has this hair? Like Michael Bolton? Real long in the back, cut short at the front and sides. And a disco 'tache. We got two tankers, he'd go out and suck shit one place, I'd be spraying it somewhere else. Business is good, but I really want him to move out, get a place of his own, but my wife takes his side, you know, I'm so selfish, Wayne is sick ...

Wayne?

Right. So Wayne starts half-emptying septic tanks, he leaves 'em half full, but he tells people they're empty. So they have to call us back sooner, they're paying us twice as much to empty their tank. I don't like this, it's like ripping these people off, families we know. We have this flaming row, and suddenly I'm sleeping on the couch, my wife throws my clothes down. Wayne bust his leg, when he was a kid, and he walks with a limp every time he thinks someone is getting on his case. So he starts limping in the house, my wife fixing him breakfast, stroking his hair.

Stroking his hair? *Ew.*

Yeah. Also, only taking half the slurry gives him half as much to spray over the potatoes, so he starts watering it down. So anyway, he gets tumbled, I don't know how, both ends of the game, and he blames me, boo hoo, you know, says I made him do it. It's my name on the trucks, and it's a real shit storm, clients threatening lawsuits, and my wife sides with her brother. So the business is over, my marriage is over, and my life, in every sense, is shit. At around this time I was staying with some friends, to give my wife the space she needed, and there was this guy who came by, who just had this incredible sense of peace and calm about him. I never met anyone who seemed so – solid, at peace with himself. He was a, a mechanic or something. No, a computer program writer. Wrote, computer programs, codes I think they call them. Anyway, I had no peace and calm in my life, I think he could tell the pain I was in. I asked him, you know, what's his secret, where do you get this peaceful calm from? And he says – Jesus. And I felt the holy peace of Our Lord come through him to me, lifting me up. He said, pray to Jesus tonight, he has a task for you. So that night in my room, my friends' spare room, I pray to Jesus, and it's like I hear his voice in my head, so clear, I can't explain, and I feel his hand on my shoulder. I really feel his hand on my shoulder in the dark.

We both stare at his hand, which he has lifted for inspection.

Jesus says, you have to find Val Cuomo. Val Cuomo? Vandals quarterback, back in the day, one of the best, multi-millionaire, has his own line of eyeware. See my glasses? These are Val Cuomo Signature Aviators, limited edition. Also he had that disco hit? Cuomo My Place? No? Anyway, Jesus told me to find Val, it's really important for both of us, our futures are linked. I found out that Val was due to show at the Sports Banquet Awards in Moscow, this is the Idaho Moscow, not the Soviet one, so I drive a slurry truck over, because Wayne needs the car on account of his leg. It takes two days, and I don't know it, but the hose comes unfixed, and I'm spraying watered-down shit all over the highway, which I get a citation for. But I got there just in time, literally, to the second, to see Mr. Cuomo, getting out his limo, literally as I was parking the truck opposite, and I'm running across the street, it's like I'm on a mission, running, running – I'm a quarterback for Jesus! I kind of do this vault, over the hood of the limo, and Val turns and, get this, he asks if I'm okay, because I landed awkwardly. How sweet is that? But this is my moment, right? So I said, Jesus has come into my life, and he told me to find you, because it's important for both of us! I gave him a business card, I think I was crying, it was very emotional. Val was listening very hard, I could see I got through to him, but he had to go inside, do the show. Also I think I stank a little because of the hose thing, clearing that up. He promised to get back to me. Then these goons, you know, bodyguards or security, are pulling me away. But I completed my mission! I don't think I ever felt so, you know, valuable. Important. I've done the Lord's work ever since. Oh, they ticketed my truck, I got a parking ticket.

He takes a natural break at this point, sucking his shake up noisily through a straw. I have cramps from silencing my laughter, wiping the tears away. When I get my breath back, I say, *did Val call back?*

No, but Jesus did. Who'd you rather have call, the Son of God or an ex-quarterback?

I think I have the answer to that, but I ask him what message the Son of God left on his machine.

He told me, go to South East Asia, because I was needed there. Am needed. Here.

I think about all this for a while, watching him bend his straw into a loop and knot it around his finger. *Does anyone ever tell you that Jesus has fucked you over?*

Krist nods slowly, pursing his lips. *Oh yeah, I get that all the time.*

We spend some time blinking at each other, leaning one way or the other, the kind of thing you think is so hilarious when you're stoned. In fact, I'm tired of being stoned, it just smears you all over the place. It's unattractive.

I hate this.

He laughs. *So do me too.*

That old guy, back at the house. Under the house.

Old guy.

Yeah. We were talking when you arrived.

Oh, that old guy.

You know him?

I know . . . a lot of old guys. Under the house?

Does he work for you? Is he a translator?

Translator? What does he translate?

He's Burmese.

Maybe he's . . . a volunteer.

Do you get many old Burmese guys volunteering?

Nah. Never happens.

It's freaking me out. I met him in Thailand.

He's following you?

No, he was here first.

Maybe you're following him.

Maybe I'm imagining him.

He gestures hypnotically. *You might be imagining* this. *Everything.*

No, I'm remembering *this. Changing little things, the quarterback's name, so, I don't know, you can't sue me or something.*

Why would I do that?

Maybe you think what I'm writing is libelous, I don't know.

Writing? What are you writing?

What I'm writing . . . is . . . it's a thriller. I'm here to research the, uh . . . the background.

And I'm in it? Can I have . . . hair? Like Michael Bolton?

We cry with laughter for a very long time. It is very painful. It subsides, and we're grateful for the relief, and then it starts again. Eventually, we're all cried out, two stoned old homeless divorced guys with no tears left. I stand up, steadying myself on the table. *I really have to find a room.*

You can stay at the house.

Yeah, I don't know.

Well, good luck. He tips me a salute and slumps sideways against the wall, dislodging a travel poster of Rome that curls over his head like a nun's hat.

THE BEGGARS IN THE STREET
RISE FROM THEIR RAGS AND LAUGH

What you do?

Russian, can't be anything else.

I don't know. What are you doing?

He jerks a thumb back over his shoulder. *Wait boss.* He produces a pint bottle of Green Label. *Want drink?*

Is it real?

He laughs, showing those bullet teeth, and reaches over behind him to flip the passenger door open. There's nothing too weird about this, white faces tend to want to talk to each other in Rangoon. I climb up, smelling the leather interior. He passes back a plastic cup with an inch of Scotch heating up an icecube. *American?*

Scotch, I say, wishing I hadn't. *It's a joke.*

The smile freezes a second, staring at me. *What you do in Yangon?*

Vacation.

His eyes have gone blank, thinking in there. I go on, because he doesn't. *What do you do?*

Russian Embassy.

You look like a soldier.

He refills his own glass and throats it back in one. His neck looks like steel pipes bolted together. *I was soldier. Afghanistan.*

Kill anyone?

Sure. American tourists. He reaches under his seat.

Suddenly, I am sick with fear. My skin is clammy, my mouth dry as dust. I want to reach for the door handle, but I can't move. My mind's racing. He lifts the gun. It's a mean-looking thing, with a stub barrel and molded resin stock and grip. He holds it upright, gently, like he's presenting a trophy.

Steyr A2, Austria. Best gun in the world.

My heart slows a little. I rinse my teeth with ice cold Green Label. I take a breath.

I make short, the – this. The barrel. And here, I take telescopic sight. Fast!

He stows it back under the seat so quick I barely see him move, like a couple of frames missing from the movie.

Fuuuuu-uuuuuuck.

The front passenger door opens and a man gets up inside, looking back at me. He's a little portly-looking, round-ish, black shiny hair with a thick-cut edge to it, like a toupée. Trim moustache, and a humorous look to him. Pale blue sport jacket over white shirt and dark tie, which he tucks under his seat belt.

He asks me a couple of questions, I give him the stock

replies, and I think I see him exchange a look with Stealth Bomber when I say *tourist.*

So! We go for a drink!

Stealth pounds the steering wheel with his fists, starts the motor, we glide off.

You're the Ambassador?

He gives a modest little chuckle, shakes his head. *I work for the Ambassador.* Stealth drives right down the middle of the street, and fast, swerving to avoid potholes, but there's no traffic, so we don't kill anyone. They talk a little in Russian, pointing down the street. With his normal human-sized boss next to him I can see exactly how big Stealth is, a back you could land a Chinook on. It's scary. We make a couple of turns, pull up outside a dark place, could be anything, anywhere. It looks closed, whatever it is. Stealth leaps out, strides to the door and pummels his fists on it, like he did on the steering wheel. He shades his eyes, peers through the small window.

I say, *it's closed,* thinking, please, let me go. Let me run screaming into the night.

That little smile. *Nowhere is closed.*

He's beating on the door again, tries the handle, rattles the door, and I think he's going to flick it off its hinges when a light goes on. He stands back, gives a quick look up and down the street, the boss gets out, I follow, drop my cup of icewater in the gutter. Stealth aims the key at the SUV, beeps the locks.

The owner of the bar, in undershirt and sweat pants, looks scared, mostly. Eager to please, exhausted, but mostly scared. He takes the chairs off a table, wipes it with a cloth, shouting back into the kitchen. We sit down, Stealth taking up one side of the table, and a boy arrives cradling three bottles of beer, glasses, and a plastic bucket of ice. He doesn't look at us, and my Russian friends don't look at him. I'm looking at everybody, at the owner, sneaking back into the kitchen, at the way the boy's hand shakes, just a little, as he pours the beer over the ice, rattling the neck against the rim of the glass.

The Boss and I have a conversation while Stealth sinks his beer and calls for more. He drinks clumsily, slopping it over the table.

So! You are a tourist in Yangon! How do you like our city?

I like it.

Why?

I like the people.

The people are happy! And do you notice – no beggars! Did you ever see a beggar in the street?

No, never! I've seen plenty. You walk the streets of Rangoon, you're tripping over beggars. Also I've seen people who would consider begging a step up the social ladder. But I'm not disagreeing with anything these people say.

The West has a very wrong view of Myanmar. It is a good country, and good for business. What is your business?

I'm a teacher. English.

Stealth tops up my glass, the foam spilling over.

Is it good business?

It's not really a business. I make very little money.

Don't you want to be rich?

I had some money once. My ex-wife has it now.

The Boss laughs. Stealth laughs. I laugh. The beggars in

the street rise from their rags and laugh. Burma is truly the Land Of Laughter, LOL.

Stealth takes a pause from sinking beers to lean at me across the table. I can smell the drink on his breath. He launches into some kind of political argument about Afghanistan that gets more slurred and more anti-US the more the empty bottles appear on the table. I never saw anyone drink so fast as this guy, it's like a Formula One car taking on fuel, the boy scurrying in with more every five minutes. I want to get out of there, but I have no reason, and no clue where I am. Also, in spite of my efforts to pace myself, I'm getting drunk, too, which I hate almost as much as getting stoned.

Suddenly, Stealth sweeps the empty bottles off the table, they bounce and roll across the boards. He plants his elbow on the table, in the arm-wrestling pose. *Wrestle*, he says. *Come on, teacher, we make wrestle.*

Are you kidding? No way I'm going to arm-wrestle you. He looks scornful, disbelieving almost. *You're a nice guy. I don't want to break your arm.*

Boss is chuckling all the time now, his shoulders jerking up and down. He's drunk, too. The boy is scrabbling on the floor, picking up bottles.

Stealth says, *What you look at, in street?*

What do I look at? The buildings, the people . . .

No, no – when I see you tonight. You look at something. In your hand.

Oh! A book.

This is the funniest thing the Boss has heard since my ex-wife. He pinches the bridge of his nose, says, *you come to Yangon to read books on the street at night? What is this book?*

I reach into my pocket, pass him my Soundbite Buddha, which I covered in leather to stop it falling apart. I'm not a vegetarian.

The Boss flips through it. *This is about Buddha.* He passes me the book, apparently satisfied, like a passport inspector. *Are you a Buddhist?*

I'm going to say *no, but* . . . then I glimpse an opportunity to get out of this, so I say, *yes, I let Buddha into my life, he's my personal savior, and I want you to meet Buddha, too. He can save you.*

The Boss's interested in me vanishes. He checks his mobile, jerks his head at his driver. *We go.*

I don't see anyone paying for the drinks. In the SUV, Boss says they'll drop me at a club he knows, I can find a girl. *Forget Buddha. A girl is better.* They can drop me in the river for all I care, if they promise not to save me. We pull up in front of what looks like an apartment building, just another brutal collapsing concrete block. There are steps up to a porch lit by a fluorescent tube, and a riveted steel door with a hatch at eye-level. I thank Boss while Stealth does his door-beating act again, the hatch opens and shuts, and I'm in. It's a shitty lobby with an open elevator, a guy sits inside on a plastic chair, his cadaverous grin the blood-red of a betel-chewer.

He beckons me in. *Dancey boom-boom!*

I consider turning on my heel, leaving, but I'd just get picked up by somebody worse. It's one of those nights. On the way up, I can feel the elevator knock against the sides of the shaft, it's like a tin can on a wire, I'm glad to step into a black-painted lobby with blacklight lettering on the wall, Cock Tail Club, and some cut-out palm trees around a badly-painted tropical sunset. I've been in worse joints. The cross-eyed woman behind the counter bends to spit betel juice in a plastic bag, and says, *three dollar*, so I ante up. She looks at the bills carefully, somehow triangulating them into focus, and returns one, pointing to the ripped corner. I find a replacement, muttering *fussy, fussy,* under my breath, but it's not unusual for less-than-perfect notes to be refused.

I push through a velvet-covered door, worn gloss black where my hand touches it. The place looks emptier than a bottle. There's a deserted dancefloor with tables around, and a bar to my right. As my eyes get used to the gloom, I make out people in the booths along the walls, groups of dark-jacketed men and trashy-looking girls perched nearby, not sharing the tables, topping up their glasses. I move to the bar, ask for vodkatonic, get the usual blank look from a bartender who must be at least thirteen, change to *vodkarocks, ice, gimme a vodka. VOD-KA. Great, thanks, Scotch is fine. No, no water, I said, hold the – doesn't matter. Fine, Scotch and water, thanks.*

When I turn back, there's a group of girls giving me the glad hello. *Anyone speak English?* I get giggles, slanted hips, but a leggy thing strides up, tosses her hair, and says something short and nasty to the girls, who slouch back off into the shadows. We exchange names, each of us using a totally unnecessary alias, but it's the form. She speaks a little English, and she looks perfect. In her twenties, I guess.

Taken a lot of trouble with her make-up, glittery eyelids, wet-gloss lipstick, the whole deal. She wears a tight denim waistcoat that's more like a bikini top, over a halter with silver stars, and a pair of frayed denim shorts she must have grown into like a tree grows into a wire fence. Add a pair of plastic fuck-me heels and hoop earrings you could jump through, and you have just the kind of girl to take back to your mother, should your mother operate a whorehouse. As a sidebar here, it should go without saying (but probably doesn't) that the interest these girls show in me isn't due to my rugged good looks and powerful sex-appeal. Here, I'm the only white customer to walk through the door, and there's no way I'll be leaving alone. If Frog was here, if *Stephen Hawking* was here, I'd get the second-stringers, but they're not and I am so this is where I win. I get the leggy one, and she's over me like a thick coat of paint. I buy her a drink that she doesn't touch, she's too busy touching me. This one is *good* at it, and due diligence brings rewards. I have a hard-on that's going to need its own cab home. And that's the problem right there; I have no idea where my hotel is and I have *forgotten its name*. I tell Brittany (whatever) this, and I sound like the dumb, drunk fuck I am. *No problem*, she says. *We take some room here.* We do the math. There's a "bar fine" to the bar for taking her out of the bar, and a room fee, which is more than I'm paying for my hotel, and she wants twenty dollars, which I know is twice what I could haggle her down to. I also know the average Burmese daily take-home pay is around fifty cents. But *not* haggling is a mistake, as it makes the seller (of anything) regret they could and should have asked for more, as well as thinking you're a sap for not trying to get a lower price. So we settle on eighteen bucks. It's hard to concentrate.

She takes me by the hand – a giddy romance! – and leads me out through the toilets to a starlit sylvan glade, where fauns frolic, and we embrace upon a grassy knoll curtained by fireflies and cushioned with pink petals.

I wake up, and she's taking a piss in the shower. I pretend to be asleep when she comes back, and watch her through slitted eyes. She sits on the bed in her frayed underwear. Without make-up, she looks closer to thirty than twenty. She meticulously folds and packs her working clothes into her handbag, puts her shoes – nested together – into a plastic bag and puts that in the handbag too. She stands and puts on her day clothes, the dull *longhi* wrap, a grubby t-shirt, her hair up in a cheap scarf. She rubs circles of cream-colored powder onto her cheeks, *thanakha*, using a plastic Barbie hand mirror. She puts the powder and mirror into a pocket on the handbag, and then the handbag goes into a white plastic bag, and she knots the handles. She sees me watching, turns away. I don't say anything as she leaves. The siren of sex left the building when she fell asleep. I turn off the lamp and lie awake until daylight filters through the dust-clogged ventilator.

PRISONERS OF SPACE AND TIME

Frog has a Docklands apartment, Canary Wharf, London. He's always complaining he's broke, but that's broke as in investment broker. There's a view over the river, white walls, a wealth of excitingly exposed brickwork, and a full wine rack. We're sitting on the deck (which is what he calls the balcony, which is more of a ledge), under a metal outdoor space heater (Londoners know space is cold), drinking white wine and watching England refusing to have anything at all to do with color and light. It's like an evil arch-villain hooked up a big corrugated tube to the city and sucked all the color out. The people we can see are all dressed in black. We're dressed in black, black and gray. We've been talking about my marriage, which has had all the color and light sucked out of it too. Frog has never been married, although every woman who steps into his apartment has seen herself as his life mate. He's London's most wantable bachelor! French good looks, long wavy hair, olive skin, a jet-set job writing features for Condé Nast, and a father who's won the *Prix Goncourt* in France for being an *auteur*. So fuck him.

He can see I'm very badly depressed (The Five Blind Boys Of Alabama could see this, it's not indicative of any sensitivity on his part), and he's suggested I go out to South East Asia with him, he wants to have a look at the Rangoon River, and also do some industry-standard whoring in Bangkok.

I can't see myself going with prostitutes, I say, the pompous prig. *I've never done it, never wanted to do it. Don't see the attraction.*

Oh, it's totally different out there. I wouldn't take a whore in London either. Out there, the first thing is, they're gorgeous. They're not old Eastern Bloc slappers. It's the most fantastic fun you can have in your life. I mean, really, fantastic, unbelievable *fun.*

Fun. When was the last time I had fun? The last time I laughed? *But, Burma . . .*

That's something else again. No fun at all.

So why go?

He gestures with his wineglass. *Incredible people, break your heart. Rangoon is like a city on the edge of the world.*

You're doing your voice-over again. I do a bad French accent. *Rangoon ees like ze ceety on zer etch of ze wuuuuurld, e-hon e-hon.*

He refills my glass. *I think you must come. Ten days. Tell wifey it's research for a new novel, you need inspiration.*

What I don't know, because I'm too fogged with depression, is that he knows exactly what he's doing. He sees my marriage more clearly than I do (standing outside something helps), and he hates to see me suffer. He knows a first trip out east taken at this time could well act as the catalyst to bring it to an end. It's a terrible risk he's taking, but what neither of us know is how my wife is setting her own snakey fuse back there in the darkness.

I'm looking at his collection while he pushes his hair about like a woman in the bathroom. There's an alcove where he displays his travel souvenirs. An African wife-beating paddle, should he ever get married. I weigh it reflectively in my hands. Swords, fireworks, weird-looking medicaments, talismans, an ironically hilarious Saddam Hussein keyring, and on the floor under the table, a box of clothes, a faded and collarless blue cotton shirt, clumsily mended with red cotton. Underneath, there's a coolie hat, the type worn by Chinese railroad workers. The hat is made of woven plastic strips, cut-up packaging perhaps, with what looks like bits of lettering.

Frog comes out of the bathroom. *Try it on.*

I put it back in the box. *I look stupid in hats. I'd look mentally ill in that one.*

On the way out, I say, *I'll need a visa, right?*

The strange thing is, a week or so back, I pick up a little book of Buddha quotes from a bookstore. I'm waiting to pay at the counter, and they have a little display of Buddhist literature by the cash register. I haven't read any of that since my teens, but I pick it up and the first thing I read is this:

"You should wander in your own space, in tune with your true nature – a space of intense alertness, with no misery and greed. This is your own space, your natural range."

This strikes me with the force of a biblical revelation –

I am *not* in my own space. I am *not* in tune with my true nature. My life is full of misery and greed – the misery is mine, but the greed is not. And intensely alert? I am numb with thick, clinging fog, clogged with gritty cobwebs. So I buy the book, and I'm dipping into it all the time. I couldn't take in any lengthy arguments or philosophies or whatever, I don't know if it's depression or what, but my attention span can be measured by a bee's wing. But these little soundbites hook me, dig their way in. The immediacy of it, like there's no time to lose:

"Let the past be, and forget the future. I will teach you that which is now."

Forget the future? How can I forget something impossible to remember? This puzzle starts me thinking about the nature of time, which Buddha has a lot to say about, either up-front or more subtly, and this is my own particular chink of light, my own fracture in the world. *How Buddha gets into me.* Buddha throws the same ball, over and over. A different spin each time, in the hope you'll catch it this way or that. The spin we call *time* (which is not *at all* what we think it is) is the throw I catch.

"I will teach you that which is now."

That which is now. There is so very much in this simple phrase it needs a book written about it. Who would write it? Where would I start? At the bookstore, or Frog's apartment? My arrival at the meditation retreat in Southern Thailand? In the Abbot's hall? Or *right now*, as I type this on the balcony of our shop-house, watching thunderheads roil above the Mekhong River? Or maybe *this* now, when you're reading these words? *Which now?* The book is written in the present tense for a reason, the narrative blown to bits for a reason.

"Without intense alertness, you are locked into time and space, a prisoner of the made world."

I know that voice. I look up. It's Old Guy. I haven't seen him for a while. He needs a shave. The cataract over his eye has grown, I think, since I first saw him. Or remember seeing him. "Come on," he says, "let's get into this. We have the time and I know the space."

We take the *motosai,* a skinny little Honda two-stroke caked with red dust, upriver, along the red dirt road out of town, the hot air not cooling as we cut through it. To the right, the banks slope down to the river. It's dry season, the river has retreated, and the fertile slopes are planted with vegetables in neat and productive parcels of land intersected by dirt paths. Little palm-leaf and bamboo shelters have sprung up to shade the workers as they bundle the produce for market. Beyond this, a series of low sandy dunes eye-lashed with dune grass, and a white sand beach where I sometimes walk Djini, who chases sand frogs and barks at the river, which looks deceptively wade-able at this point, all the way to Laos, that low treeline horizon.

After a while, Old Guy taps my shoulder, and waves his hand to stop. There's nothing. Overgrown bushes to the left, and, here, a steep grassy bank down to the river. He strides off into the bushes, and I guess I have to follow. The bushes are heavy with pink and white flowers – this was a garden, and my feet find a broken brick path under the dead leaves. I see the flash of Old Guy's coolie hat, push the branches aside to a bamboo gate, wired shut, but sagging enough to climb through. There's a little wooden house in the trees, octagonal, with a blue tin roof. Old Guy is climbing a bamboo ladder to the second floor, which is open on all sides. Birds whistle and creak, broken windchimes clink in the lazy breeze from the river. I climb the ladder. Up here, the floor is planked to the center from each side of the octagon, and the radial roof beams are strung with dead electrical wiring, and there's the scent of teak. Somebody's little retreat, long abandoned, but Old Guy has evidently made himself at home. A new hammock is strung across an angle, the concertina of postcards from Angkor Wat is pinned to the wall, and I see my missing Sudoku Extreme III book on the floor and a couple of empty Leo bottles in a corner. He gets into the hammock, not as elegantly as he should with all the practice he's getting, and settles in, peering over the bushes to the river. I sit nearby, leaning against the rail. I pick up my sudoku book. He's completed most of the puzzles, in his wavery hand, without showing his workings, like I have to do. They're very clean, no crossing out.

Wow, you're good at this.

He shrugs. "Nothing to it. People don't spend any time thinking *about* time, because it's pointless, of no use or value, intellectual masturbation."

Your potty mouth.

"They would say time is something we have to live with, there's nothing we can do about it, it's just there, we all get old and die, so thinking about it is a waste of it. They wouldn't see the point of investigating it. So, why bother?"

Buddha says, "be attentive to this present moment, forget tomorrow, let the past be. Be in the now." *He says it in slightly different ways each time, but it all comes down to the nature of this* now, *understanding it, being in it, being attentive to it. If that isn't to do with time, I don't know what is.*

"And the nature of this *now* is continuous change. Why are you waving?"

I'm waving goodbye to the people who've hung on grimly up to this point, hoping for more sleaze, or rants about tourists and white women. They're going to skip this stuff, because they're lazy-assed prurient masturbators, robbed of their capacity to think by the internet.

Wait a second, I want to take notes. I open the sudoku book at the back, scribble the ballpoint pen to get it started. I think I see a little smile on Old Guy's face, he's flattered to have his Mystic Insights recorded. He's enjoying his guru role, but he'd never admit it.

"Ready? In the West, you have a real need to define, to describe, to categorise, and to do this, you have to hold things still to look at them. And this is why you have great difficulty with the idea of a constantly changing instant, the moment in flux. That's *f-l-u-x.*"

Wait a minute . . . d-e-f-i-n-e . . .

"Our common model of time, as a railway track we're moving along, is Flat Earth thinking, inadequate, primitive, and misleading. We're not sharing a fixed time track, ticking by at the same speed. Our now isn't a point on a line with a beginning and an end. Our *now* is a point on a cycle. Well, it's the point on many intersecting, interdependent cycles. Everything is changing, turning. The change is a cycle, not a line with a beginning, a middle and an end, and it does not tick like a clock."

He waits for me to catch up. In spite of his deconstruction of time, this takes a lot of it.

"Everything is coming to be, ceasing to be. Everything has its own cycle, but they're not all turning at the same rate. This is obvious to anyone who spends a day and a night observing the natural world. In fact, thinking of a cycle as a circle doesn't help that much, it doesn't have a shape. It's turning, changing. Thinking of it as a circle is convenient, but not accurate. It's the simplest way we can visualise it. The yin-yang symbol, the Buddhist wheel, they only stand in for the reality, which you can't draw."

That's why you threw your drawing away.

"There is no future, no past. All there is, is this moment, changing. That's all we have and all we are and all there is."

But the Facebook demographic are going to spit their latté through their nose at that. They can remember yesterday, and they made plans to meet at the mall tomorrow, so this no past, no future *line is bullshit. You're going to have to do better.*

"I don't have to, because I can't. There is no better. The past does not exist now, *that's why it's called the past.* It's gone! Not here! Does not exist! It exists only in memory, a mental activity which we'll get to later."

If we remember.

"The future is not *now*, by definition, so it does not exist now, either. It exists only as a mental concept, supported by the invention of the division of time into so-called units of measurement. You can point to next week on the calendar, but that is not proof of its existence, only the existence of the calendar. The ordinary definitions of past and future prove their non-existence."

No, it doesn't. They don't. We know that yesterday existed yesterday, *because here's the DVD we rented yesterday. We know tomorrow will exist* tomorrow, *because that's when the DVD is due back. This is the reality of organised human life on the planet, and no airy-fairy notion of yours is going to change that reality.*

"Saying *yesterday existed yesterday* is saying the past existed in the past, and as there can be no proof of the past's existence, because its very definition negates its existence, your argument is fallacious."

F-l-u-x . . .

"Using the railway track model of time, we're moving into the future and leaving the past behind, right?"

Yes.

"If the model's true, the past is retreating *in front of us*. We can only see the past. Doesn't this strike you as strange? If we're on a train moving into the future, why are we all facing backwards?"

Because . . . we bought the wrong tickets?

"But are we, in fact, watching the past recede? What are we watching?"

We're watching what happens right now.

"Right. So what is the future for? What does it do? What does it hold?"

It, uh . . . it's what will happen. This little house will get knocked down and they'll build a whorehouse, with a big-ass gold statue of you in the lobby picking your nose.

"And these events are waiting for us up the track? Behind us, like a country we are going to travel through?"

Hmm. If the future's waiting for us up on the track, but we just can't see it yet, it means ... the future will have already existed by the time we get to it. Which means that the future's in the past. Which is nuts.

"But if the future *isn't* some kind of storehouse of events, waiting for us, what is it?"

And why is nobody on this goddamn train asking for his money back?

"We're all flat-earthers, cave dwellers, when it comes to understanding time. It is not a measured, or measurable, serial universe, no matter what the latest fashion in physics would have you believe. It's a cyclical universe. Some egghead once prided himself on the conceit that space is curved. He was nearly right. Space *turns*. Everything turns. There's a big institution in Switzerland where particle physicists – as they like to call themselves these days – are building a big machine to locate the Big Bang, which they fondly believe to be the beginning of the universe. These clowns even think they'll be able to point to a place on the calendar when this happened. If any one of them had sat under a tree and observed the natural world for a while, and reflected on it, he'd have reached the conclusion that this universe – for want of a better name – has its cycle, like everything else, and the Big Bang is not the linear beginning of time, nor the ending of it, but a point on a cycle, and this point – creation, destruction, alpha, omega – is not fixed but changing, turning, in tune with everything else."

"Man is the only creature on the planet to worry about next Tuesday. The past and the future do not exist *now*, by definition. Simplify that statement. The past and the future do not exist. The *now* is implicit in the use of the present tense *exist*. With them out of the picture, there is only the *now*, which Buddha experienced. What's stopping you seeing this is, firstly, memory, a mental activity you call *the past*. And thinking about the future, which is a mental activity based on extrapolating information from the past. We spend most of our mental energy remembering the past and anticipating the future. The other big stumbling-block is our inability to grasp the idea of the constantly-changing point or instant or moment. We can't understand this at all, because we think changes take place over time, as we move along the railway track. We think the moment, the instant, is unchanging, fixed like a photograph."

Okay, explain that, because you could use the photograph, or even better, a single frame from a movie reel, as evidence that the instant doesn't change, that time is a succession of frozen moments.

"You think a photograph captures the moment? Freezes it in time? No. It's just a photograph, on its own coming to be/ceasing to be cycle. There's not an infinite succession of different instants we can freeze and preserve, different nows, there is only one now, this one, and it's always changing. If there were a series, you could say there's a frame missing between any two on the movie reel. So you could run the film faster, take twice as many *nows*. But you could still say that there are other images between those, and others between those, towards infinity. If it's a series, how does one image, one frame, one instant, leap to the next? You can always subdivide a clock's tick, make it smaller and smaller, divide the smallest fraction of a second into an even smaller fraction. The primary unit of time does not exist. The universe turns, but it does not tick."

I know we're leading up to something here, that this talk about time really isn't about time at all, and there's an important step we have to make, but I sense the Old Guy is tiring, and me too.

"It's the classical three-act story format – beginning, middle, end. We all like to be told a satisfying story. Once upon a time they lived happily ever after. But life and time are not like that, and that's one of the reasons life can be so unsatisfying. Always struggling for the happy ending which never comes. When Buddha says forget the future, he means forget *about* it, forget the happy ending, stop thinking about it, worrying about it. Thinking about the past and the future clouds the present moment, and everything you need to know is in *this* instant. This instant is the same wherever you are. It's all the same instant. You don't have to be in a monastery or on top of a mountain to be in it. Although if it helps, why not."

He puts his hand across his eyes, thinking something through. He's mouthing the words, while he gets them right. Then he looks up at nothing. His cloudy old eye like the moon.

"An understanding of time is an understanding of the nature of things, not their duration."

I'm eyeing the empty bottles while he's saying this and he reads my mind.

"If you want a beer, there's some cooling, in the river." He waves out over the trees.

Thanks. Love one. I don't move. For maybe a full minute of measured time, neither of us does, then he starts to get out the hammock, but winces, holding his back. It's his old trick.

I'd go, I say, *but I don't know where they're hidden, do I? And knowing you, and knowing the needle-eyed fishermen round here, they're well hidden, right?*

He sighs, swings down from the hammock, and shuffles over to the ladder, muttering something impolite in Burmese, for all I know. And I hear him fart on the way down.

I add his quote *an understanding of time is an understanding of the nature of things, not their duration* to my notes, then look back through the book, to admire his sudoku skill.

And I see first one wrong number, then another. Then another. He's just filled them in any old way.

TALKING TRASH WITH THE REPTILES

I'm staying in a rented house that backs onto the river that runs (much too energetic a word) through Siem Reap. There's no A/C and it's hot, the unlined metal roof sucks the heat into the second floor bedroom, you could bake bricks. It cools down a little after midnight, enough for me to sleep naked and uncovered for three or four hours, before snapping awake to sob and writhe in despair for a while. This pays for a refreshing pre-dawn black-out. The bed is a split bamboo platform with a mattress about as thick as a ham sandwich. The shutters over the unglazed windows hinge at the top, and mosquitoes are my most faithful companions. I've become pretty adept at snatching them out of the air, but some enable their hyperspace mode when attacked. I can be certain I've caught the bugger, and scrunch my fist up hard, but when I open it, the thing's disappeared. That's strange enough, but even stranger, my fist has disappeared, too. The house is a guest-house for wildlife. I only get to see the small geckoes, which freeze cunningly on the wall when you look at them, convinced they've become invisible. The big guy I never see, but he's up in the beams somewhere, I hear his loud mating call or territorial claim or whatever it is. It starts with a curious glottal stutter while he pumps himself up, then there's a sound like a rubber frog imitating a bird; a series of descending croaks, *geh-ko*, of diminishing force. The more croaks, the stronger the male, and it's never more than nine. Cambodians lay bets when they hear a gecko clearing its throat. Cheered on by me, my guy usually manages seven or eight before coughing to a halt. I can almost see him shaking his head, saying, *nuts, I'm too old for this shit.* One time I see a small, pale scorpion scuttle across the bedroom floor. There are regular inspections by frogs, and a wiry viper sprang guiltily through a window as I entered, as if I'd caught it masturbating. Cockroaches adorn the floor like leaves blown from a New England fall. I'm just passing through this place like these guys, no point in getting all proprietorial and trying to sweep them out.

Down on the first floor, mostly open, there's a block-built washroom with a ceramic hole-in-the-ground toilet and a showerhead on a plastic hose that doubles as an ass-gun. It's taken me a while, but I prefer hosing my ass to the Western method of scraping it with toilet paper, a horrible and dirty thing to do, when you think about it. Westerners' bathrooms may be spotless, but we walk around with crotted-up buttcracks all the time, it's no wonder Asians think we're dirty. That and our body odor and foot stink from wearing trainers and socks. They can smell all this, and it's offensive to them. Consider that next time you deal with an Asian hotel clerk or cabdriver. You don't wash your ass, you smell like shit. Plus, I've learned that shaving under a cold shower, using cheap soap and a disposable plastic razor, is as efficient as the elaborate shaving-soap/brush ritual I used to pamper my pan with. This personal regime helps me concentrate for my big important working breakfast at the Blue Pumpkin, honing motivational wordage for Krist's website while having a yogurt and shameful fantasies about the waitresses.

I tidy the yard, bagging up the usual flotsam of plastic bottles, polythene bags, and miscellaneous Cambodian crap. I'm surprised anyone can set off a landmine through the carpet of litter that covers the country, or maybe that's the idea, make it safe for hikers by adding a spongy non-biodegradable protective crust. Once I bag the trash, I have nowhere to put it. So I leave it in the street next to an overflowing garbage can made out of rubber tires in the misty-eyed hope that the crack Siem Reap garbage team will deal with it expeditiously. Garbage is occupying the town right now, there's a big recycling *initiative* at the Foreign Correspondent's Club, which involves stringing a net dam across the river a couple of hundred yards upstream from the FCC, which fronts it, so all the litter backs up where the poor people live, and the rich white people enjoying a chilled Chardonnay at the FCC can look out on a clean stretch of river and say they *made a difference.*

Tonight it's the official opening of this public cleanliness program, and Krist gets me an invite, so I have my good shirt publicly cleansed, anoint my temples with fragrant balm, and ankle– upriver, past the houses that make mine look like the White House, like they're about to tip their occupants right into the river, past the stinking crocodile farm where clay-colored monsters doze in concrete tanks, undisturbed even by the clods of earth I toss at them, to the twinkling lights of the FCC, a classier crocodile farm for upmarket reptiles; keen young interns, doing good to do well, government officers in military uniform, and occasional movie stars shopping for last-minute souvenir orphans. The building is architecturally significant because it was built over fifty years ago and is still standing. It used to be the French governor's mansion, back when the French could still kick the shit out of a desperately poor and disorganised Third World nation (seeing French tourists having to bite the bullet and speak English when they order in restaurants here in "Indo-Chine" is a pleasure). It's now a hotel and restaurant, and no real Foreign Correspondent could afford to billet here, so there are no sweating reporters in crumpled linen tapping their portable Remingtons on the balcony. It's clean, cool, and elegant, but above all, it's smug, and tonight is a glittering celebration of smugness. The river is strung with lanterns and there's a spectacular dragon made of recycled plastic waste set on poles in the middle of the river and lit with fairy lights. Poor, colourfully-dressed people huddle at the gates to gaze at the rich people inside, where seats have been set up in front of a stage. Liveried flunkies move through the crowd, and I grab a couple of glasses of champagne as they pass. I see people I've seen around town, or in the Blue Pumpkin, but nobody I know. Maybe I can make some new friends and invite them back to wrestle crocodiles.

Baddha

Here's one. She's got a bunch of jewels round her throat as delicate as a chain round a ship's bollard, and her blonde hair is teased into that stiff windswept casual style. She says something about not thinking we've been introduced? She's Nancy Barry? The outreach consultant for UNESCO? And what brings me to her town. The only time she doesn't make a sentence sound like a question is when it is one? I tell her I'm helping Julius Krist's association? They're dancing here tonight? And where are the whores. No, I don't say that. The whores are scuffing their heels at the Leaping Lizard bar, where I'd be if the drinks were free.

I was admiring the dragon, in the river, I say. *Very beautiful.*

Oh, our Apalala! I was one of the team, she says proudly. *Over six thousand plastic bottles!*

A . . . palala?

That's the Buddhist term. She's our iconic water spirit.

You're a Buddhist?

I teach a women's meditation class here at the FCC.

I didn't know meditation was gender-specific. I say this nicely, in the spirit of honest inquiry, but I'm spoiling for a fight.

We approach it from a woman's perspective.

Wow. How do you do that? I mean, I thought that the aim of meditation was to empty the mind of perspectives.

Nancy Barry's smile is showing the strain. *We set it in a woman's context.*

Scented candles. I nod understandingly, *leotards,* but Nancy Barry is looking over my shoulder, her eyes searching for someone else to charm. But I haven't finished. *What's going to happen to it when the recycling initiative is over?*

I'm sorry?

Your iconic dragon, when they take it down. What's going to happen to your six thousand iconic plastic bottles?

Well, I guess . . .

Maybe it'll get swept away when they open the dam.

Dam?

Sure. They put a net across the river upstream to hold the garbage back. Up there, where the poor people meditate. When you've all flown back to Brussels or wherever, they're going to release all the crap that's built up behind it. Like a frothing tide of plastic waste surging past the FCC, carrying your Apalala to the sea! One for YouTube!

Nancy Barry moves away. Someone is tapping the mic up on stage. Maybe because I'm relatively tall and have distinguished silver locks, I'm led to the front row. Maybe they think I'm old and deaf, I don't know. I spot Krist a few rows back, sitting next to his boss, and we grin at each other. A photographer takes a few pictures of the uniformed dignitaries in the front row, so I lean into shot, looking appropriately caring and dignified. Then it's time for a few endless speeches in Khmer, so I occupy myself with my Buddha Soundbite book, chasing the *coming to be, ceasing to be* trope through its pages, because I'm convinced this is as intense a distillation of what he experienced as it's possible to formulate. It's one of his phrases that gets deeper the more you look into it. But you have to look. You have to investigate and reflect, to plant the words like seeds and tend them. If you just read what he said like you're reading this sentence, you're not going to get anything out of it other than a reinforcement of the perspective you approach it from. Scented candles. Leotards.

Baddha

And now Nancy Barry takes the mic, thanks everybody whose name is on her list, and emcees the evening's educational entertainment, all from her very special perspective as a woman. There's a fashion parade, Khmer boys and girls wearing clothes made out of trash, which is fine and fun, but it's going to be a hard sell to the poor, *wear your trash, poor people!* or to the rich, *wear poor people's trash*! But I get it, we're shifting the paradigm, thinking outside the square, opening possibilities. Either that or we're opening up new avenues of UN funding to pay administrative salaries, and fattening the résumés of all the interns and volunteers and outreach consultants associated with the project. Also, it's free entertainment for the Khmer in the street and his extended family, gazing in at all the wonderfulness without a trace of the righteous indignation I'm feeling on his behalf.

Then there's the dancing, Krist's LCSOBA troupe. And I have to look away and blink, because every time I see them I tear up. There's a row of heartbreakingly beautiful girls in terrible old iron wheelchairs, some on splintery wooden crutches, and they're beautifully dressed in traditional Khmer clothes, purple and pink and gold, flowers in their hair, and they dance, as the Old Guy said, with what they have, which is everything. Tonight they'll sleep on the floor of a dirty room with a broken fan and cockroaches the size of their lovely little hands. Still, Nancy Barry has her suite at the FCC, so it's not a totally inhumane situation we have here, no point in being cynical.

Most of the cripples (is that a bad word? why?) at LCSOBA have injuries from motorcycle accidents, or from using machinery. Only one or two are injured by land-mines, but getting funding and donations for land-mine injuries is easier, relatively, because land-mines are an *issue* westerners can get into, and ordinary accidents just aren't sexy enough, don't have the delicious hand-wringing pull of guilt that land-mines do. But motorcycle injuries are endemic and often lethal. Nobody wears a helmet, and motorbikes – ratty little 50cc two-strokes – are overloaded with extended families (five-up is common, sometimes six), livestock, produce, whatever. Add alcohol, a total lack of awareness of other road users, poor or no street lighting, brutal potholes, and non-existent insurance, and you have a workable formula for killing and maiming thousands of luckless Cambodian sons of bitches every year. But tonight, the focus is on creative recycling of waste materials towards a sustainable eco-environment, initiating a motivational engine for pro-active change, and I'm sick of it. I arrange to meet Krist at the Lizard after he's taken the dancers back in the truck. Nancy Barry cuts in to congratulate him. Modest guy that he is, he runs his hand back over his bald head and grins awkwardly. He thinks of himself as just a driver, a driver for Jesus. Nancy Barry calls the dancers *darlings*, and I do puke fingers behind her back for his benefit.

The Leaping Lizard is a bar down an alley in the Old Town, run by the World's Most Stoned Human Being. I don't think he's had a clear head since Altamont. You can get a contact high just by looking at his name in the phone book. There's always a charm bracelet of hookers draped around the lamp on the corner, but this is an area of activity I've neglected for a while. For one thing, my money is running out. For another, I have a place with its own toilet, and I'd have hookers piling up in the yard. And for another, I have pecker fatigue. It just wants to be let alone. In fact, it's gone on vacation. It left a note in my pubic hair, *back in four weeks*, and was last seen flagging down a tuk-tuk on Airport Road. I hope it comes home tan and raring to get back to work, but in the meantime, I'm learning how to breathe.

The big mistake in this meditation is breathing deep, in a kind of yogically calming way. Breathe through your nose, not your mouth, and focus your closed-eye attention on the tip of your nose. Don't follow the breath down into your lungs and back, you'll get lost. Stay at the tip of the nose, and don't breathe deliberately and wilfully, just be aware of your breathing at the tip of your nose. And that's it. Why should you subscribe to this seemingly banal activity? It's free, and it's not harmful, and it doesn't bother anybody. Those are good enough reasons alone, but it's also an *in* to being aware of the moment, to being in the instant while it changes, and no amount of intellectual understanding is going to do this for you. It's *letting it happen*, not thinking or analysing. Find somewhere comfortable but not sleepy, sit upright without support, relax your body, and let the breathing thing happen. Ten minutes a day, five in the morning, five in the evening. You should really do this, because it's proving too much for me. I'll do anything to avoid it. Clear the yard again, rewrite that paragraph about corporate sponsorship packages, go for a yogurt and a nap at the Blue Pumpkin. Or meet my Jesus Nut Chum for a light snack at the Shitfaced Pizza Company, or a tasty beverage at the Lizard. We don't have much in common other than the traits shared by all the white guys drifting around South East Asia in the wake of a savage divorce, wide-eyed with the discovery of the slender, gentle femininity here, and bitter at being ripped off and fucked over by white women. These ugly sentiments form a common bond between us, Krist and me, as we pass the dutchie on the left hand side at the bar of the Lizard.

How's the wife? I say. He has a beautiful Khmer girlfriend who wants to get married, preferably to him if he doesn't spend too much time circling his toe in the hot sand and dimpling prettily.

He grimaces. *We had a fight.*

Oh. I drop the subject. *How about that Jesus thing you have going for you?*

Jesus – he takes a long crackling drag on the joint, and his voice sounds like it's squeezing through the neck of a balloon – *is all I have.*

Oh, come on. He fucked you over, and he's gone. Seriously – when was the last time he called?

He didn't call. He doesn't have to use the phone, *he's Jesus.*

Okay, when did he speak to you last?

This would be Idaho, so, three years ago.

And you pray every day, right?

Sure. Three, four times a day.

And your prayer is what, you're asking for something?

Sure. I ask for forgiveness.

For what? Being ripped off by your ex-wife and her brother? Helping cripples?

I'm beginning to think . . . there's a possibility . . . he's not her brother. They've been seen in town, restaurants, picking

146

out drapes, like they're newlyweds. I pray to God he's not her brother, anyway, for their souls' sake.

I'm glad you figured this out, because I was going to tell you.

You knew? About Wayne and Roberta?

Well, yeah. If that's her name. Roberta?

They say the husband is always the last to know.

Also, work with me on this – the computer guy? Guy that writes codes for computers, Mister Peace of God.

What about him?

You remember his voice? What does his voice sounds like?

Ye-ahhh . . . uhhhh . . .

Does he sound anything like – Jesus? To your personal knowledge? Hmm?

He thinks about this for a while, squinting as he conjures voices from the past. Then he turns to look at me, narrowing his eyes, and he recoils slightly, holding himself erect and distant.

I see what you're doing here, he says. *It's a test of faith.*

He presses his hands together in prayer, squeezes his eyes shut. *Thank you Jesus for testing my faith, thank you for making my friend here an instrument of your will.*

I'm staring at him when he opens his eyes. *Heads up to the Son of God – I'm really going to tap his nuts if he makes me the instrument of his will again. Tell him, next time, find someone who gives a shit about what his old man says.*

Ah, he says. *That's why he chose you, my friend. He's working through you.*

I'm signaling for more drinks while he says this, we're

benefitting from the Lizard's relaxed Happy Hour policy to chase the FCC Champagne with some *vodkalox*.

So, I say, as we moisten our beaks, *do you buy into in this Rapture shit? The Second Coming?*

The joint has gone out. He flicks a disposable lighter, the flare cutting deep lines in his face.

Nah. That's a little flakey for me.

SLEEPWALKING OVER BROKEN GLASS

Nui won't come into downtown Bangkok, where we usually meet, at the Siam Centre or the Emporium mall. It's been a year since her last night on the town with me. I'm passing through on my way back from Burma, my failed attempt to find Nu Win. I'd shown his photograph around other cab drivers, but there are thousands of men who fly a hack for a day or two and then try to scrape up some cash doing something else, so my grubby photograph meets with blank looks. The telephone number he gave me was disconnected, no signal at all. I try hiring a cab for the day but couldn't remember the route to the temple, and my driver was a toothless betel-chewing rogue who levered another five bucks out of me before he'd take me back to town. This was the *you can't go home again* thing happening. I knew it was wrong, trying to repeat the experience, but once you've seen Shangri-La, you'll crawl over broken glass to get back.

So Nui. I'm waiting for her at the Victory Monument BTS,

the elevated Skytrain station, and I'm still crawling over the broken glass. I have a vague plan to go to Phnom Penh, and up through Cambodia to Laos, but that's about all I have. I'm staying in a 200 baht windowless room off Silom, with a door I had to buy a padlock for and three beds blatantly refuting the Goldilocks theory. In spite of the supernumerary cribs, there's no question of entertaining ladyfriends, hosting Book Club meetings, or idle afternoons spent just pottering around straightening pictures, and the less time I spend awake in that room the better it looks. I'm taking Xanax to help me sleep. It's not the real thing, it's a cheap knock-off I get on the Sukhumvit Road, one of those hole-in-the-wall pharmacies where they hide the illegal stuff in herbal remedy boxes. This particular medication is used by evil ladyboys to drug their victims so they can relieve them of their wallet and phone, and it's also the sleeping pill of choice for the would-be suicide, and it's turned my brain to mush. The panic attacks are gone, but so is the sex drive, and the will to live. I call Nui because my mobile is about to die on me and I'm not going to top it up. I just want to know if she's okay, but she doesn't want to talk on the phone, says we should meet.

I'm waiting on the elevated walkway outside the station, leaning on the rail, looking down at the brightly-colored traffic and the people, and thinking about how different it is from Rangoon, the footbridge over the Mahabandoola Road intersection, looking at the Sule Pagoda in the hyper-chromatic blur of Burmese sunset. The Sule Pagoda is the site of regular monk-clubbing and citizen-slaughtering carried out by the junta to keep the streets free for their tanks and motorcades. It's beautiful, but dwarfed by the junta's brutal highrise narcotechture. Which is more than can be said for Bangkok's Victory Monument, a fascist-style obelisk commemorating an absurd WWII Field Marshal's vanity. To their credit, Thais hate the fucking thing, too. Unfortunately, unlike a lot of Thai architecture, it hasn't yet fallen over or been demolished to make way for a Tesco Lotus superstore. It's more important, and universally known, as a bus station, and to my knowledge no monks or poor people or students have been gunned down here. You'd have to get a cab to Thammasat University to see where the blood flowed, the altogether more discreet memorial to the students massacred and mutilated in 1976 by the para-military *Red Guars* (massively funded by the US) with a far greater corpse-count than the handful of soldiers "commemorated" by the Victory Monument.

Thinking about this stuff isn't making me any happier, as I watch the good Thai people, and some government workers, coming up the steps to catch the Skytrain, but I think it's information I'd rather have than not. Soldiers march to misery, whatever flag they wave.

So. Nui. I *always* have to wait for Nui. Chromosomically correct or not, she has this quintessentially feminine trait encoded in her g-for-genome string. I'm expecting a more casual version of the cover model I last saw outside the Chinese temple, when we'd both taken cabs in different directions. Maybe she'll have a kind of Jackie O. Hyannisport thing going for her. I never saw her in anything that wasn't immaculate, and I look like I feel. I've lost weight I can't afford, my clothes need a wash and then incinerating, and I need a shave and a haircut, and maybe I should get myself incinerated too. I look like a gristly, bristly red-nosed bum, and I'm surprised and disappointed the citizens aren't dropping spare change at my feet. I'm thinking maybe Nui knows how I am, in her witchy voodoo queen way, and doesn't like the idea of being seen in a nice place with a piece of white trash leaning up against her shuddering every so often. But my main problem right now isn't personal grooming for successfulness, which I could care less about. In addition to burning me out, Rahu has found time to burn out the transformer for my MacBook, and the price of a replacement will be a major bite out of my dwindling living expenses. If I had a PC, I could pick up a transformer for a couple of hundred baht on any street market. In fact, I can find a PC for less than the price of a Macintosh transformer, but the last thing I want to do is upset Steve Jobs, I don't want to loosen the bolts on the boilerplate over his white-hot vat of plasma-fury. So I'm not writing, and I can't lose myself in this complex narrative I'm constructing, about someone I'd like to be but never can. I miss these lost hours like an addict misses a fix. I have nothing to do, no purpose, and perversely, this is something I don't want to change right now. Because I've lost very nearly everything, had it all stripped away, carried off by carrion crows, and I'm interested in what's left, what you are when you stop being a worker, a writer, a whatever.

So I do what I do whenever I have a moment to spare, which is all the time, I reach for my Buddha Soundbite book and open it at random.

"There is walking to be done, and a path to follow, but there is no walker."

Baddha

Like all Buddha's mind-tattoos, these words are deep-dyed, indelible, glow-in-the-dark. In my *nah-vel* (which has ceased to go anywhere, like me), I use Walker as my hero's name, because of my attachment to this dense and intense quote.

I've been deserted by Old Guy, for some reason. Haven't seen him for a while, although I occasionally think I see his coolie-hatted head in a crowd. I need him now, or I'm just going to be talking to myself, so I'm going to have to conjure him up, like magic. Pretend he's here. See? Here he is, leaning on the rail at my side, noisily sucking a black jelly drink through a straw. He looks shockingly out of place here, among the commuting office workers, like the Ghost of Old Siam, but nobody seems to notice.

"You look terrible."

Why, thank you, old man.

He takes my book from me and looks at the passage I underlined.

"There is walking to be done, and a path to follow, but there is no walker," he says, passing the book back. He finishes his drink, smacking his lips in satisfaction. "This isn't the Parable of the Pedestrian." He's looking for a trashcan for his empty bottle. "There's an obvious connection with the *way*, the path to truth, but this is one of Buddhism's more romantic images, bringing to mind the barefoot hermit climbing the mountain with his staff. That's *so* not you."

He surreptitiously tosses the bottle over behind him, down onto the sidewalk, and we both move from the rail for a few seconds in case it bounces off a Thai skull.

"In Buddha's phrase, walking represents activity, doing.

We fondly believe there is an *I* doing all the walking, the sitting, the eating, the thinking. *I* am doing this, *I* am doing that. Buddha saw that the *I* claiming responsibility for the action, owning the action, is an imposter, a fraud, a shadow who – apparently – flits from action to action, reinventing himself all the time to cover his tracks."

He rubs his palms together in pleasurable anticipation of the truckload of bullshit he's going to back up to my front door.

"Imagine a room full of people, they all look the same."

It's a Scientology convention.

"Everybody in the room is motionless, standing still, except one, who is walking around."

He's serving tasty snacks and beverages.

"He's just walking. That's the only way you can distinguish him from the others."

Blacking out with boredom here.

"If I ask you, where is the walker? What do you do?"

I point to the guy walking.

"Okay. Now he stops walking, stands still like the others. Point to the walker."

Holy crap! He disappeared!

"You can't point to the walker. The walker, as a distinct, discrete identity outside the act of walking, does not exist." He lifts his forefinger, and my nerves are so shot I flinch. "Same people, same room. Someone else starts walking. Where is the walker?"

Scientologists are nuts.

"When someone walks, he's the walker. When he sits, he's the sitter. When he talks, he's the talker. This equation can and must be simplified, because it contains a term with no value or effect. The term is *he*. Reduce it to there *is* walking, there *is* standing, there *is* sitting. There is no walker behind the walking, no stander outside of the standing, no sitter doing the sitting. There is just the activity, the act. Extend this principle to thinking. Thinking is an activity, it's doing. So – there's no thinker doing the thinking, just the thinking."

I think, therefore I'm not.

"Normally, we're multi-tasking on a huge scale. In addition to all the bodily activity that goes on regardless of our awareness or control, we're thinking, feeling, using our sense organs, balancing, carrying, writing, talking, listening, driving a car, eating ..." He backs off a little to see me better. "Washing, showering, shaving, using soap, doing our laundry. For example."

I've been busy.

"More than you know. You're whirling with activity. So much so, it's impossible to see the vacuum at the centre of this whirlpool. Don't get tricked by the *just being* thing. Buddhists have a tendency to revere *being*, as if it's some pure and precious state. But *being* is only another activity. We say, *I* exist, *I* am, but again you can cut out the middle-man. There *is* existing, there *is* being. There's nobody doing it. There is no wizard behind the red curtain, no ghost in the machine, no puppeteer pulling the strings. No actor. There are only acts, actions, activity, from a universal scale to the human scale to the sub-atomic scale. In scientific fact, there is no such thing as a thing, there are only events, actions. The universe happens."

The hippies got that right, at least. It's a happening scene, man.

"What you recognise as, say, a table -"

Whoah. Could we use an apple? It's my favorite metaphorical device.

"What you recognise as an apple, a distinct and separate object in space, is a complex activity, or combination of activities, that suggest the idea of an apple in your mind. What you call an apple is the label we give to a snapshot of the cycle that includes the apple falling from the tree, rotting away, the seed taking root and growing into a tree and producing more apples. An apple is not separate from that cycle, it's part of it. Is there anything behind this cycle? Anyone pedaling the apple tree cycle around? Of course not. Is there anything behind the cycle of a sun? A rock? A human being? Anyone doing the being? Who beats your heart?"

Thinking this is a rhetorical question, I wait for him to go on.

"Come on, who beats your heart?"

It's an automatic motor reaction. Nobody beats their heart.

"Who grows you?"

It's a, well, it's automatic, at cellular level. I don't grow me.

"Who processes food in your gut?"

Okay, I get it. But there are many functions I consciously control, like I use my legs for walking, my brain for thinking.

"So where does this *you* come in, this *conscious controller* who is so noticeably absent when it comes to essential activities such as growth, circulation, breathing, and digestion? Why the sudden necessity for someone behind the scenes when it comes to the brain?"

Because these are functions I have to be able to control.

"So where is this *I* located? From where do you control and monitor the billions and billions of interdependent events and systems necessary to the life of the human being?"

Somewhere in the brain. It's like a tiny control room, with DNA-sized CCTV and dials the diameter of an atom. I'm in there, drinking coffee from the smallest mug in the universe and listening to this stupid conversation on headphones made out of hollowed-out electrons.

"Okay, fair enough. And this omniscient micro-dwarf, this *you*, flicking all the nano-switches, presumably he doesn't make these decisions at random, but after thought. Or he's un-necessary, and out of a job. So he'll need a brain to use for thinking, only it'll be half the size of a neutrino."

This is the most retarded conversation I ever had.

"There is conversing, and a conversation, but there is no converser."

Buddha's always pitching the same ball, but I always leave my catcher's mitt in the car.

Listen, I'd love to smack some more Zen-lite ideas around, but I really have to go stand over there and wait for Nui.

"She's not coming."

What, she sent you with a message?

He puts out his hand. "Twenty baht, for the train."

You promise to be on the next one, I'll give you fifty.

He picks the note out of my hand. "Something to think about while you're waiting," he says, "*This* world, this ordinary hum-drum everyday normal work-a-day world," he gestures around him, the people walking by, the station architecture, "*this* world is the magical, miraculous, mythic, monstrous, mystical world. Buddha is the ultimate pragmatist, the seer-through of flim-flammery, smasher of smoke and mirrors and voodoo ju-ju, the great breaker of spells. If you're happy sleepwalking in fairyland, you don't need him, and you don't need me."

He walks off toward the change booth, his cheap flip-flops clapping against his heels. He is the walker, I am the sleepwalker, and I'm sleepwalking over broken glass. I turn away before I see him disappear.

So. Nui.

CRAZY BILLY CALLS

First, don't get mad with me for taking *your* computer and hijacking *your* book. I won't be around to see your anger, and the only person that will suffer from it will be you. Second, you can delete this, or leave it in, or change it to suit your needs, whatever you want. I haven't touched the writing you've already done, even though I was tempted to improve some of the speeches you have me make. You can't remember everything I say word for word; unfortunately the oral tradition, so accurate and reliable, has been lost. But the words you give me to speak are close enough, and don't misrepresent me, so rather than start to tinker here and there (and believe me, I was tempted), I haven't touched a thing. Well, yes, I changed your horrible American use of a *zed* in words like *specialize* to an *s*. I really can't stand that particular *Americanization*, and the time and effort spent in weeding them out has made the book less harsh on the eye. On mine, anyway.

I admire your cheek of "having to invent" my appearance at the Victory Monument, by the way. I'd been waiting for you all morning, as you well know, and as for deserting you, I am always hopping up and down trying to get your attention. You don't mention me serving you champagne at the FCC, but maybe that's because I wasn't wearing my signature riceworker clothes, and all Asians look alike to you? You also don't mention me giving you a ticking off in Rangoon. That's my home town, and you were using it as some kind of backdrop for your stupid drama quest to find Nu Win, which I told you was hopeless and pointless. I'm *always* here for you. Because you're an idiot. But anyone reading this isn't going to see that, they're just going to think you drag me in whenever you're tired of writing about sex and drugs and whatever, and that you've oh-so-graciously and modestly given me your *wise man* lines to speak.

Okay, rant over.

I understand the disjointed narrative construction of this book reflects not only your state of mind but also gets across something of what you need to say about the nature of time, and how your use of the present tense is intended as a constant reminder to the reader to be in the present moment. But the lack of concern for telling a story leaves a gaping hole, and *that's why I'm here*. I'm not here to flatten your boxes or clean up after your dog or open the shop shutters in the morning and close them at night (bending to do that has hurt my back, something you seem to find a sly work-avoidance tactic of mine). I don't mind doing this, I understand I'm living in your house and sharing your food. But you should, and could, be getting more out of me. My appearances are like subtitles, or footnotes, a kind of "philosophical seasoning", where they should be the core of the book. Although you do go on about *this is not about you*, that's mostly what all this is about. So that's why I'm here, tapping at your computer like a short-sighted hen, while you're off buying stock.

When I lived across the river from Rangoon, I had a hammock over the water, and it was quite a trick swinging out into it. Once I was in, I'd spend most of the day there. I'd have a couple of beers in a net bag in the river I could lift up by a string, and I'd take some rice and a chicken foot or whatever. I'd watch the boats on the river, the children playing, the cooking smoke coming up through the trees from my village. I was happy, I suppose. I'd always avoided the trouble over the river. I'd always been able to, even when I was studying English at university, when we still had a university worthy of the name. I was luckier than some of my friends. I don't think you'll ever understand why keeping your head down is the major preoccupation of the Burmese people. So when I saw you coming across the river, with that absurd Frenchman standing like he was leading a naval exercise, I thought, here are people who have never had to duck. I know now it was a shame you hadn't learned, because you really got hit, didn't you?

But this isn't about you.

You're rightly wary of the word *enlightenment*, but that's what all this is about, what happened to Buddha under the Bodhi tree, and it's something I want to write about, for you, because you seem to be skirting around it, dealing with other things, like most people do. Someone once told me, a real traveller, not a tourist like you, that there wasn't a single enlightened man left in Tibet, and I suspect you could cast the net a lot wider. Non-Buddhists think it's beyond their interest or ability or authority to worry about Buddha's enlightenment, and no Buddhist I've ever met has shown any evidence of being able to think intelligently or perceptively about the subject. They mostly recite tired old clichés or brush it off as unthinkable, or, worse, pretend to *know* but be unable to transmit this insight.

It's only by stretching language to its limits that you can discover the limits of language, and you don't need to use specialist Buddhist terms for this, in fact it's better if you avoid them altogether. That doesn't make it any easier, just more approachable. It's still the hardest thing in the world to think about. I'm not concerned with your hypothetical reader, either. You can sugar the pill for him if you want, interpolate some of your "wise-ass" retorts, or invent some colourful detail to bring the scene to life (*why* did you give me a missing tooth?! I'll never understand that. Aren't I memorable enough with a full set? Or does a missing tooth make me conform better to your *poor Asian* stereotype?)

What happened to Siddhartha Gautama under the Bodhi tree turned him into the Buddha. Enlightenment or awakening or realisation are just labels we give to this *what happened*. He'd tried all the traditional Buddhist techniques, and found them adequate tools for making him contented, and a better person, but they didn't go far enough, they weren't revelatory. Buddhists will wag their fingers at this point, as if they've caught you out, and tell you it was his Buddhist/Yogic training that made his enlightenment possible, that led up to it, paved the way. If this was the case, Buddha would say so, and outline the steps so we could follow in them to Buddhahood. But he *doesn't*.

He specifically says he does not teach a system, *any* system, because the truth cannot be broken down into a system. Traditional Buddhist/Yogic techniques are nothing if not systems. This is something Buddhists, with their mental and physical trappings, find it impossible to deal with. The fact that Buddha does not specify or recommend or teach doing what they do. Throw away your monk's robes, your scriptures, your meditation program. Because they have nothing to do with Buddha's enlightenment, and it was this that made him Buddha.

Buddha doesn't spend a lot of time describing his enlightenment, but his brevity and conciseness allow us to go through it step by step:

"I came to a forest grove by a river, and sat under a big tree, sure that this was the right place for realisation."

He deliberately choses a spot to sit and work through what he knows he has to work through. This is in itself amazing. He doesn't know what he's going to do, or what's going to happen, but he knows this is the place and the time for *realisation,* which is a better word than enlightenment, but didn't catch on, for some reason.

So what happens next?

"All the conditions of the world came into my mind, one after another . . ."

Already, he's left the rest of us behind. He's off the map. We can understand the story so far, how this man has been a prince and a monk, and still knows there's something missing from life, and how he chooses the place and the time to find out what this something is, and how he sits down under a tree by a river ... and then he loses us. As soon as he tries to describe what happens in words, we – him, us, everybody – come up against the limits of language.

The first thing he does is throw us in at the deep end. "All the conditions of the world." We have to understand how and why he uses the word *conditions*. He calls the world, this world, this universe, the *conditioned* world. It means *caused*. He's talking about the causes and effects of the world, how every effect has a cause. Every event is conditioned by a complex set of other events, or conditions, or causes. Every thing/event is brought about by a particular set of conditions that could result in no other outcome. You don't get bread if you bake bricks. This is at once a very simple thing to understand, but the ramifications are extraordinary, if you think them through.

We ascribe a lot of life to chance, to randomness. These are labels we apply to something with causes we can't see and don't understand. The throw of a pair of dice, as an example. How those dice come to rest, the numbers they show, is the exact result of a series of interlocking and complex conditions that include; their position at rest in the cup, before the cup is shaken; the forces acting upon them and their relationship to the geometry of the surfaces in the cup as they are shaken; the spin and velocity imparted to them as they leave the cup; the angle and force of their impact with the table, and so on. If we could measure these forces and do the calculations, we would know that the way the dice come to rest is not at all by chance, but completely determined by the factors involved in the throw. *That result was the only possible outcome for that throw.* We only call it luck, or random, because we can't see and don't understand the conditions behind it. I use dice as an analogy for any and every possible event. Supposedly random computer activity is also determined by a set of conditions (the exact play of electrical current), although this is harder to visualise than throwing dice.

Once having disposed of the lazy conceit of randomness, we can tackle the issue of free will. Much pointless agonising is done over whether it exists, or if everything is predetermined. The simple and true answer is yes, we do have free will, but no, we don't. We have free will in the sense that we can make any decision we like, do whatever we like, within the limits of our capabilities. But this decision, *whatever it is,* will have been exactly determined by the set of conditions that informs it, and this set includes the reasons for our "decision" and the limits set by our capabilities.

The world is the way it is because it can be no other way. There has never been a crossroads, a choice, with multiple destinies, parallel universes, decided by luck or will. The universe we inhabit right now is the only possible universe. You are the only possible you. Nothing has gone wrong, there are no mistakes in the way things turned out, there's been no luck, good or bad. Fate may be decided on the spin of a coin, but that spin is already determined by its own set of conditions. You could not be "better" than you are, or "worse", richer or poorer, fatter or skinnier. There is a natural fairness and rightness to the universe, and the way things are, a justice beyond the magic theater we call law.

So when Buddha says "all the conditions of the world" he's talking about the causes for everything in the universe, and he's not talking about the idea of the conditioned world, which anybody can understand.

"All the conditions of the world came into my mind, one after another . . ."

There's no reason to suppose he's being inaccurate, or lying. This is very precise. He's not talking about *an understanding of the conditioned nature of the universe*, which these words of mine can realise in anyone reading them, with a bit of thought. He's talking about a serial succession of all the causes that form the natural world, coming into his mind one after the other. This serial succession is very important, and as far as I know is not given enough or any attention by Buddhists or anybody else. It's glossed over, or misunderstood.

"All the conditions of the world came into my mind, one after another."

This is Buddha's description of his realisation. There are countless words in the Pali canon, but this short phrase is the reason for their existence – without this happening, no Buddha happens. *This is the throw that results in Buddha.* To my knowledge – but I'm no scholar or authority – it's Buddha's only description of his enlightenment, all he can say about it.

It's not an instantaneous, blinding light kind of revelation. It's not Buddha's *eureka*! moment. It's a process, or procession. *One after the other.* He says *one by one*. A succession implies more than one, but is it a finite series? Are there, say, nine conditions in the world? This isn't an idle question, and it needs answering. If there were any comprehensible number of conditions, Buddha would have named them, categorised them, so we could learn them. Even a hundred thousand conditions wouldn't have been beyond the capabilities of the oral system of learning and recording they used in Buddha's time (there was no alphabet for the language used in that part of the world, so transcription was impossible, and the oral tradition was well established and practised, and certainly more reliable than committing information to the hard disk of a computer). So we have to assume the number of these conditions was not fixed, not finite, that the conditions that cause the universe cannot be counted. That they are *numberless*. He does not say he counted all the conditions of the world, and there are three and a half billion of them, and then they end, that's it, the complete set. All he says is, they came into his mind one by one. So we're presented with the seeming impossibility of an infinite number of conditions coming into his mind, *one by one*. Surely if this is the case, he'd still be sitting under the tree?

We need to understand infinity. And to do this you don't need to be a mathematician. In fact, it helps, because mathematicians don't know what numbers are. Terms like *infinity* and *eternity* (the same thing) are not their exclusive property, although they want you to believe they are. Mathematicians are the priesthood of an occult religion, and like all priests, they love to parade the richness of their knowledge against the poverty of your own – the humble crowd parts for the passing of the Pope. The more complex the equation (the liturgical incantation), and the more people excluded from understanding it, the happier the priest, and the more status he accrues.

One of the big cults the mathematical priesthood propagates is *infinity*, and how it's necessarily incomprehensible to the lay person. We're brought up to be baffled by the idea of infinity, but the idea of something being *finite* – which we're quite happy with – is actually the stupid, lazy, mad and misleading concept. The idea that anything can spring into existence from nothing, and then disappear back into it, goes against reason, and also, coincidentally, the so-called laws of physics.

If something is finite, it has an end, and the existence of an end presupposes the existence of a beginning, and the *end* and the *beginning* cannot exist without a *middle* to separate them, otherwise they'd be the same thing. 1,2,3, or A,B,C, or birth, life, death, it doesn't matter what you call them. So we're back to the tired old fraud of linear thinking. Nothing in the world has come from nothing, and nothing in the world disappears into nothing. Matter is energy constantly transformed, and nothing is lost. Fact. The idea of *finity* is based on nothing observable in the real world. It's an airy mathematical conceit, a fairy story, a mythological demon. Whereas infinity is *all* there is. It's everything, and it is very real, not a mathematician's fantasy. There is nothing else, and we don't need to start counting to understand it. There's only everything, and as such it's numberless. So Buddha's words, "one after another" don't imply counting, they mean (again) the constantly changing moment. Eternal instantaneous flux.

What did Buddha do, presented with this spectacle? Did he sit back and watch the show, in awe of the infinite majesty of the universe? Perhaps with a bowl of popcorn?

"All the conditions of the world came into my mind, one after another, and as they came they were penetrated and put down."

Each of these conditions (and we're still struggling with exactly what he means here by *conditions*, and will continue to struggle) is *penetrated and put down*. He sees through each condition, sees into its true nature, sees it for what it is, and in doing so can put it aside, forget about it, move on to the next. What he's seeing, and what he's telling us, is that all the causes/conditions of the world are linked, and cause and condition each other. It's like a chain where each link forms the conditions for the next, and so creates it. He sees *infinity* as the ever-changing instant, the conditions for the world recombining, always creating new sets of conditions. This infinite but one-by-one process is another way of describing the cyclical nature of things. He got a glimpse of the universe turning. He didn't lose himself in it, become dispersed atomic matter, he saw the world as it is, and spent the rest of his life trying to help us get a glimpse of it, too.

Why?

"All the conditions of the world came into my mind, one after another, and as they came they were penetrated and put down. In this way, eventually, a knowledge and insight arose, and I knew this was the changeless, the unconditioned."

Knowing the world as it is, and not as we think it is, does not in itself constitute Buddhahood. As clear as human perception has to be to realise this (as opposed to *understand*, which you and I can do), it's not enough. Buddha, in knowing the impermanent, ever-changing nature of the world, saw *that which does not change*, that which does not turn, that which is unborn and undying. It's this that freed him, that made him Buddha.

"All the conditions of the world came into my mind, one after another, and as they came they were penetrated and put down. In this way, eventually, a knowledge and insight arose, and I knew this was the changeless, the unconditioned. This was freedom."

"Composed and at peace, I broke apart, like a shell of armour, all that makes the self. The nature of all things is empty and calm and devoid of self. In truth, there is no individual being, no beginning, middle or end. Everything is an illusion, a vision or a dream. All beings in the world exist beyond the limits of language; their true nature is like the infinity of space."

There's a lot more I need to say, especially about this breaking down the shell of self, the whole idea of breakage, and the ideas of emptiness and illusion, which are widely misunderstood, but I'm tired and my eye aches. You'll be back any minute, so I'm going to finish here. I'll give you a couple of days to read it. Some of it may be above your head – please ask me if anything is unclear. If you decide to use it as the basis for a chapter, I'd suggest calling it "Glimpses Of Eternity – A Meditation On Buddha's Description Of His Awakening" but of course it's your book, call it whatever you want. I've flattened the boxes and tied them up, and taken *loi baht* from the cashbox for food.

Oh – Crazy Billy called.

KIND OF OPIATE SEX HAZE

There's nowhere like Soi Sii. Daytime, it's just another Bangkok street, scuzzier than most, School Of Crap architecture strung together with electricity cables, like sutures on a dirty scar. Nighttime, it's Santa's magic grotto for overweight, sweaty elves. You turn off the Sukhumvit Road into a microclimate of sweltering sleaze and funk. Thick-waisted white guys nurse beers at the rail to watch the passing show. Cripples, elephants and amputees, starving beggars and foodsellers, cane-tapping crooners hooked to battery amps, grinning dwarves, spittle-lipped Jehovas testifying in sweat-heavy shirts, bullet-headed porn thugs, and ordinary guys in space, their eyes like planets, holding hands with their one true Thai love, their wives and lives forgotten in the bone-deep soak of sex. And the girls everywhere; tramp-stamp tatts and whale-tail thongs, strappy tops and dangling bags, doing the broken-hip heel-clack slut-step in frayed sequin shorts, jeans tighter than paint, skirts short as a sigh, the girls and the half-girls, hand to hair, looking for the look, the hook, the short-time john with the bone and the baht ... this is Bangkok, the city LA would be if it had any balls at all. This is the whorehouse at the end of the universe, so swagger a little, white boy, do that testosterone strut down the miracle mile, because the crap you have to put up with is a million miles away, and here you're the King of the Hill.

Frog strides under the filthy neon into the Nana Entertainment Plaza, like a Foreign Legion captain inspecting a garrison. I follow, past the open-fronted bars, full of laughter and noise, past the spirit house (cluttered with votive offerings, bottles of soda, cigarettes, flowers) and up the escalator to the first floor. We navigate the narrow balcony, Frog good naturedly fending off the "hello girls" at the velvet curtains who spring from their seats to grab him. *Hansum man! Welcome!* I have assumed my mantle of invisibility in his shadow, as usual. I've lost my Bangkok virginity several times, catching up with stuff I should have done thirty years before, but tonight, he says, we're up for something different, or how he said it, *différent*, with a little Gallic pinch of his forefinger and thumb, *e-hon e-hon e-hon*. We go up some steps to a bar I haven't been to before, with unusually tall girls at the curtain competing in a breast-growing race. They seem to know Frog, their faces light up like neon, and we're escorted inside. There's the usual tiered seating opposite a stage, which is elaborate and multi-levelled, with fake rocks and real chrome poles and mirrors. And there's the usual mirrors up behind the seating, so the dancers can look at themselves, which go-go dancers like to do, and who can blame them. If I looked like them, I'd be all over myself *all* the time, I'd never get out the shower, I'd die of hunger in there soaping myself up. Go-go dancers aren't exactly dancers. They mostly do a tired, bored kind of shuffle, with one hand grabbing the pole in case they feel faint. If they weren't sex on a stick, it would be as interesting as watching someone strap-hanging on a bus. These particular dancers are taller than usual, and many have the kind of breasts thirteen year-old boys draw on toilet doors. Frog orders drinks from the mamasan, raises his eyebrows at me.

You like?

What's not to?

Well, some don't.

What do you mean? Who?

Men who think it's gay.

There's maybe a dozen customers in the place. They don't look gay. A couple have dancers in their laps.

What's gay?

Fucking a katoey.

You mean – these are . . .?

Frog nods, his eyes wide in a devilish grin. *Oooooooooooooh yeah.*

I stare at the dancers on the stage, at their crotches, which are barely covered by g-strings.

What, with cocks and nutsacks?

Frog laughs. *There's a bar in Patpong with post-ops, if that's your thing, but here they're all, uh, un-cut. The real thing, if you like.*

Where the hell they keep their junk? Tucked up their asses?

Katoeys are the big, big secret in Bangkok. Any man who's been here a few times gets into it, business types, the athletic American college boys, family men, the bar-owners, the totally straight guys with girlfriends, the police, the soldiers, all of them. But nobody talks about it.

The dancers nearest us are performing for our benefit, doing their best moves, and they're pretty good. They're also pretty unambiguous. It's not like you could misread the options they signal you. They all wear numbered buttons, the idea being you can ask the mamasan (in this place, a guy with ducky blonde curls) for that number to come and share a tasty beverage with you, chat about whatever comes to mind. But like in every other bar, you can do this by eye contact, a smile and a nod, actions I'm being careful to avoid.

So how do you know they do it?

You see them here, and other places. And you get introduced, like I'm introducing you tonight.

Now he's told me, I imagine I can tell that few of these creatures are not all they seem to be, or more than they seem to be. But I really didn't have a clue, coming in. And there's a few who are, I have to admit, stunning. It's weird, but it's exciting. Am I gay?

Which one am I going to be introduced to?

Oh, she doesn't work here. She doesn't have to work the bars. This is just for some fun and a few drinks. I set it all up, she'll come to your room. Midnight.

What, you set me up on a blind date with a dude in a dress? Gee, thanks.

You don't want her, I'll take her. Believe me, you'll want her.

Baddha

Our drinks arrive, and so do a couple of, uh, girls. Frog has two, in fact, but mine is already more than I can handle. The social etiquette we follow is courtly ritual of delicate *nuances*. We shake hands, make up names, I ask if she'd like a drink, and we fuck each other silly in a short-time hotel. There are some other things that happen, but they're not important. What is important is that *technically* I'm fucking a boy with breasts, which surprises me. It re-wires my head. We both have a good time, she (I'm sorry, ladies, but *she* is the word that works) fixes her make-up, which got smeared up against the shower wall, and goes back to work, and I wander out into the NEP in a kind of opiate sex haze. None of this was meant to happen. Just a few sociable drinks then back to the hotel to get my cherry popped by the Queen of the Night. But I'm done. It's eleven o'clock, Soi Sii is a boiling sump of pheromones, and I need a drink. I find a place at the rail of the Golden Bar where I can watch the activity at the Nana car park and order a beer, brushing off an old Chinaman trying to sell me something from the street. Fuck *off*! My beer arrives attached to a girl I take back to my room before I finish it. I can't stop myself. She's giggly and cute and what the hell. This is Bangkok, where less is so very *not* more, where too much is never enough. I hustle her out of my room before the bell tolls midnight, clean the place up a little, flush the condoms, kick my crusted shorts under the bed, rinse the shower, change a pillow for the one in the closet, and add refreshing floral accents to the ambience by douching the semen-heavy air with what's left of my cologne.

Around one o'clock maybe, I fall asleep with the TV on,

some movie about dumb American teen sluts getting slaughtered in the woods for being dumb American teen sluts. It's only breakfast time, toward noon, that I notice the card slipped under the door. It's a business card, expensively printed on linen-finish stock. There's a tiny embossed lotus flower centred above some elegant type, a mobile number, and a name. Nui.

HOW ABOUT THAT YOGURT
FOR EPHEMERALITY

I do not feel good. I'm staring at my bed, at the thin mattress. There's a big dark oval, about the length of my body. I bend to sniff it. Not piss, I haven't started senile incontinence, which is a relief. But it's soaked, the mattress glistens as I press it. I lick my fingertip, salt. Sweat. I feel dizzy, steady myself against the wall. I feel weak. Maybe I overdid the health drinks yesterday with Krist. Point of fact, I didn't feel too great yesterday, put it down to the brutal heat and existential *ennui*. I drag the mattress to the stairs and push it over, thinking, I'll hang it and me both out to dry and we'll be fine. Now I have to sit down on the bed, the activity wore me out. Fuck – I have *something*. AIDS? I did get a mite careless back there in Bangkok.

Shit. I have AIDS. I'm going to die. It's a hundred per cent certain. In a matchwood shack on a polluted river in Cambodia, my thin frame blotched with festering pustules

177

and weeping open sores. My Great Novel tragically unfinished.

Oh, woes.

Not exactly the glittering academic and professional career set up for me, but the dice fall exactly as they're thrown. Yeah, I asked for this. I thought I had nothing left to live for and fucked some whores and I got my end sticky and I am *going to die*. I curl up on the hard bed. I feel clammy, a little nauseous, my arms itch, my bones ache, but I mainly feel weak, as if I drained all my strength into the mattress. I don't have too many options. I count them off. One, lie down and die. And ... that's it. I can't think offhand of anything else that's workable. I don't have a phone. I have no transport other than skinny old legs which have just crumpled under me like drinking straws. It's not like anyone's going to miss me at the office. I'm fucked, Rahu has won. He kicked the shit out of me and then he made me eat it.

But a weird kind of peace comes over me. I'm too weak to be able to do much else than breathe, and it's restful. The sunlight slices through the shutters, I can hear the sound of traffic from the other side of the river, the road into the Old Town, the day starting to get busy.

I close my eyes. I want to talk to Krist, tell him some of the writing I did for his web site is good to go. I want to talk to Nui, say goodbye, say thank you. Tell her it's her eyes I can still see. I wish my ex-wife was by my bedside. I'd hold her hand and tell her there's no hatred left, but she should go fuck herself anyway just as if there was a shitload of it.

I should drink.

Baddha

Water. Lots of it. Rehydrate. There's a bottle somewhere. I can not move. I feel like a voodoo doll, pins in me. I feel something at my throat, touch it. The *Rudraksha*, my mystical protection. So much for *that* shit. But who knows, maybe it's worked for me so far, exhausted its powers. It's all I'm wearing, and the thought comes to me that they'll find me here, eventually, naked and stinking, bloated with my own gases, eyes crowded with flies. The dead cat at the temple gates. Where I come in is where I go out.

Breathe. *Breathe*, dammit.

It's hard to tell, but I drift in and out of consciousness for quite a while. I hallucinate an old Chinaman who appears in my room and sits cross-legged by the bed. He says it's important I remember what he tells me, but that's all that I *can* remember, how important it is I don't forget. I cling to that. Okay, I got it. *Do. Not. Forget.*

When I get clear enough to know for sure that I am conscious, I'm in a different room. Painted concrete walls, glass windows, and a noisy aircon. A plastic crucifix, the type with a Jesus stuck to it, above the door. The bed's comfortable, and I'm wearing baggy boxer shorts and a tee. An I.V. tube runs into my arm from a bottle hooked to a nail in the wall above my head.

When I wake up again, I see Julius Krist, as if in a vision, his bald head surrounded by the saintly aureola of a flyspecked ceiling lamp.

You rascal, you, he says. *You had us worried there.*

I cough, trying to find my voice. He fumbles with a plastic tumbler, lifts my head, and I sip the warm water. *What do I have?*

Dengue fever.

Dengue fever? Shit – how?

Mosquito bite, probably. We got a medic in to look at you, I didn't get you to hospital because there's not a lot you can do for Dengue fever, you just have to ride it out, see if it kills you. Plus, I don't know if you have medical insurance, and this kind of thing can mount up.

How long have . . .

Day and a night here. Before that, I dunno. You've been doing a lot of mumbling.

Please, don't tell me you prayed for me, okay? I'm still weak.

Okay, I won't tell you. Hungry?

Almost.

Good. I'll get some rice sent up, maybe a little fish?

Sounds good. Oh – do me a favor? The Jesus souvenir over the door? It's depressing the shit out of me.

So I'm set up in the guest room at LCSOBA, the air conditioning on wheeze, and I'm propped up in bed, my laptop on the folding plastic tray I eat my meals off. I type out a lot of notes, stuff that's been going round my head I can maybe put into my novel, but it's all in bits. I write something about the Fall from Eden which comes out of nowhere. I'm getting frustrated with this when there's a knock on the door. It's him again, the old guy I spoke to under the house the day I got here. He's holding out a bottle of yogurt from the Blue Pumpkin.

"I thought you might like this. It's not cold any more."

Thanks. The top's off, there's a straw in the neck. *Did you drink some?*

He shrugs. "I tasted it."

He places it carefully on the floor by the bed. *Hey – could you get the door? The air conditioning?*

He shuts the door, pulls up the plastic garden chair, brushes it off, and sits with his knees together, his hands resting on them. "When was the last time you saw me?"

Here, at the house.

"Do you remember what we talked about? What I said?"

I try to remember. *Something about Buddha?*

"Something about Buddha." He looks at me for a long moment. "Do you remember a few days ago? At your house?"

What, being sick?

"We talked. Well, I talked, mostly."

This makes me feel angry, which I barely have strength for. *At my place? You were there?* I have to control my voice. *You came to see me when I was fucking dying, and all you did was lecture me about Buddha? It didn't occur to you to get help?*

"Of course it did. That's why I was there." He takes off his hat, runs his hand over the frosty bristle that covers his scalp. I can see the muscles stretch in his neck. "I gave you the best medicine I could. But I'm guessing you remember none of it, right?"

No, I don't, and I don't care. I don't know what gives you the right to keep turning up and lecturing me about Buddha any time you feel like it.

"You do."

Huh?

"Listen, we have a problem. You don't have the capacity

to remember on one hearing, it goes in one ear and out of the other. You must write down what I tell you, or it is lost."

Thanks for the offer, but I already have two writing projects, for your information. I'm writing web site content for the association, and I'm also writing a novel. I am a published novelist, so if you want a typist to take dictation, I am regretfully unavailable. And if you don't mind, you interrupted my work. Thanks for the yogurt, and bye-bye.

He nods toward the bottle on the floor. "You going to drink that?"

No, okay, I say testily. *You finish it.* I have to wait while he sucks it up through the straw. It's a thick drink, and it takes him quite a while, his cheeks hollowing alarmingly. I pretend to immerse myself in my writing, as if he wasn't there, but I can hear him slurp and gurgle and swallow. Eventually he's finished. Or I think he has. Then he smacks his lips and sighs in satisfaction. Then he wipes the bottle out with his finger, sucks it clean. Then he wipes his finger on his pants. Then he carefully puts the bottle back on the floor. Then he sits with his hands on his knees again.

Have you quite finished?

"What are you working on?"

I don't answer for a while, type out something meaningless, frowning. *Nothing. Notes. I, you know, I rough in ideas. Part of the creative process.*

"Read it to me."

It's just stuff going through my head.

"Humor me."

I shake my head in a wide-eyed, this-is-fucking-stupid

way, and tilt back the screen of the laptop. *The Fall, our casting out from the Eden of childhood, is not in the eating of the forbidden fruit, but in the naming and counting of it. "Understanding" the natural world, paradise, in this way puts it at a distance. We are truly cast out from the garden, and not in any metaphorical or allegorical sense. Things are not what they seem.*

I close the laptop. *I told you it was stupid.*

"Not stupid at all. As stars, a lamp, a mirage, as dewdrops or a bubble, a dream, a lightning flash, a cloud, so one should see conditioned things. You should take notes."

I'm not taking fucking notes from a snaggle-toothed old Burmese field laborer. No offence.

"None taken. Ready? Everything, from the sun our planet orbits, to a tiny dewdrop, everything is ephemeral, unlasting, impermanent. They are events, not objects. To see the world as events is to see it as it is – things happening, not things with any permanent reality in themselves. Wonder at it, but don't mistake it for permanent, fixed reality. All this – look around you – is a firework display."

I look around the room. *It's a pretty dull firework display.*

"Really? It's wonderful. Everything that has a beginning and an end in time is wonderful and magical *because of that*. Everything, and everything is an event, has a beginning and an end in time, and it is this very quality of eternally *coming to be, ceasing to be* that makes our world magical and wonderful. Things are events and are magical, unreal, and fantastic because they seemingly appear out of nowhere and disappear into nothing. Not only the spectacular cosmic events of the universe, the black holes and suns and galaxies

– but the mundane objects we see around us, this chair, the bottle of yogurt-"

Yeah. How about that yogurt for ephemerality.

"are at an atomic level merely a complex play of energy, a combination of forces too subtle for us to appreciate. Nothing has more substance than a rainbow."

I gesture mystically. *It's all an illusion.*

"Yes, but not in the commonly misunderstood way. People think that Buddha says everything's an illusion in the sense that none of it is real or of any significance. They couldn't be more wrong."

That's people for you.

"If there's one corny Buddhist stereotype that everyone's familiar with it's the notion that this world is illusory, unreal. What Buddha means by illusion refers to everything that has a beginning and an ending *in time*. That is, every damn *thing* in existence. Buddha called this world – this universe – illusory purely because of its impermanence. The very idea of things coming to be and ceasing to be is magical. This is the magical world – the world as you perceive it, not the world as it is. The world as you perceive it is like a dazzling froth apparently whipped up from nothing, then passing into nothing. When Buddha says the world is empty, he means empty of your ideas, of preconceptions, of thinking. It's our thinking that fills it up, obscures it."

I pretend to have fallen asleep. After a while I hear the door open and close, and then I really do fall asleep.

When I wake up, I see my Buddha Soundbite book on the chair with the yogurt straw marking a place. The old guy marked a passage with a tick in the margin:

"Don't think I say that things are nonexistent, cut off from life, unimportant. I never say such a thing. The awakened mind does not deny objects or say that they are unreal. But a thing, a self, is not so in essence but only in idea. The names self, person, object, are names only. Everything in the world is like this, and you should have confidence in their essence without names."

I copy this out after my perplexing out-of-nowhere paragraph about the Fall from Eden, thinking about apples, my favorite metaphorical device.

Later, I'm talking with Krist. We're sitting on the busted couch under the house, watching the lights come on along Airport Road, the lurid greens and violets of the karaoke bars showing through the trees. He's telling me the thing about Dengue fever is that it kicks the shit out of your immune system. Once you catch it, it's not like your system uses it as a gym to get stronger and punch out the next invasion of viral visigoths.

What, I can get it again?

Yeah.

There's no, like, vaccine?

Uh-uh.

So, you're telling me . . .

I'm telling you, if I was you, I wouldn't hang around somewhere where people are dying from Dengue fever.

So that's it. The little life I have here is over, Dengue fever claimed a fatality of sorts, and it's thanks for the yogurt and bye-bye. The sound of the girls singing comes from the back of the house, laughter. A gecko up in the roof somewhere kickstarts his voice box, manages a respectable eight cries before stuttering to a halt.

Do me a favor, Jules?

Sure.

Say a little prayer for me.

He grins, that big lopsided Midwest grin.

I punch his arm. *Just kidding*, I say. *Save them for yourself.*

CRAWLING OFF THE JESUS TARP

I get up at around six, shower, make a pot of green tea while Djini barks little reminders at me. I drink my tea at the kitchen table, give my wife a tickle as she passes. She's a shy lady and it gives us both pleasure. Sometimes I chase her round the shop, if there's no customers, making tickle fingers. It's already hot by the time I get Djini's lead on, and she insists on biting it and leading the way, so people can see it's her taking me for a walk. So she takes me to the waste ground near the temple, where I sit on a rock in the shade and watch her race around and, if she's lucky, find some elephant shit to eat, or a dead toad or old fish to roll around in, anything that offends my human sensibilities. Sometimes I dip into my Buddha Soundbite book, but I mostly know it off by heart by now, which is a bad thing, because my mind races ahead to complete the phrase, like it's showing off, and I no longer think them through. This is one of the reasons I've started writing this Buddha crap, because it seems like a logical step, moves it forward, keeps it alive.

When Djini has made herself loathsome to her obvious satisfaction, I try to catch her to put her lead on, but she just has to be a big grown-up wolf and run back home by herself, heart-stoppingly weaving through tuk-tuks and motorcycles. She hides under the shelves in the shop, and I crouch down, my knees popping like firecrackers, to give her a half-hearted ticking-off.

Old Guy once tells me a great story about a zen dude being asked *does a dog have Buddha-nature?* And the zen dude says, *mu*, which is kind of Japanese for *no*. Now this trite little exchange has been the subject of endless show-off debate by people who think they're smart, but Old Guy tells me *mu* means *fuck off with your dumb questions*, and it's the only time I ever hear him curse. It's not like this stupid question doesn't have an answer – nobody or nothing *has* a Buddha-nature. It is not a possession or an attribute. This is why the question is stupid, and also why the discussion it "inspired" is also stupid, and why Buddhists are stupid for wasting time on it. ALBs love to waste time on shit like this, outsmarting each other with mystic profundities. Does a dog have Buddha-nature? Better ask a dog than a Buddhist.

Now, routinely, I'd notice Old Guy hanging around until I toss him a few baht for his breakfast. Today, he's not here. He's been absent since hi-jacking my book and writing a chapter himself, which I'm not too pleased about. In addition to the questionable ethics of the act, he's smeared up the screen. I can tell he was eating fish and sticky rice while he was typing, it's all over the keyboard. My lovely white computer looks like a used airline meal tray. I've found the best way to clean fish and sticky rice off a Macintosh keyboard is to use a damp dishwashing sponge and detergent. You give everything a good scrub, and a wipe with the cloth hanging by the sink. This also flushes out the colony of tiny, biting ants making a home for themselves under the keys, and maybe it rinses off the hard disk as well. I make a mental note to email Steve Jobs about this. So I sit out on the caged-in balcony at the back of the shop, next to the laundry rack, and add some material to my Buddha book for a while, but I need Old Guy's input to kickstart the Cosmic Theme. And I start resenting the fact that I need him to write my own book. And it's right now, when my feelings about him are at their lowest, that he decides to turn up. This makes it worse, because he knows I like to be left alone here, and also he has to walk through my bedroom, which I don't like, because there's usually some of my wife's underwear lying about. He's eating something, finishing off some fruit, and spits the pips out through the cyclone fencing that prevents hostile intruders from swarming up the side of the house and stealing my laundry. I don't say anything, keep typing, hoping he'll sense my mood and creep deferentially away. He wipes his hands on his pants legs.

"So? What did you think about it?"

Think about what?

"My contribution to your book."

I'm sorry?

"I added some content, you know, wrote a chapter."

You did? I didn't see it. Atone for your transgressions, Old Guy!

"You must have. Three or four days ago."

I make a pretence of scrolling back up through the document. *Nope, nothing here.*

He frowns. Got him! "Are you sure? I spent a lot of time on it. While you were off buying stock in Mukdahan."

What did you save it as?

He looks puzzled, repeats the question.

Yeah, if you didn't save it to the directory as an RTF file, the default settings revert to the original. This is bullshit, but I want him to suffer.

"What, you mean, it's gone?"

Nothing in the world is permanent, I say, with an airy gesture. *Words are just dust on the winds of time.*

"Let me see that."

I snap the laptop shut. *No. And you have some goddamn nerve interfering with my book. You could have wiped everything.*

"Without me, your self-vaunted writing would be nothing but a tawdry tale of sex and drugs. It's me that provides the real content and the value."

I'm sick of this. *Listen, you know what? I re-read a lot of your input. Even when sexed up by me it's a drag to get through. Great long stretches of head scratching pseudo-profundity. If it wasn't for the sex and the drugs, there'd be nothing here. And all my stuff is* real, *not pie-in-the sky philosophy.*

Old Guy pointlessly adjusts his coolie hat, staring out across the bushes and the palm trees and the tin roofs. "Pie-in-the-sky philosophy. Is that how you really feel?"

I've gone too far to back down. I can feel my heart beat. *Yeah.*

He turns and goes into the house. I shout after him, *Don't let the door hit you in the ass on the way out.* As soon as he's gone, I know I was wrong. But fuck it, he has no right to take control of my book, gaze at my wife's underwear, eat my fucking fruit.

I try to shake off my bad mood, get back into my book. I'm up to the part in Vientiane, in Lao PDR, where I find an old copy of my first novel in a used bookstore. It's quite an emotional Kodak moment for me, and I want to do it justice, bring to play all the sensitivity at my disposal. The scene has to resonate with the reader. But all I can think about is Old Guy. I close my laptop, take it into the bedroom, and plug it in to recharge. The recharger and the keyboard are hot to the touch. The floor beneath my feet is hot. I'm hot. This is good. I eat the heat out here, never get tired of it. Wear a short-sleeve shirt every day of the year. And no, it's not boring, like the LA climate. Thai climate has its seasons and peculiarities, but the heat is a constant. Sometimes its enough just to be part of that heat, sit and let it do its good work through my bones. Right now, though, I am my own micro-climate of bad weather. I take the *motosai* to the river, looking for Old Guy. His hammock under the boardwalk is slack as my nutsack in a sauna, but I see some crushed-up paper back there in the dark, and retrieve it, flatten it out. It's his crappy drawing of the yin-yang symbol. I put it in my pocket, just for tidiness. Then I get back on the *moto-sai* and head upriver, just to feel the hot air blast into me. No particular place to go. The Mekhong is low, really low. People are saying it's the Chinese, damming it back in their own country way upriver, and I'd put nothing past John Chinaman.

It wouldn't surprise me if they're using it to cool plutonium before releasing it over the border, bulldozing their own girl-babies into it. All the big fuck-off nations, Russia, the US, China, giving the rest of the world the finger, the erect I, the Big Number One.

I'm fucking menstrual. A bad mood is a very, very useful thing to have, a gift, according to Old Guy, who says attentiveness to the moment is attentiveness to how you are, how you feel, as much as anything else. To be aware of it, watch it come and go in the moment of forever changes. Good moods don't present you with a challenge, you're not motivated to take a step back. If you're happy, you're happy, and why spoil a good thing? But a bad mood is like a bad dog, and you're responsible for it. You're not the bad dog, although it seems that way. You identify with it, even give it a poke, get it growling and frothing at the mouth. But it's possible to see this beast for what it is, and to realise in this seeing that it's *not you*, and the beast is gone. There's a defect in language that suggests we are what we feel, and it's a defect encouraged by those Californian self-help shit-eaters telling you to *be* the anger! Don't deny it! We say, *I am angry*. That's the equation, self = anger. This is like saying you are your nose. *Be* your nose! If I learned anything from Old Guy, it's an understanding of self that is very helpful. Moods are like the weather, always changing, and none of them contains the *I* or represents the *I* better than any other, and identifying *oneself* – yes, *oneself*, here's a thing, another clue in the book of magic spells we call "grammar" – but wait! here's another correspondence hitting me in the face: *grammar/grimoire*. It's the same word!

And we still don't get it! And now back to *oneself*, the British Queen's snooty use of *one*. Beautiful! The first person – I am 1. The mark on the cave wall, the trace of blood left by the finger, or the line in the sand – cross this, you cross me, pal! All the troubles of the world come from making this mark. The mark means possession, ownership, making your mark on the world. Dividing it up. This is a great truth – by counting to one you create division.

I may have learned this attentiveness-to-moods thing from Old Guy, but I'm fucked if I can put it into practice. I'm gunning the motorcycle hard down the red dirt road, grit in my teeth, every muscle in my body tight. I'm a bad dog. In this beautiful place, I am an ugly thing.

But it's all blown away by the time I stop at the house in the forest, the storm has passed. I'm regretting that *pie in the sky* line I shot at him. I just want to see him again, shoot the breeze. Maybe apologise. Perhaps the old fraud's up there cheating at sudoku. I push through the heavy leaves, climb the ladder. No, he's not here, and the hammock's gone, the place looks deserted. From here, I can't see the river, the water's so low, just the beach sloping up to one of the long midstream islands, crossed by thin blue lines of plastic water pipe. Smoke from charcoal fires twists into the cloudless sky – see? Air, earth, fire, water . . . I hope Book Clubs dig this good stuff out because it's lost on the general reader (and they don't get any more general than you).

In my gut, suddenly, I know he's gone. Gone like a train. Maybe it's my woman's intuition. Maybe it's the sixth sense, an almost supernatural, instinctive thing beyond rational thought. Maybe it's the words I'M GONE scrawled in pencil on the rail.

Well, he comes and he goes. Coming to be, ceasing to be. This is what he does. Popping up when I need him least and disappearing when he's needed. I check my watch. I have to get back to my part-time gig teaching Business English at the temple.

I get to the schoolroom in the temple grounds as the monks straggle in. A couple of them are already sitting at the battered seats. One of them is sleeping, his chin on his chest, and I leave him be. These guys are up at four in the morning, filing through the streets for their rice. The other guy plugs in his laptop and checks his email or his Facebook page or whatever. Maybe he's selling amulets on eBay. I wait while they settle down. They chat, check their mobiles, some get out scruffy notebooks or torn sheets of paper. One or two still have the course notes I wrote and copied for them. The thing is, I'm here to teach these guys Business English, but their grasp of the language is so feeble that terms like *office* and *desk* are Business vocabulary. The monks are all from Lao PDR, aged around eighteen to forty, and the one thing they have in common with 99% of the outside world is an obsession with the outside world, and a complete disinterest in Buddha. They're tapping into it by wi-fi and portable phones, meeting girls on dating sites, and probably looking at porn like everyone else. I don't generalise from the group I'm familiar with that every monk in Thailand can't wait to pick up their graduation papers and step into a pair of polyester pants, but it's still a mystery to me that not one of them is interested in talking about Buddha. They can recite, if pushed hard, the Four Noble Truths, the Five Hindrances, the Seven Factors of Enlightenment, the Nine Rings of the Nazgul, and some other tired old Buddhist shopping lists (ALBs love these! Collect the set!), but as to actual *thought* – reflection, inquiry, meditation; there is no evidence of that at all, and this isn't something limited to this temple, this class, nor even this country. And it is, frankly, fucking depressing.

I say, *good afternoon, monks,* loud enough to get their attention. They mumble, *good afternoon, Ajarn,* which is Thai for teacher. To start the class, get them listening in English, I always tell them a little story about my life (why I'm here is probably the greatest mystery they confront in the temple), and today I tell them about Old Guy, this old Burmese laborer who's attached himself to me. Already I'm losing their interest, anything to do with Burma is elephant crap to these guys, and when I tell them he teaches me about Buddha it's like I've freed them from any involvement at all, and they start talking and joking with each other, and some go to cluster round the laptop open on the back row.

I have a choice here. Be stern and authoritative, tell them to get back to their desks and listen, or do a flounce. I opt for the flounce. I walk out, which is the right and very Thai option. With a smile on my face. My one Good Student follows me, *Ajarn! Ajarn! Where you go?* I tell him I'm going home, because I don't want to play at *Ajarn* any more. I tell him to drop by the store any time if he'd like to polish his English conversation. And I tell him if he sees an old man in a coolie hat and riceworker blues, with one good eye, tell him I'm looking for him.

I take a calming stroll around town in my fatuous *Ajarn* polyesters, getting the usual broad grins and hello-hellos from the citizens, which I return. This never fails to pick me up, just the good humor of the place. I have an eye out (weird saying) for Old Guy all the time. I duck into the internet shop to see if he's playing World of Warcraft online, which I know he enjoys. Don't see his coolie hat. I go down to the river, under the boardwalk again. I try the market, because it's closing, and he sometimes pockets fruit past-its-sell-by-date. He's not there. I'm thinking maybe I should tape up photocopy posters, *MISSING: ANNOYING, SMUG, FREELOADING OLD MYSTIC. Distinguishing marks: MISSING TOOTH. NO TEETH AT ALL. Warning! Has power to BORE TO DEATH. If found, kick in ass and send to Ajarn Farang.*

I get home, shower, sit on the balcony with my laptop, cracking my knuckles. Who needs him anyway? I got published without him three times, I can do it again.

I drift off.

Yeah. My first novel. Who'd have thought I'd find it here? I'm in Vientiane, capital city of Lao PDR, in a second-hand bookstore. It's a first edition, too. And I'm in a dilemma; buy it or leave it? I don't keep copies of my books with me, and it would be nice to have. But the idea of this battered bit of me finding its way here *before I do* is too magical and beautiful to mess with. I should leave it for someone else to discover. I'm looking for a phrasebook, so I can learn a little Lao, but there isn't a lot of choice, mostly badly-photocopied and antiquated, concentrating on the loopy alphabet, with fucked-up menu English written by somebody with a Vietnamese-English dictionary. But here it is, snuggling alongside the land-fill Dean Koontz and Dan Brown, the bright blue spine I know so well. I laugh out loud. Not because it's a funny book (it is, delightfully so), but through sheer surprise and happiness. I'm the only customer in the shop, but the girl at the counter looks up. I wave the book at her over the shelving. *My book!* She looks puzzled. Maybe she thinks I'm saying I own it, it's been stolen. *I wrote it!* Nope, not registering at all. Oh well. I calm down a little, thumb through it, the familiar phrases – *damn*, I'm good! And it's been much read, too. The spine is cracked almost to white, and the pages are pleasingly thumbed. I gently put it back on the shelf, smile at it goofily. I wish I had a pen, I'd write what just happened on the title page. I remember when it was published, the thrill of seeing it on bookstore shelves. I make a mental note never to go back into that Vientiane store in my life, because I don't want to see my book still there, waiting for someone to buy it like the last puppy in the pet store. That would kill the little flame that's just been lit, the little flame in the fog. I've been in a kind of slow-motion novocain cloud, attentive to nothing, but that chance meeting with my book, so very far from home, is like a confirmation that I'm on the right path, that things are happening as they should, and for the good, somehow. So I walk out of the bookstore and into the dimming afternoon streets, feeling a whole lot better than I have for a long time.

Vientiane doesn't do bustle and hustle. It's a capital city that feels like a backwater town. Dogs sleep in the street, if you had a car you could park it right in front of wherever you were going, if a dog hadn't got there before you. I have a three-dollar room in a guesthouse, and all I do is walk around and eat, and Vientiane is fine for both, although the restaurants (some with genuine European *khwi-siin*) are a little beyond my budget. There's great bakery, so I'm slowly putting on weight I lost from Dengue fever, I no longer look like a twisted antenna with laundry thrown at it. And seeing that tatty paperback makes me want to celebrate the fact that I'm still around too, so I head for the swanky (for these parts) Italian restaurant, with the swanky menu in a swanky glass case by the swanky door with the swanky dimpled glass. I'm going to swank out on red wine, for the first time since coming out here, and I'm going to plow through a big plate of pasta and scarf as many packets of breadsticks as I can grab, because *I am a published novelist.* I turn the corner, by the coffee stand where I have my morning coffee, and there's a tug at my pants pocket. Thinking its one of the massage girls from next door, I turn with a grin on my face, which stiffens into a grimace. It's Old Guy, sitting alone at one of the tables.

"You wanted me?"

Wanted you? Why?

"You were looking for me."

The last time I saw him was Siem Reap, maybe a couple of months back.

I frown. *I really don't think so. Why did you think that?*

"A monk told me. One of your students."

He's being oblique again. I sigh, pull out a chair opposite him and sit down. If I go to the restaurant now, he'll just follow me and I'll end up paying for him. He wouldn't be embarrassed about being in a swanky restaurant wearing Chinese railroad laborer's clothes.

"I saw your book, in the bookshop. Nice."

He gets me off guard. I'm about to say something like, yeah, they get all over, when it hits me. *How long have you been here?*

"Oh – would you like a coffee? She's closing up, I think."

No, wait. When did you get to Vientiane?

"Today."

And you've had time to browse the bookstores?

"Of course not. I saw you wave it about, shouting you were the author. Couldn't miss that."

He's trying to get the girl's eye, so I signal her for a coffee, saying *make that two* at a suggestive cough from Old Guy that's about as subtle as a submarine klaxon. I watch the girl prepare the coffee, grind the beans, make a professional job of it. Lao coffee is the best in the world, there's nothing that comes close. It amazes me how such a small country can't get prosperous on just this crop. In addition to their synapse-poppingly great coffee, they make one of the best beers in the world, imaginatively named Beer Lao, which, with a label that didn't stink and some marketing and distribution, could also be a world-beating brand, making the people rich. But no. They pride themselves on their production of *cement*. The displays of wealth you see here – the massive Champagne-silver and piano-black SUVs, the palatial homes – are bought on credit, with downpayments from government salaries or the black market. It's a People's Democracy, see, which means the government workers shuffle papers in air-conditioned offices on behalf of the farmers breaking their backs in the fields. I try not to think about this political stuff too much, because it makes me grind my teeth to a bitter paste in my mouth, and I can't say back home is that much of an improvement, either. At least out here, you have miracles to distract you. Like the girl working the espresso machine. Straight-backed, slender, her long hair bundled up in pins, a profile from a temple bas-relief. She works and moves with a featherlight grace that I've never seen in a white woman, and if this sounds sexist or racist, it's also the truth. I can, and do, get massive pleasure watching women out here do anything; ride motorbikes, walk, slip out of their shoes without breaking step, hold parasols against the sun. They dignify everything they do. I'm not lusting after them *all* the time, being a breathing machine for my dick, it's such a gentle pleasure to watch them, and what multiplies that pleasure is the smile I get if they see me watching. They don't come over and start yelling at me, or call the cops, like that one time in the mall at Hanover. They're pleased I like looking at them. A little moment to sweeten the day. She brings our coffees over, Americanos, and I say thank you in Lao, get the smile.

"You're looking better," Old Guy says, rotating his cup in the saucer. "I really thought I'd lost you back there."

You're a tough guy to shake off. I take a sip of the coffee. The only coffee in the world that tastes as good as it smells. Buy some today!

"Can I ask you a question?"

What, another one?

"Can you remember what we spoke about, back in Siem Reap?"

Baddha

No. Not that I'm trying.

"What *are* you trying to do?"

Right now, I'm trying to sell Lao coffee to my demographic.

"Do you remember why you came out here? I mean, this part of the world?"

His voice is gentle, but there's an edge to it. I notice the sun's down, the sky looks like a cheap hippie tie-dye. Good question, and one that *Frog done brung me* doesn't answer.

Come on, I say, let's let the girl finish up here. We drain our coffees, and even Old Guy's bad eye has a glint to it, like a cheap Zircon ring. We do a walk-and-talk to the river, to catch the last of the sunset. Why did I come out here? Herman Hesse? Jimi Hendrix? My first hit of acid, at sixteen? My second, a week later? Sergeant Pepper? Jack Kerouac?

Yeah, there it is. Let's put the blame on Jack, the pansy-ass Catholic mummy's boy.

On The Road, I say. *Read that when I was thirteen, and it changed everything. Didn't make anything easier, just made me dissatisfied with everything I had, made me hate and fear everything that was being lined up for me. Infected me with the yearning virus, I guess. I bought a bedroll and a backpack from the Army Surplus store, and it stood in the corner of my room for five years. I put in a Swiss Army knife, a compass, and the books I'd need on the road.* On The Road, *of course.* Zen Flesh Zen Bones. Love's Body. The Tibetan Book Of The Dead. The Journey To The East. The I Ching.

Old Guy laughs. He has a great laugh, like it's wriggling out of him. It makes him squirm, like he's being tickled. I don't know what he finds so funny, but it doesn't matter, I'm getting a contact high.

Books meant a lot back then! We used to pass them around. Do kids read books like that today? I don't think so. Books are dead, it's a dying thing. But yeah, Jack Kerouac, the son-of-a-bitch. He's why I'm here.

We walk on in silence. Infra-red clouds rip into fiery rags above our heads, stars piercing ink-purple depths. And that lazy moon, rocking on its back, yellow as the sun.

We got so much absolutely right back then. Blowing your mind, freaking out – phrases that got big yoks from the creeps and geeks who never did either. They won, of course, the guys that stuck to their desks and sneered – the lawyers, the bankers, the bean-counters, the virtual computer nerds. It's their world. Even out here, Buddha's footsteps have been crushed by SUV tires.

I guess it was inevitable it all went so badly wrong, I don't know. I went as badly wrong as any of it. Played the career game, became the corporate whore, the fake family man. Forgot Buddha's nudge in my ribs. Forgot the bedroll and the books. Worse, forgot the dissatisfaction, the urge to escape. I thought it was all over, dead with the death of the sixties, memories of foolish times, a box of old magazines and records. A little nostalgia for the old folks. I was sleeping, telling myself this was real, grown-up, life. This is what we're here for, the career, the rewards, the friends with shoes like yours, the standard of living, the shared jokes, the culture of entertainment and passing the time. But all of that stuff, it's just distraction, isn't it?

A nod from Old Guy. I hold his arm to stop him stepping into a *moto-sai* taking the curve on the wrong side.

When I came to Burma, and that little something happened,

that's when I saw I'd been distracted for too long, and that the distractions were killing me. And at the same time the sex thing – I know that's a distraction, but you need to do it to know it. I came out here to get my mind blown. To freak out. Uh – what was your question again?

I'm suddenly conscious of how much taller I am than Old Guy. You look at him in a rice field, or a hammock, he doesn't look small. Here, it makes me feel awkward, and I realise I'm walking in a Julius Krist-style ducked-head crouch. We get to the Mekhong, and a last sliver of sun fuses out over Thailand. The clouds start to disperse, their work done. We sit on the bank, the grassy slope down to the black water, already dimpled with stars.

When I went back West, after coming out here the first time, it was like it had been replaced with a cheap CGI simulation while I was away. I recognised everything, but it was fake, a shoddy show patched together out of vague memories, if I turned my head quick enough I'd see the world-constructors hurriedly erecting a street scene with ropes. I was standing at the gate of my house, paying off the cab from the airport. It was early evening, and the lights were on and the curtains closed. I could hear her kids laugh, and her barking at the kids to be quiet, like people I didn't know. And the house, which I'd invested love and money and time and work in, looked like a pile of bricks in a field of bricks. So that was a grim scene, hearing the cab drive away and standing there with my travel bag and my gift bag in the cramped dead-end street in front of a cramped dead-end family home that was neither home nor family, knowing I had to intrude into a set-up where I had no place and no role, walk in and give out the gifts, the sailor returned from the sea and no welcoming fire in the hearth. I knew all this, and I still didn't know enough to throw the gift bag over the gate and grab the next flight back to Bangkok, because I didn't know that this fake life was out to kill me.

Does that answer your question? Because you can't go home again.

We're quiet for a while.

No – it was much earlier, I say. And the scene's as clear to me now as if it was yesterday, the feeling's as intense. *When I was a little kid, four or five, on a family vacation, I was on the beach playing, and this guy comes up, smiling, says, hey, you want to sing with us? And he takes my hand and leads me to a tarp pegged into the sand, where there are a bunch of kids corralled, singing about Jesus. They give me a songbook, and I sit at the end of the line, feeling bad, feeling weird.* I can feel that hot canvas under me. *I mouth the words for a line or two, then I close the book and creep away, like I'm doing something wrong, but it's the right thing to do. I'm worried about the songbook, just leaving it there, if they're going to get mad at me. I didn't think so at the time, but it took courage, there's a lot of coercion in a situation like that, I was the littlest guy, you know?*

I look at Old Guy. *That's why I'm here. Still crawling off the tarp.*

"The bean-counters, like your ex-wife, always win," he says at last, tossing a pebble into the water, "but *what* they win is worthless, and you don't need it. A pile of bricks in a field of bricks. You're still not singing from their songbook. And that's exhausted me, metaphorically speaking."

Baddha

We throw stones into the water until it bores us.
You feel like freaking out on fettuccini? I say, *blowing your mind on a bottle of wine?*

TASTY BEVERAGES IN THE
HOUSE OF PAIN

Early days at the Tower Of Babel on the Petchburi Road, and I'm hooking up with a contact here in Bangkok, Terry, a friend of a friend. The friend in the middle is a record producer (as they used to be called) back in the States, who I've written some sleevenotes for (as they used to be called). The guy he's introduced me to used to be the drummer in a UK heavy metal band, pretty obscure but known to me, and now he's a painter here, a portraitist, he's had a commission from a minor member of the extended Thai royal family, and he's a successful businessman. He has a studio on Thong Lo, which is an upmarket and stylish street with neo-classical gated communities, chillout bars and flouncy wedding boutiques, just around the corner (and a world away) from my crib.

So I walk, ignoring the offers of death rides from the *moto-sai* taxi drivers popping Red Bulls and amphetamines at the intersection. Nobody walks in Bangkok, and for a reason – the sidewalks are obstacle courses of telephone poles, streetlamps, fuseboxes, advertising, and signage. Brutalised trees. Knee-high pipework, tilting drain covers, broken paviors, food carts, and parked vehicles. Head-high electricity cables and knife-edged roof extensions and more food carts. Billboard-sized pictures of the King. Sleeping dogs, concrete "street furniture", and spirit houses. Steps to bridges to the other equally unusable sidewalk. And flagpoles. Everything except pedestrians, a word without a direct translation into Thai. So I mostly walk in the road, weaving and diving, until I get to Terry's condo, a lah-de-dah post-modern deal with that "subverting the inside/outside paradigm" thing that gets architects incontinent with their own cleverness, the empty square window arches and the tree. Fucking architects. I buzz myself up. Terry's apartment is the penthouse, with a great sloping north-facing wall of glass.

Hey, I say. *You can see my house from here.* I can, too, the dark ziggurat Babylonian head looming over the Petchburi Road, pierced by mean little lights. You can see the ledge on its shoulder where I sit and sob like a baby. Keep looking, you might see me disappear. I turn away.

Terry has dark hair, in a Jeff Beck cut, wears a green polo shirt with a Jaguar logo, khaki dockers, and a big fuck-off amulet on a heavy gold chain. I left my sandals at the door, we're both barefoot on the waxed "natural" cement floor. He's a few years older than me, in much better shape, tough-looking, muscular. A very serious guy, I notice, no hint of laughter in his heavy-set face. Doesn't hold eye contact. He shows off his latest work in progress, a highly-colored and terrifyingly life-size portrait of a Thai general whose name sounds like Pongipornsupermariokart, but I may have that wrong. Terry proudly tells me he's a *personal* friend. As opposed to *real*, maybe. When Thai soldiers are promoted to General they undergo a secret surgical process which shrinks their skin to their skulls, and he's caught that tight shine perfectly. The guy is clearly incapable of smiling or opening his eyes further than slits. Thailand is sometimes called a democracy, sometimes a kingdom, but the truth is that, like its neighbors, it's run by the Generals. All the major decisions of governance, including who governs, are made in back rooms by a few brass hats acting in their best interests. And Terry gets a big girl-boner painting pictures of his hi-so *friends*.

There's garish symbols in the background of the painting, and patterns of stars joined by white lines. *All these,* Terry says, pointing, *are astrological symbols. The whole painting's a very detailed astrological reading.* He speaks in a North London accent, not posh. It suddenly occurs to me that he's waiting for my judgement on his painting, almost impatient for it.

Great picture, I say. I'd like to say, you really *nailed* the mean-ass motherfucker. Terry nods, as if I've given the right answer, asks if I'd like a drink. He calls out in Thai and sits in the middle of the leather couch, legs splayed, tapping his fingers on his knees, and it's then I see the drummer. Drummers are boxers, they hit things for a living. I take a chair at an angle to him, and a young Thai woman shuffles in, her head down. Terry says, *coffee*, and she curtsies and leaves almost walking sideways.

He nods after her, more of a twitch, rubs his nose with the back of his forefinger. *The wife.*

There's a pause while the domestic situation here tightens around me. Then he reaches behind him to a glass-topped table, picks up a thick stack of A4 paper. He tosses it into my lap, it almost winds me.

Here it is.

This is the supposed screenplay for a movie based on Terry's life he wants me to re-write. I check the page number on the last page. *Yeah, uh . . . Terry? This is nearly six hundred pages long?*

He says nothing, his face set.

Scripts work out about a minute of screen time a page, I say. *So this is a ten-hour movie.*

His eyebrows lift slightly in surprise. *A minute a page?*

Yeah. First drafts generally run about a hundred and twenty pages, a couple hours, and that'll most likely be cut. I'm skimming the script. I know Terry's had an incredible life, and this is an incredibly bad script, page after page of detailed description and bursts of dull dialog. It's typed in one of those curly typefaces people think are elegant and sophisticated, and the formatting's all over the place. It's horrible, a perfect example of how not to write and present a movie script, and everyone's going to run away from it screaming. He must be able to see this in my face, I've never been good at hiding my feelings. His wife comes in with a tray, and she actually crouches and shuffles the last couple of yards on her knees, and puts the tray on a side table, offering it up like she's at a temple. Terry drums his big thighs, poppadom-poppadom. She gives this painful smile and half-crouches out, without looking at us, and as she turns her head I get a glimpse of what she's hiding under her hair, a bandage over her eye. This is the House of Pain.

Well, he says, *that's why you're here.* His eyes hold mine, briefly. *You're the expert.*

I sip my coffee, too sweet, I think there's Carnation milk in it, Thai style, but I'm grateful for the thinking time even if it fails to qualify as a *drink*. All I said on the phone was, I'll have a look at it, which I've done. I really don't want to look at it any more.

Terry, I say, *this needs more work than I can put into it right now.*

He gives this little joyless laugh of disbelief. *What's more important than this?*

I'm working on my novel.

He waves a hand dismissively, with a vestigial lip curl. *Forget that. This is going to be a big movie, it's the opportunity of a lifetime for you.*

I've had a lifetime of opportunities like this, surefire movies to catapult me into the big time, and I've worked my ass off for good will and promises, like an idiot, and I'm not going to do it again.

Terry looks at his watch, a heavy gold Rolex, like he wants me to look at it too. *Okay, I have to meet my man. Bring the script.* He stands and walks to the door, slipping into his deck shoes. I have no idea where we're going or why, but there's not a lot of choice. I'm grateful I don't have to finish my *drink*, anyway.

In the cab, I'm trying to reconcile the old coke-snorting British rocker and the society painter, the groupie of the generals, so I ask him how he got into painting, and he tells me a story I'm partly familiar with, how he went to Art School, designed the group's album covers, and drumming was never the big thing in his life. I tell him I still have the 'World War Crimes' album, the one with the banned cover, his painting of Field Marshall Montgomery bayoneting a baby. *Oh yeah*, he says, *first album we made any money on. Nice little earner.*

He's keener to talk about the high society he mixes with here, how he has resident's status, doesn't need a visa, and I get it, he's a big fucking cheese and I'm nobody, being given this wonderful opportunity that I clearly don't appreciate.

Terry speaks in quick, fluent Thai to the cabdriver, and we pull over, somewhere in Silom.

I never have this bloke round my flat, he says, walking quickly into a hotel lobby. *I can't be seen with him, understand?*

I nod. I don't understand. Terry thumbs the elevator button and stares up at the floor numbers, jingling loose change in the pockets of his Dockers. The hotel's a definite step up from mine, but it's still skanky, the carpet worn shiny and taped in front of the elevator doors, and when they open a skank topples out, spilling her bag and giggling. She's a mess. I instinctively bend to help her, get a look up her skirt, but Terry pushes past and starts jabbing buttons, so I leave her scrabbling for her keys and phone. Terry's change-jingling continues in the otherwise silent elevator, which smells of cheap skank.

In the narrow corridor, the door's opened by a guy with

frizzy black hair, like a grandmother's permanent, with a slight purple haze to it where the light shines through, and a long, lined face, dark eyes set close together. He's wearing a black nylon soccer vest and sweat pants, and the cheap perfume lingers here, too.

Terryyyyy! he says, spreading his arms. *Babyyyy!*

Terry pushes through without saying anything, leaving me unintroduced.

I'm, ah, working with Terry.

Good for you, man. I'm Charles.

I place his accent. Australian. We go through into his apartment, which has been styled by David Lynch, like a serial killer's basement. Viper nests of dirty clothes, food spillage, old newspapers, crimped beer cans, funerary ash trays, scraps of paper tacked to the walls, and exhausted air fresheners, the kind cabdrivers hook on rear-view mirrors, hanging from the lopsided ceiling lamp. The air smells of ash, stale fart, with lingering topnotes of skank juice. Thin curtains sag from wire coat hangers twisted together. It makes me homesick for my dim hollow of a room. Terry kicks some clothes to the floor and sits in the middle of the couch. Charles fetches a taped packet from the refrigerator by the bathroom door, and he and Terry do their business.

I'm looking at a stack of crisp new paperbacks on the floor, and I know who this guy is, Charles Hardaker, self-published writer of a series of shit Bangkok crime novels. I always wondered how he funded his hobby, thought of him as a rich playboy, an image the now ludicrous jacket photos encourage, him in a tux, hair waxed back. He's a dealer, Terry's *bloke*.

Baddha

Terry tells him I'm working on his movie, like it's a done deal. I've still got the script under my arm, but I'm rapidly drifting away from understanding why I'm even sharing airspace with these people. Terry rolls a joint while Charles takes a big frothy horse-piss, totally audible through the open bathroom door.

Terry, I say, *I'll take a look at the script, but what I propose is, strip everything back to an outline, seven pages that tell the story. Start from scratch. I can commit to that. Okay? Then you can get a screenwriter involved, or start trying to raise capital, you'll have something you can work with, show around.*

Terry freezes, the unlit joint between his fat fingers, considering what I've just said. Charles comes in, stands with his hands on his hips. White chest hair curls through the open weave of his shirt.

I'm not paying you for that, Terry says eventually, as if *that* is ten minutes' nosepicking, and I'm trying to rip him off. *But I'll give you a reading.*

Reading this – I weigh the script in my hands – *and digging out the story, getting the people doing what they need to do, is going to take a couple of weeks. It's a lot of work.*

Give me your date and time of birth, I'll give you a reading and get a nice piece made for you, something to change your luck.

I'm thinking, a nice piece? What's a nice piece? But I say, *fine, I could use some good luck, I'll be in touch. We're neighbors!* I nod to Charles on the way out. He looks blank, like he's thinking of something else, or nothing at all.

In the elevator on the way down, I'm kicking my ass about

how I let myself float into situations, go along with people I don't know. All the time telling myself I'm doing the right thing, doing what I want, and I'm in control. But I'm just getting sucked into whirlpools, with less control than a styrofoam cup. Of all the things I don't have, a fucking clue ranks up there with a house in Aspen and an Oscar speech to rehearse.

I ride the Skytrain to the end of the line, watching the lights of the city come on against a dirty orange sky. I don't want to go back to my empty room, and after the serial killer décor it's a pleasure to sit in the cool, clean, quiet train with the cool, clean, quiet Thai people. The comfort of trains, being carried, the lulling rhythm, poppadom-poppadom. Terry's fists on his thighs, the dead weight of the script in my lap, and I don't know if I should go with it or not. If I make a nice job of the outline, which I'm already thinking through, maybe he'll pay me upfront to write the screenplay. If he does, I'll forget about my novel for a while. Which I'm going to have to do for a few days anyway. Get my astrology reading and my nice piece. And I start feeling bad about feeling (and probably acting) superior to Charles. At least he has books in the bookstores, and the money to put them there. I can't get a deal cleaning publisher's toilets, and I can't even scrape up the ante to join the elite corps of self-published Bangkok scribes.

At Mo Chit, I cross the platform, get the next train back, and I start to look through the script, because I want to impress the nice piece next to me. You may think this is another wretchedness indicator, confirming your low opinion of me, but I like to think of it as a positive attribute, hope springing eternal in an old man's undershorts, and this is something we're just going to have to agree to disagree on. And it's a measure of the shallowness of your judgement that the nice piece – a university girl – and me have a pleasant and informed conversation about Hollywood in the seventies all the way to her station, and she gives me her mobile for my number, but my phone's back in my room being recharged, and I can't remember my number, and I certainly can't remember hers, although I tell her I will. Numbers aren't my strong point. Numbers and . . . something else.

My time spent with the girl has given me PLB (Preliminary Loin Buzz), so I give myself a wipe down with a damp cloth back at my crib, adorn myself in my good jeans and a new tee with fold marks showing, crack a blue pill with my thumbnail and pop a quarter, and I'm just scooping up some cash for a night of giddy romance when the phone trills. The voice is thin, old-sounding. I don't recognise it, nor the slight accent.

"You're a hard man to pin down."

What? Who is this?

"You don't remember me."

I wait a moment, but he doesn't talk. *Right. Listen, I've enjoyed our little chat, but I really have to go wait in the lobby.*

"Inside, outside."

He's just given me the password. There's a sudden chill in the room.

Who is this?

"It doesn't matter. Get your Buddha book, the little one. This is important."

It's right by the phone. *Why? What is this?*

"Page sixty-six, two kinds of happiness."

The line goes dead, and I even frown at the handset, like they do in movies, replacing it thoughtfully.

Page sixty-six:

"There are two kinds of happiness; that of an uncommitted life of sensual pleasures, and that of a life committed to a new consciousness. This is the greater happiness."

I take the book out onto the balcony. The apartment is windowless, a door leads to a small open space with a sink and a faucet, where I've installed a plastic garden chair and strung a line for my clothes. I sit in the chair, hearing the grind and grate and honk of the Petchburi Road four floors down (not enough to make a drop certain death, thankfully), and I stare at the quote in the light from the street and I think about this. The voice said *you don't remember me*, which means we've met. He knows about inside-outside, and he knows about my Buddha book. And he clearly knows I'm leading the life of the lesser happiness. This should creep me out, how anyone but me knows these things, but it doesn't.

Buddha's not a fire-breathing moralist. He freely admits that sensual pleasures bring you happiness. But if you're after a greater happiness, commit yourself to a new consciousness. He doesn't say, come unto me and ye shall be saved, he says, focus on opening your head, dude. And I've been neglecting that flip of the bottle-opener, I've just been drinking the beer.

But what am I to do? There's no denying the PLB, the viper-like strength of the lesser happiness, and I'll be damned if I'm going to stay in my room and meditate now I'm all bauched up, ready to get righteously debauched. I'll get back into the new consciousness thing tomorrow, I promise. As I'm leaving the room, the phone sounds again. I let it ring.

I go to Baccara on Soi Cowboy, nurse a vodkalox looking up through the glass ceiling at the underwear-forgetting dancers in their Uni-girl uniforms. It may be the lesser happiness, but it's an area I feel I should fully exhaust before committing myself to a greater one. A girl in a blue bikini with badge number 23 sits next to me. She's not an Isaan girl, she has the straight nose and narrower face of Ayutthaya, these girls consider themselves a cut above their country cousins. Her name is Apple, and mine is suddenly Charles. I buy her a "lady drink", which is small and sweet and expensive, like her, and while we talk her hand works in my crotch, and she has a malicious little grip, and my cock uncurls in my pants, I have to shift a little to get comfortable. Her other hand is at her pussy, something you don't see many bar girls do, she's squeezing, pinching, her eyes nearly closed, biting her lower lip. She has a heavy-lidded, sullen look, black lip gloss, black gloss hair, black gloss nails, perfect skin and a total lack of issues, total commitment to the lesser happiness. Everything you're so very *not* going to get in a woman in a bar in Topeka, Kansas. For instance. Going by the book, she asks what I do, and I say I'm a writer, Bangkok stories, I've written *A Call Girl Calls*, *Bangkok Bang Cock*, and *Luck Be A Ladyboy Tonight*. I'm making myself laugh, anyway, but bar girls aren't called bookstore girls for a reason, so we move on to subjects of more interest, like what I want to do to her and for how long and how much. We arrive at a compromise, I can do anything I want all night long for three thousand baht. But I say I can do anything I want *and* everything I can in an hour or so, including a power nap, so two thousand baht short-time. Taking a girl long-time sounds cosy but means paying them to sleep in your bed and sneak out early in the morning, without waking you for the promised breakfast straightener. I pay the bar fine to the mamasan while Apple (my favorite metaphorical device) trots off to get dressed. It's always a nice moment, seeing them wearing clothes for the first time. She wears white shorts, really very white and really very short, and a doll-size black vinyl biker jacket over a silver halter top, and her bag is shiny black with straps and buckles. I stand here looking at her, I'm going to go off in my shorts, so we walk hand-in-hand like starcrossed lovers down Cowboy to the short-time hotel, because my crib is too depressing for sex with anyone but myself.

She takes a shower while I lock and load, tearing the foil on the rubber and putting it under the pillow. Fumbling for the damn thing while you're kneeling over her is a real turnoff. She comes out of the bathroom, like they do, modestly wrapped in a white towel. Usually they slip between the sheets like this, too. Hookers are bashful. So I brush past her, copping a nice feel, and take my shower, and I'm drying off, admiring my beautiful tensile boner in the mirror, when Apple comes in, and she's wearing her tight push-up bra and nothing else. She has a nude pussy and a nasty look in her eye. She pushes me back until I'm sitting on the toilet, and she straddles me, her hands on my shoulders and her tits in my face, like a lapdancer. I play along, my hands loose at my sides. She backs off a little to look down, and her hand goes between her legs and she starts to piss, a hot silver stream she aims precisely over my cock and balls. I'm breathing obscenities, and she squats and takes the head of my dripping-wet cock in the shiny black O of her lips. I feel her suck and slide hard, and I come, deep in the back of her throat, and she keeps sucking, and she's swallowing, gulping it back, and she lifts off, shakes her hair, come shining on her lip, gives me a dirty look, her pink tongue pierced with a silver stud.

This is stupid. I never did this without a rubber before. And I'm gazing at her in wonder, my cock stiffening in her hand, when there's a knock at the door into the corridor, a polite little tap-tap-tap. I have other things to think about. I pinch her nipples out of her bra so they harden against the lace edge. She says, *be still*, turns around, straddles me, reaches around to soap up my cock, and works the head into her ass, and she grunts, freezes for a moment, then drops down the oily shaft until she's sitting in my lap, my cock deep in her, she's breathing heavy, and now she arcs back, her face next to mine, her arms above her head, and I work her breasts, and the knocking on the door gets louder, and she grinds her ass in my lap, clenching my cock like a fist, and the knocking at the door is now a hammering, and it's the second coming, the beautiful spastic rapture of the near-death orgasm.

Then there's silence.

She lifts off, after a while, popping my cock from the hot grip of her ass. She's clean, but going bareback was a dumb thing to do, and I'll get myself checked out at the clinic.

She's taking the second shower when I peek into the empty corridor. There's something on the floor. I bend to pick it up; it's the wooden bottle-opener I brought from Burma. I sometimes keep it in my pocket, like a totem. I must have dropped it. But it's fallen across the threshold, like someone leant it against the door. This is a detail that means nothing to me now, I'm in that opiate sex haze.

Later, back in my bare room, sleepless in the Bangkok heat on a bed hopping with my own demons, I remember the only two words she spoke in the short-time hotel: *be still*.

I reach for my glasses, and my book. I underlined it so I can find it easily:

"If your mind becomes firm like a rock, and no longer shakes, in a world where everything is shaking, your mind will be your greatest friend, and suffering will not come your way."

Be still. Somewhere out there, Nui stretches under someone's shuddering body weight, her eyes far away. *Be still*. High above Thong Lo, the Queen of the House of Pain lies alone in a king-size bed, her bandage soaked with tears and the silence winding around her like a rope. *Be still*. All the shaking, lonely souls in the city of starless night, be still, be still.

NOSE SHIELD LOGIC

Old Guy hasn't been by the store since our argument. Okay, *my* argument, a couple weeks back. I make the rounds of his haunts occasionally, but I'm reconciled to him being gone, and it's a strange feeling, like he never existed. Nuts, I know. Plus, I'm having to do all the boring and menial tasks I set him, flattening the cardboard boxes we buy our increasingly unsaleable stock in, sweeping the floor. But at least I have Crazy Billy for conversation. He passed through town a month back, liked the look and feel, and came back. He's got a room at the Chai Von Hotel, which is a very grand name, and an even grander sign, for what is the only old guest house left in the town, and he's bargained them down to a hundred-fifty baht a night, less than five dollars, as cheap as you'll get around here. The Chai Von is all timber, two stories high, with a balcony on the second that runs across the width of the building. No glass in the windows, just wooden shutters, and the frontage is faded turquoise paint, with a red and gold sign. Beautiful, for all the reasons the owner would never understand. At street level, the doors are concertina'd back during the day, and you can see into the lobby, the usual dark clutter of overlarge and uncomfortable furniture, pictures and motorcycle parts, dusty display cases, whatever happens to drift up there. It was where I found Old Guy when he first arrived, and he looked very at home drifted up in the age-old oriental crap. Crazy Billy less so.

He's about five-eleven, holds himself like he's built and buff, but he's straining to suck in belly flab. I've seen him morph like a balloon animal when we pass a group of girls on the street. He's nearly handsome, a kind of collegiate thing going for him, like a poor man's (hah!) Tom Cruise, exactly the type that gets Asian women throwing their daughters at him from balconies. His eyes are blue, with a twinkle in them, but they're a little too close together. His hair is light brown, near blonde, but there's dandruff on the shoulders of his shirt. He's mid-thirties, out of Santa Barbara, with a management degree, but in California they print business studies diplomas on milk cartons. So why is this eminently marriageable, Thai-speaking, super-qualified US *hansum man*, staying in the cheapest room in a backwater town?

The answer to that starts with the nose shield.

It's the first thing I notice about him, probably the first thing anybody notices about him. It has a hypnotic focal effect. If I ever rob a bank, I'm going to do it naked, just a nose shield. *What did he look like, ma'am? Uh . . . he wore a nose shield?* He's made it himself out of white card, precisely cut and angled, taped to the bridge of his sunglasses. He stops his mountain bike clunker in the street, where I'm sitting in front of the Chai Von waiting for the parade. There's a big parade in town every few months, with Apsara dancers, school bands, parade floats, traditional music, drunkards, Thai cowboys on horseback, local katoey-kwai ("buffalo ladyboys") glamming it up, the works. Parading is a big Thai thing they love to do, and I've got myself a nice table in the shade to watch it go by. White guys here are rare and precious, so we tend to say hello. Crazy Billy gives me this big grin, leans in for a handshake.

Hi! I'm Billy!

I say hello, ask him to join me at the concrete table, and he orders a beer, in Thai. All the time I'm looking at this nose shield, and I can't help but mention it.

Nice nose shield, Billy.

Stops my nose from burning in the sun. Like yours did.

He helpfully points at my nose. It's true I have a red schnozzle, but I think if it's a choice between that and wielding origami proboscis armor, I'll take the sunburn and the hell with it. He tells me what you already know about him, so I ask him why he's passing through, and he tells me something so vague and uninteresting and flat-out ambagious that I can't remember a word of it. I'm also distracted by something else, something as unignorable as his rhinal solar protection device, but less amusing. He stinks. There are great dark patches of sweat under his arms, and it's not atomiser mist of dew from the fairy dell. If I notice it, it's sure to knock the average Thai over at twenty paces, although they are way too polite to gag into their hand in front of you. So I'm weighing all these factors way before I know he's crazier than a weekend at the office. We watch the parade, which is very damn fine and spectacular, and he pedals off with a big charm grin competing for attention with his UV nasal carapace.

I think that's the last I'll see of him, but as most of what I think is wrong, it's no surprise to see him cycle up to the store a couple of weeks later. I notice another Crazy Billy styling first – the seat on his bicycle is back-to-front, and I'm scared to ask why, fearing a blunt denial. He's taken a room at the mythic Chai Von Hotel, and he's dropped by to invite me to a game of chess on the balcony in the evening.

This is the busiest my social calendar has been since moving here, and I lay out my clothes on the bed in a tizzy of anticipation. Should I wear the faded black tee? Or the off-white? They're the same color, it hardly matters.

Old Guy looks in on me at this point.

"Meeting your new friend?"

There's a hint of jealousy in his voice, but maybe I'm imagining it.

Playing chess. I pull on the gray tee. It's the only one I have.

"Horrible game."

Why?

"No such thing as a healthy chess player."

It's not a fucking fitness regime.

"Why do you swear so much?"

I shrug. *My vocabulary is fucked?*

"Words," he says thoughtfully, "is your business."

Yeah. And business is bad. Wordage is glutting the market

right now, worthless as Burmese banknotes. People want moving pictures on their phones, shit blowing up, people falling over at weddings, kittens, porn. You know, cool stuff. There's a generation that'll spend their entire lives gazing at glowing rectangles, and they think reading books is like shoveling coal, and the hell with them.

"Can we talk?"

On the balcony. I have ten minutes.

"Thank you for finding time in your day."

Fucking fuck off.

We make ourselves comfortable on the hard bench on the balcony.

"How's the book coming on?"

The book about you?

"I notice you're not putting much time into it these days."

A writer's work is ninety per cent up here. I tap my head sagely.

"That's what I mean."

No point lying to this guy. *It's just a, I don't know. A fallow period. Letting things gestate.*

"You're not carrying your Buddha book with you."

Nope. I'll be honest, I'm tired of the whole business. There are no results. I've achieved nothing except understanding some of the things Buddha said, getting my own "in" without signing up for anything. The shit may be spread a little more thinly than a few years back, but life is still a shit sandwich. The store's losing money. I have no income. I can see why people pray to Buddha, even if he's not listening. When you need help, when you're hurting, faith and prayer make sense, make you feel better. Cosmic understanding, with which I am awash, doesn't. Prayer is an instinctive act, and it invokes your god. Faith and religion and belief and Jesus and God and Allah and great golden statues of Buddha were all thrown up in the wake of prayer, to make sense of it. Who the fuck else are we praying to? But all this thinking and meditating and understanding and attentiveness and getting glimpses, what's the fucking point? What you going to do? Stroll around smiling serenely because you know the world we create is a fictive device? That we're all struggling in the mud for the wrong things? That the whole fucking set-up – families, education, money, science, art, work, religion, culture, politics, entertainment – all this stuff is nothing more than a bunch of magic spells? That there's absolutely no solid foundation to any of it, the whole deal is smoke and mirrors? How does that knowledge help anything?

"You prayed, back on the Petchburi Road."

I had nothing else to do.

"Did you get your prayers answered?"

No.

It's not like I was asking for a Porsche. Prayer is like a shout, sudden and short and strong and wordless, if possible. If it's not that, it's not praying, it's talking to yourself. If you're asking for something, that's not praying, that's begging. If your wretched pleading seemingly scores, then it's a miracle, God is great, and you offer up boundless thanks for his prompt attention to your dossier. Plus you feel fabulous, because you have a Special Relationship with the creator of the universe, he *likes* you. If your shameless grovelling goes unanswered, you make up some holy-ass reason why your prayers weren't answered. It's God's will, it's for the best, it's a test of faith, whatever lame excuse you can scrape up to strengthen your fatuous belief in the non-existent all-knowing godhead of your own making. God is made in the image of man, not the other way round.

Sometimes prayer is all you can do – which is, absolutely, nothing. But you do it anyway. At a certain point you do it anyway, and there's the thing. You don't meditate at times like that, you're not attentive to the forever-changing instant at times like that, you don't do a breathing exercise. You pray. You think the Holocaust victims weren't praying their asses off? Great God in Heaven do some fucking smiting with these Nazis already! You think that the tortured kids in Darfur aren't praying to die as soon as possible, like now? That's prayer, from the depths of suffering, and it doesn't get answered.

"Prayer is just a word. Strip the act of the name. It's the same act as meditation. There is no difference. The prayer you're talking about, the wordless cry for help, is meditation under extreme pressure. The meditation you're talking about is prayer under no pressure. Can't you see the cycle here? The total distress, the reflective calm? They're states of mind. They're both the changing instant in the state-of-mind cycle. The strange thing is, even when calm is available to us, with very little work, most of us opt to complicate things, and get stressed, out of choice."

Tell that to the women being bayoneted in Nigeria. Comfort them with Buddha's release from suffering.

"Oh, please. If you cared about them you'd go and do something for them. I mean, you *can*. Buddha can't, he's dead. All you want to do is whine about how bad business

227

is. And you keep talking about *results*. You're getting no *results*. Prayer, meditation, all this Buddha crap, brings no *results*. What results would you like to see?"

That one's got me. An airplane hangar full of Porsches? That's what famous comedian and showbiz personality Jerry Seinfeld opted for. When the day came, and he could have everything he wanted, he was ready with the answer, he'd thought it through. *Gimme an airplane hangar full of Porsches.* Comedians! But how about a more winning personality? OMG! I could totally have, like, a *gazillion* Facebook friends, and how cool would that be, LOL!

Hmm . . . a bouncy castle full of oiled cheerleaders?

Eternal peace for all mankind?

My ex-wife tragically crushed by a careening dirigible? That works.

A good night's sleep?

Eggs Benedict?

Nuts.

A book that sells, I say.

It's honest, but dumb. We both know it's stupid. Expecting results from this frustrating, interior, and endless process is like expecting to pick up souvenirs on an acid trip. A kaleidoscopic fragment of the ineffable void to put on your coffee table. *Smuggled this little doohickey back from Angkor Wat. I seen one go for five million dollars on eBay? But I ain't sellin' this baby. Memories are priceless.*

Old Guy lifts his legs and hooks his big monkey-like toes in the cyclone fence that prevents us escaping in case of fire.

"Question. Which experience means more to you, the

228

moment with the Abbot back in Burma, or the time with the prostitute with the black lipstick back in Bangkok?"

My face distorts in puzzlement. Prostitute? *Black lipstick?*

"You took her short-time from Baccara on Cowboy."

I'm trying to remember. I took a lot of short-time prostitutes, maybe a few with black lipstick, but I can't remember one specifically.

Any other distinguishing features?

"You tell me."

Well, since I can't remember the particular girl you're talking about, I'd have to say the time with the abbot back in Burma. That means more to me. What's your point?

"You just made it for me. You can remember that, even though you can't describe it. I have a feeling you could describe your time with the prostitute accurately."

Did I have a good time?

"At the time."

Give me a clue.

Old Guy stands, reaches into the pocket of his shirt and tosses my Burmese bottle opener into my lap.

"You dropped this, I think."

The doors of memory swing open at that peculiar wooden key, fatally distracting me from the chessboard a little later, and Crazy Billy gloats over two swift victories, helpfully replaying my errors for me. I get that a lot.

Crazy Billy hangs around town for a few weeks, and the list of things he has allergies to grows every day. He can't wear anything but natural cotton, because. He can't eat bread, because. He can't use soap, because. He can't be in an air-conditioned room, because. He can't touch newsprint or cats, because. He can't use toothpaste, because. It's becoming rapidly obvious why he travels alone. But it's a change for me to talk American with a smart guy, even if he's a crazy smart guy. We sit on the balcony of the Chai Von, play some chess, drink some beer, and Crazy Billy waves and twinkles at the womenfolk as they pass in the busy street, cartoon hearts popping in the air around them, little shiny pink gum-bubbles, pop-pop-pop. Forget it, ladies. You couldn't share a balcony with the guy without wrapping your head in a wet towel.

I'm starting my own religion, he says.

You do that.

Easyanity.

Right.

Religion is too severe, too demanding.

Not yours, I'm guessing. Check.

I'm serious. A new religion. Why not? He interposes his knight. I restrain myself from punching the air and shouting *YOU DIE!* in my Terminator voice.

I've written about it, he goes on. *Not really a book, more like my thoughts, with people I've met, a little autobiographical material. My friends say I could get it published.*

Publishers are blowing up balloons as we speak. I finesse a pawn move, so silkily beautiful you'd want to buy it a Manhattan and a mink stole.

People need to worship, it's a fundamental instinct, but they find that whole church-going rigaramole inconvenient. They'll be able to pray on the internet. I have a slogan – Easyanity – Redemption With A Click!

Rigaramole? Shouldn't that be rigamarole? *Will there be statues of yourself?*

Baddha

If that's what the worshippers want – why not?

Hmmm. I don't know. Buddha tells me the statue thing is crap, basically. Check.

Maybe Buddha is wrong?

This idea appeals to him, and he gets obnoxious about it, leaning into me and pointing, like this is a revolutionary stance he's taking, something new and challenging.

No, think about it, really – what if BUDDHA was WRONG?

My white bishop slants from a distant thicket of pawns, *wreaking* his fatally compromised king's side defence, and its mate in two, should he choose to hang in there for the humiliation. He pretends not to notice my gloat spillage all over the board, but I know how much he's hurting when he tips over his king in resignation. As we reset the pieces, I get sage-like on his ass.

Right and wrong are your terms, not Buddha's, Billy.

Maybe my terms are right, and his are wrong! Ever think about that?

I sigh heavily. *No, Billy.*

He's started to hawk up phlegm in the back of his throat, *PFFFNNNOOORRRKK,* and I've learned this is a craziness attack warning, probably brought on by the chess defeat.

Please do not spit into the street, Billy.

He looks offended, disbelieving. *What would you do if you had a great ball of green phlegm in your throat? PFFFFNNNNOOOOOORRRRRRKKKKKK. You want it on the table?*

I stand and move away from the balcony rail. *Goodnight, Crazy Billy.* I take the back stairs, I'm not walking under that balcony.

KNOCK YOURSELF OUT

Crazy Billy is no replacement for Old Guy. I can't bounce thoughts off him in the same way, and he doesn't tell me anything I have to work at. I've been working on that fragment about the Fall from Eden (just names, no Christianity implied or intended) I started during my convalescence from Dengue fever back in Siem Reap.

Buddha, again and again, hammers home this thing about words being only words, with no independent reality or meaning in themselves; "It is a defect in language that words suggest permanent realities," and so on. Why? Because language is one of the obstacles, perhaps the greatest, to seeing the world as it is. And seeing the true world is part of enlightenment. And you can do this, if you look where Buddha's pointing, and not at his golden finger.

Buddha sees through the world we create to the true world, which is untouched by the systems we impose on it. We accept our systems to be the true world. The strongest,

232

most pervasive system we've invented is language. Numbers, counting and calculation and measurement, are a function of language. If we don't name "one", and "two," and create names for all the tough math that follows, it doesn't exist. Mathematicians would have you believe that math is the pure science, as close as man can get to abstract truth, a kind of wordless mysticism, but that's bullshit. Numbers are words. And words is (running gag – not a typo) magic. Not magic in the Vegas show sense, or scary death metal pentagram magic, *real* magic. Magic that's so subtle and familiar and powerful we're unaware of the spells we cast every day. There's no wizard hypnotically waving his magic wand at us, no secret cabal of mind-controlling Illuminati bending our wills to their own hideous agenda. We do it ourselves. You're doing it right now.

Language is invocation, and every word is a spell. Grammar is grimoire – the book of spells. If this is a little too etymological for you (and I espouse the eschewal of obfuscation) – how about the word *spell*? How could you have not noticed that one? Right in your face, all the time.

By speaking (*spelling*) the word "one" we conjure up the idea of singularity. "Two" creates duality, and so on. Before we say (*spell*) the words, there are no numbers anywhere in the world. There are not *two* of anything, nor even *one*. Quantity does not exist in the universe. There's not a lot of anything, a little bit of something else, a third of this, fifteen gazillion of that. Measurement, based on repetitions of absolute values, does not exist outside our imaginations. The universe does not count itself, does not measure itself, does not describe itself, does not name itself. We do these things. We perform this magical act every day through language, and it prevents us from seeing things as they are, and not as we think they are. And it gets weirder – by "counting" to One, by making the bloody mark on the cave wall, the line in the sand, proclaiming the *I*, *spelling the First Person*, we already create division, we place ourselves apart from the world by making our mark on it. Counting to one is already counting too far.

Here's a charming picture of Soccer Mom teaching her rosy-cheeked youngster the rudiments of math in a sunny suburban garden, probably Santa Barbara. She's set out a row of bright red apples (everybody's favorite metaphorical device), and she's already cast the apple naming spell, so Little Kyle can invoke the idea of the apple without seeing one. Now she's teaching Little Kyle to learn their *other* secret names as he moves his finger along the line. This spell is One. Spell it O-N-E. This is Two, this is . . . the spell is cast. Little Kyle can skip around the garden casting this spell on stones, flowers, everything in the garden.

But he's not in the garden any more. Little Kyle is in the Stock Market, with one blonde wife blowing the help in the pool house, two hybrids in the garage, three kids on Ritalin, four heart attacks, and five inches of ladyboy tube steak down his throat on a stopover in Bangkok. Numbers is his business.

The loving mother casts a magical spell over her happy child in the Magical Garden of the Gingerbread House. She's not talking about apples at all, but she's under the same spell herself.

We weren't thrown out of Eden for eating the apple, but

for naming it, for counting it. A rose is not a rose is not a rose. A rose is a word is a word is a word, is a spell. It has nothing to do with the real garden, where there are no roses at all. This is how the apple is poisoned, by naming it. "Understanding" the natural world through language puts it at an almost uncrossable distance – we are truly cast out from the garden, and not in any metaphorical or allegorical sense. We've locked the gate behind us and thrown away the key.

Don't mistake the finger pointing at the moon for the moon. The finger (the indicator, the signpost) is the word "moon". We mistake the finger for the moon *all the time*. The supreme irony of Buddha's awakening is that words is the only tool at his disposal to tell us about the state beyond them. This is why he continually reminds us of the limits of language. Language is speaking spells, and every spell is a sleeping spell, that's what spells do. Words are spells, but they're also signposts. They are not in themselves truth, but they can point to it.

"Nothing in the world can be finally explained, it can only be experienced."

Same ball, different spin. Explanation is a function of language. Experience is the wordless state of awareness. So what is it that is experienced, if it is nothing that can be explained? It's *quality*, or to give it a fancy-sounding mystical Buddhist term, *suchness*. There is no quantity in the universe – there is only quality. Unmeasurable, undefinable, nameless essence – the quality of existence, the character of things, the nature of stuff. The lino in the linoleum. What makes string so stringy, and water so wet. And to get at this you have to leave words (and the words we call numbers) behind. People have been trying to crack this particular nut for centuries, and there's a little *word,* a short *spell,* that's associated with this enterprise, a terrible syllable I'm afraid to type, because it opens up a flood of crap, and this crap comes from you, not the word.

Zen isn't, and never can be, what you think it is. That's why it's called zen. Zen is a name for something that has no name, three meaningless letters in meaningless combination, pointing to nothing (LOL!). There are already perfectly good words for *calm* and *tranquil*: *calm* and *tranquil*. The calmness that everyone associates with the zen brand is a result of zen happening, not the way to get it to happen. Crack the shell to get at the nut. *Break* the spell. It can't be thought out of there, like talking a guy down from a ledge. It can't be prayed out, meditated out, yoga'd out, *niced* out. The old zen masters beat their students awake with their staffs. One said *If I hear one more monk mention Buddha, I'm going to wash his mouth out with soap.* And another: *If you see Buddha on the road, kill him.*

Buddha is a signpost on the road. Go where he points, *get moving,* don't stand there gazing at the fucking signpost like you've arrived.

ON THE BUFFALO TRAMPOLINE

I don't know if Old Guy knew it, but what he said about Nui not showing at the Skytrain station is true in a way I don't expect, because I don't recognise her at first. She's put on weight, and she's wearing scuzzy no-style clothes, loose shorts, grubby tee, and she's cut her own hair, apparently without a mirror, and she's not wearing make-up. I'm baffled, and disappointed, and she must sense this in her witchy way, but she doesn't show it. She smiles, and her eyes are still lotus pools or whatever, and she says she wants me to come home with her. Not to live with her, or even to fuck, she just wants me to see how she is now. She's quiet and respectful, and I get a sense of her saying, this is me, I'm not who you thought I was, and you can know me or not, I don't care. It's a very steady, calming thing, absolutely rock-like. It's impressive. She was always that.

We get a bus out to the 'burbs somewhere, I couldn't even point to it on a map. Differences between Bangkok suburbs, once you're out of the money, are impossible to pick up. A vast, crumbling, cable-tangled, horizontal Tetris game of low-rise concrete apartment blocks, covered markets, slab-sided superstores and choking thoroughfares, with no architectural distinction or variety. Edging through traffic at geological pace (*never* run for a bus in Bangkok – stroll to the next stop and wait for it to catch up with you), Nui tells me she's been clean since the last time we met, our last night on the town. No ya-baa, no alcohol, no fucking, no nothing. She gave her beautiful clothes away – *they don't fit me anymore!*

She shares a single-storey three-room house on a small scruffy street where people live their lives outside, not locked up inside, and this is an in-your-face defining difference between rich and poor. Clothes hang in the street to dry, big old underpants and worn-out bras and faded tee shirts, and it's the same as your neighbor's, no secrets here, including Victoria's. We sit on the bed – the low wooden platform where most of the big things in Thai life happen – in front of the house and watch barefoot kids parade from house to house, rulers of their own cartoon-colored kingdom, caught up in hologram trading cards and iridescent spinning tops. Nui's relatives – a shadowy confusion of cousins and half-sisters and nephews and nieces – move around, say hello, sleep on the floor in the cool of the house. They're interested in me, but polite, not a pain in the ass. They ask how old I am, and they're surprised, because I look so young. Again. An older guy than me stops by to show off his hair-dye job, and everyone laughs with him, because he fell asleep under it and dyed his scalp black too, you can see the paint line. There's an over-riding feeling of comfort and ease, of everybody and everything accepted for what it is, nothing to get steamed about.

We go to the covered market on somebody's moto-sai, me rattling the loose gearage with my toe, Nui correctly side-saddle behind. I don't have papers, or a helmet, and if we're stopped I'll put a hundred baht into the cop's glove. No big deal.

There's nothing in this world that looks cool and clean, it's a mess of junk, tangled nets of wiring, rasping trucks and mosquito motorcycles, potholed concrete roadways, cannibalised advertising. There's no visual harmony or beauty in anything. It's everything that Switzerland isn't, and all the better for it. The beauty and the quality of life here is in the recognition that these things don't matter, they're not more important than any individual human life. People know this shit (the world) is temporary, like they are. Palmleaf shacks, where life *happens*. And it always happens now. Nobody's preparing for their careers or pensions or death, there's only today, and today the farang buys lunch.

Later, Nui and I are lying in the back room, which looks like a storeroom for broken furniture, a stack of cobwebbed TVs in the corner. The fan's busted, it's too hot too move. The bed feels like it was used as a trampoline by a buffalo, a dust bowl covered with rugs.

Nui takes it from the top. These are her words, close as I can recall.

I was about eight or nine when I knew what I was. I could see how people were, the differences, and I could see where

I fit. In Thailand, it's not shameful, nobody hides it or feels guilty or makes a problem out of it. I'm lucky, I was always pretty and slim, so girls' clothes always looked good on me. But school was always a problem, I was difficult. I was always at the hair salon or the beauty salon to watch them working. They let me help, fetch things, clean equipment. It was fun. But I wanted the clothes, the shoes, the bags. I started to get greedy and impatient. I got a job doing nails, but I wanted to be hi-so, not a country girl, so when I was fifteen I went to Bangkok to live with my cousin and started working in the bars, because the money is good and you can meet rich men. I was a hello girl, sitting at the door, because I was always the most beautiful, but I didn't take any customers. I was working in girl clubs, not katoey clubs, but I moved to the katoey clubs, and started taking customers, because I needed the money for these.

She cups her breasts, looking down at them.

When I was the most beautiful woman in Bangkok, I came home, and I bought a Seven-11 for my mother, and a motorbike for my brother. But I couldn't live there, I was a snob, so I tried living in the south for a while, Phuket, with a farang, in a beautiful house, but he was stupid and boring. He kept saying "all right, darlin'?" and falling asleep in front of the TV all the time, so I got an agent on the internet, and moved back to Bangkok. I was there for a long time before I met you. A man promised to marry me, to take me home to Holland. He was a pilot for KLM, very handsome, young. I think I was in love. If I wasn't, I should have been, because he was perfect. He sent me money every week, and every time he had a stopover we were together. I told him I was waiting for him, but I couldn't stop working, it was easy, and there was always a call from the agency. I was getting three or four thousand baht a time, plus tips and gifts. And I loved being fucked by handsome men in fabulous hotel rooms! So my boyfriend suddenly stopped calling, and the money stopped, and I couldn't contact him, he didn't answer my emails. I thought he found out I was still working, someone told him. Katoeys can be very bad like that, very jealous and spiteful. But then I went to a mor doo, a fortune teller, and he told me I was in love with a married man. One hundred percent. I got very depressed. I was taking ya-baa, sometimes cocaine if the customer knew how to ask for some, the agency would do that through me. I came back here for a while, and I was trouble for everybody, always fighting with my family, so I went back working in the clubs, and then the agency again. I was a mess.

You didn't look like a mess.

Inside, I was a mess. I hated my customers, because they had all this money. I hated me, because nobody wanted me, they wanted my tits and my ass and my cock. I couldn't stop, I had nowhere to go. And I was seeing my friends die . . .

You hated me?

No. You were the first to tell me I was talking bullshit. When I told you I was waiting for you. Nobody ever did that. You didn't try to own me, and you didn't make promises.

What made you quit?

Buddha. I'm happier being good.

I get up on my elbow, look at her. *Do your card trick.*

She blows out her cheeks. *I don't have any cards.*

I reach into my pocket for the fresh deck I brought with me, tear off the seal.

One time, she says sternly, wagging her finger.

She sits crosslegged as I shuffle, thoroughly, and cut the deck a few times. She fans the deck and I put my finger in, sneak a look at that card, put it back and shuffle again. She holds the deck in her lap, looking me in the eye.

This is not as easy as it sounds, it's unsettling. Nui sees right inside me, and here's the proof. After a few seconds, she says, *seven of diamonds.* And it is.

Go on, I say. *One more time.*

No, she says.

Please. Once more. The last time.

She smiles. *No cards.*

A card trick without cards?

Think of a card.

I think the ace of hearts would be the brightest, simplest, and most obvious choice, so I make an effort to visualise something else, deciding on the eight of clubs, because it's one of those anonymous, characterless cards.

Those eyes again, inside-outside. Then she closes them. *Eight of clubs. But it's not the one you wanted. You wanted the ace of hearts. That's your card.*

I flop back on the bed, feeling the sweat stick my shirt to my chest, suddenly icewater. *Do me a favor.*

What?

Don't ever, ever, do that again.

A SPY IN THE HOUSE OF LOVE

I hang around Vientiane checking at the post office for Frog's promised shipment of LSD until I realise the flimsy envelope the floppy-haired cretin sent it in has fallen through the cracks in the postal system. You don't put a return address on something like that. I have the option of going back to Bangkok and scoring some from Charles Hardaker's refrigerator, but I don't want it that badly. It feels like time to move on, not back.

I'm still considering the invitation of a Thai woman I met at the post office to visit her, but I don't know if it was meant in the Thai way, as a pleasant thing to say with no commitment behind it, or as a real invitation. She was in Vientiane with her sister buying coffee to sell in Thailand, but she didn't seem too hopeful it would make her rich. She writes her address for me on a page from a Hello Kitty notebook, and I tell her I'll say hello if I'm passing through. There's nothing in this meeting to suggest we'll be living together for the rest of our lives in a couple of months. That surprises us both.

I buy a ticket for the bus north to Luang Prabang, foolishly turning up at the bus station on time. The bus pulls in an hour late, which is okay, but it's already full, which is not. And a full bus in Lao PDR is *full* – people sit on little plastic stools crammed in the aisle, and the roof is piled with stuff, car tires, produce, taped-up plastic sacks, motorcycles, anything at all. In my stiff-assed Western way I wave my ticket at the guy in the little office, pointing at the bus. He says, *next bus, hundred percent, sure,* so I wait a couple of hours for the next bus, which looks as if it has been hit by a meteor storm of cabbages. There's a man-high layer of them netted on top of the bus, which is as full inside as the last bus. They've even crammed cabbages inside the engine compartment at the back. There's no clearance between the worn-out tires and the wheel arches, and it pulls out in a sharp stink of rubber and singed cabbage. I glower at the guy in the office, saying *a hundred per cent,* and he gives me a greasy look. For him, this is job satisfaction, sticking it to the white man. When I get that, a pressure valve releases, and I give him a real smile, mentally thanking him for giving me the opportunity to not be an asshole. If you can not be an asshole when everything is screaming at you to claim your right to be one, you've learned everything Buddha has to teach. The rest of it, the core of it, the stuff I'm trying to get at, he freely admits isn't teachable.

It occurs to me that the transformed Buddha doesn't have much to say about his awakening, or that all that can be said, can be said relatively quickly. But he gets this huge following, and he has to give value for money, so he works in the easier teachings, a lot of which already exist, to bulk out his material. Here's how to live a good life, here's a few categories, a few definitions, a few parables, something to chew on. It's not like he was hiding the core of his experience, he was totally open about it, but it's hard to grasp, and like he says, you have to do the work yourself, which nobody finds attractive. People like being *given* things: rules, commandments, categories. Things to say and do. Most of this material (and there's vast acres of it, like Dean Koontz books), boil down to *don't be an asshole*. Life is full of opportunities to practice that, but we rarely grasp them.

I eventually get a bus late afternoon, and it grinds north, stopping only to pick up a cloud of flies at a food stop in the jungle where there's nothing but muddy buckets of eels and black bulb-like innards on bamboo skewers. I'm wishing I'd brought a bag of bakery from Vientiane, but I'm perversely enjoying myself. Everyone's having such a great time, piling off the bus, piling back on. I even eat some of the stuff that's offered me, miming *it's delicious but I'm full, no more, thank you*. They all look healthy enough on it, and have no difficulty sleeping as the bus bounces and slews up into the hills, while I spastic about on my seat over the wheel-arch, head whiplashing, water spilling in my lap, micro-vomiting into my mouth.

We hit Luang Prabang about two in the morning, and I find a comfortless bench in the bus station to huddle on – it's *freezing fucking cold* – and I'm just drifting off into a nauseous shuddering motion sickness coma when a young guy holds my shoulder and asks if I *want loom*.

I want loom more than I want world peace right now, so I climb onto his bike, nearly lurching off the other side, and we weave through what seems to be toy-town and he deposits me at a courtyard of nice little cabins built of Lego. They're all dark, and for all I know occupied by nomads, but he pushes open a door and flicks on the light for me. Then he just stands there grinning at how wonderful everything is until I give him a couple of scrunched-up dollar bills. I fall onto the bed, which is like falling onto the back of a wardrobe, and black out.

Early morning is when the monks make their rounds, and local people donate rice. It's a common ritual all over the continent. The line of orange-robed monks, silent and barefoot in the dawn light, is a beautiful thing to see. It's also a hard thing to see, on account of the tourists filling the streets for the photo opportunity. A very humble and dignified event has been changed into a circus in Luang Prabang, and it's horrifying, makes me ashamed to be a Westerner. You want to destroy a place, first thing you do is stick a World Heritage Site flag in it, which turns it into an unmissable add-to-cart item on the tourist trail. No amount of funding is going to preserve the unique qualities destroyed by its qualification for World Heritage Site status. At Angkor Wat, another location blighted by the World Heritage people, tourists make themselves look idiotic against the setting of the temples, here, they compromise and embarrass the monks, who they massively outnumber, and it's a harsh and ugly thing to see. Tourists feel no shame, that's evident. The world is here for their entertainment. And camera. As far as I can see I'm the only tourist without one. That's the most important thing, the photographs. The happy snappers line the route and lean in close, like it's the Tour de France, some even asking the monks to turn, or smile, or hold it right there. The serious art photographers, grim-faced, have set up tripod and bazooka-like camera early for that hazy zoom lens shot that'll show everyone exactly how great an artist they are. An American serious art photographer (dressed as Steven Spielberg) is waving and shouting at some Koreans coming between him and the monks. When they move away, and he's grunted into his camera a few times, I speak to him.

Unbelievable, those guys just standing in front of you like that.

Yeah, he says, *fucking snapshot tourists, pain in the ass.*
I didn't mean them, I meant the monks.

I leave him puzzling this one over, or not.

The camera fetish is a terrible thing. It's like tourists can't see where they are until they see the pictures. Here's a picture of me, at the temple! Here's a picture of me, at the market! Here's a picture of me, on a mountain! On a bus! In a restaurant! With what's-his-name! And monks are the most photogenic of subjects. From the cute neophyte in the shade of a parasol, to the wrinkled sage sitting cross-legged in the temple, they lend an exotic accent to any on-line photo album! Here's me with some monks! LOL!

I get to Luang Prabang too late. I miss it by maybe a decade. The Rough Planet ethos (the HIV of tourism) has wreaked its awful havoc on what must have been a very special place. The main street of the old town on the hill is a cutesy parade of all the usual fake services catering to the usual middle-class white tourists, slouching heavily through the streets *simpering* at the simple but honest townsfolk as they go about their time-honored crafts of mixing blueberry smoothies and rebooting internet connections.

I spend the day scowling at tourists, which is a foolish way to pass the time when you're a tourist. We *climb* to the temple on the hill, *admire* the spectacular view, *marvel* at Buddha's footprint. We *explore* the quaint lanes of the old town, *sample* the local cuisine, and *haggle* at the night market. We don't get to *fuck* any of the local hookers, though. The nightlife area, a block of bars and restaurants on the other side of the temple hill, seems as gay as a weekend in Paris. It's Boy's Town, but for boys. I sink a couple of vodkalox, still in scowl mode, half-expecting Old Guy to show. What does he do, where does he go, when he's not giving me the Buddha crap? I have no idea. Probably not to a gay bar festooned with twinkling homosexuals. Some of whom, I have to admit in my relaxed vodkalox mood, are disturbingly pretty.

You don't remember me? he says. He sits on the bar stool next to mine.

Uh, no.

His smile is glad as an ad. *Motosai from bus station. Take loom.*

It's him, but he's cuted himself up for a night on the town. There's maybe a little make-up around the eyes, and his hair is gelled up, and he's wearing a scoop-neck tee with some glitter on it and skinny jeans, and black nailpolish. He's a knockout.

Name Spy, he says, and does a little *wai*. I'm aware this is a hook, but what the fuck. I buy him a lady drink and ask him where the girls are. He says he'll take me to a girl bar, but first he has to try to scam me out of a few bucks. He doesn't say that, but I recognise the form. He says he's very sad today, because his mother is in hospital. *Ah-hah.* Hospital expensive. *Uh-huh.* He's good at this, I like watching him work. I lie about my life, too. I tell him I'm happily married, I'm a professional ice-skater, I'm twenty-seven years old. I pay for the drinks and we climb on his motosai and head out of town, which is where they keep the girls. By the time we get to his bar, which looks like the back of a barn, the night's gotten cold, and Spy is shivering as we sit at a concrete table. I ask him if he has a coat, and he says no. A girl brings our drinks, a "whisky" in a plastic tumbler for me and a Spy, suitably enough, for him. These are the only drinks they have, apparently, and no ice to warm them up, either. He nods at the waitress, asks if I like her. *Not really.* I've scanned the establishment with my hooker detector, and the needle's hardly twitching. The few girls here are mostly with boyfriends or in groups, and there's as much atmosphere as you can expect from hanging fairy lights on the back of a barn. Nobody looks at me, although I'm the only foreigner in the place. I was having a better time in the gay bar. I tell Spy I have a sweater for him, and get him to taxi me back to First Homosexual Experience Cottages, where the proprietor, a dark-faced woman with a tooth that sticks out from the corner of her mouth, gives me a corrosive look as I ask for my key, and gets Spy to sign the guest book. *I have a, uh, sweater for him*, I say, miming pulling on a knitwear garment. She turns away in disgust.

Spy likes the cottage, sitting on the bed and smiling around the room as I find the sweater in my bag. When I hold it up, I see he's already under the coverlet, giggling, and his jeans are over the back of the chair.

Hot! he says.

You'll be hotter in this, on your way home, I say, throwing the sweater at his face.

Home no have, he says, folding the sweater carefully on his chest.

Bullshit.

Sleep bus station.

I'm sitting on the bed now, admiring the ease with which he insinuated himself into it. He holds up an index finger with a black-painted nail.

One hour! He mimes a knock on the door. *Guest, one hour can, one night cannot.*

I ask him if he's kidding me about where he sleeps. He tells me he and a couple of other guys share a loom near the bus station, where they sometimes fall asleep waiting for business. They share clothes, the motorcycle, everything. Get money from tourists how they can, taxi, guide, sex with both women and men. White women travelling in pairs are good, he says, nodding appreciatively. But I know this already – the WWWI has manipulated sex tourism into a males-exploiting-females issue, keeping very quiet about their own harmless little holiday indulgences. I get into bed with my clothes on, because I'm cold, and I'm paying for the bed. I have a secret agenda here, and maybe it's not so secret, maybe Spy has picked up the signals. When one flips the switch in one's head that allows one to fuck a *katoey*, one inevitably asks oneself if what one is really turned on by are dudes. You know, strip away the ninety-nine percent of the *katoey* that's more feminine than anything you've ever done back home, and you're left with man junk, and that has to be homo, right? So this is some fieldwork I'm doing on behalf of all the straight-arrow alpha-male types who secretly fuck *katoeys*, or would like to, but secretly worry about their secret faggotry. Spy's hand moves to my crotch. I instinctively flinch, then relax. If it happens, it happens, I tell myself. Let the guy do his job. But it doesn't happen. I'm more interested by what he's telling me, which is his story. Trouble and hard times, a life that makes my own problems seem like bad moods. And he was a monk for five years, out there being photogenic at sun-up. When I ask him what he learned as a monk, he says, *how to cold, how to hungry.* He's stopped hooking, spinning out lures, so I say, *surely, there was something about Buddha, something you picked up?* He thinks for a while and tells me about a discussion he had with the other monks. They were defining or describing true peace. When it came to Spy's turn, he said, *you go toilet, you bad inside, you make shit, and you are relax. True peace.*

I look at him, staring up at the ceiling. Buddha would have been proud of him. He's as truthful as language allows us to get. So I ask him if his mother really in hospital. His eyes – all that's visible of him above the comforter – squeeze shut, and he's quiet for a moment. *I don't know,* he says. I wish with all my heart I hadn't asked.

A fist hammers on the thin door, and pokey-tooth-lady calls out something bad-tempered. Spy swings his legs out of bed and into his jeans, then puts on the sweater with real pleasure. It's a little too big, but he loves it, hugging himself. I give him twenty bucks and he gives me a *wai*, eyes downcast. When he's gone, I can't even work up a bully wank.

So next morning I bid farewell to lofty Luang Prabang, mystic mountain-top refuge of the Far East. I hike down to the bus station, hoping I don't meet Spy because I suspect he'll put the bite on me again, and I'm worrying that my *making a difference* has destroyed the economic micro-climate. Not being hungry and cold is unsustainable, right?

When I climb on the first bus out of town, negotiating the vegetable matter rolling in the aisle, I don't know if I'm happy or disappointed to see that plastic coolie hat. Old Guy's kept a seat for me. He's pecking at a styrofoam tray of IDM (indeterminate nutritive matter) in his lap, so I get my notebook out of my bag and flip through my scribbles, ignoring his labored chewing. I write *spy in the house of love* on a fresh page and underline it.

"I hope you're writing down what I say," he says. I write down *I hope you're writing down what I say*, and show it to him. He gives a delighted little laugh, stamping his feet like a little kid, and goes back to working on whatever he's got in his mouth. It's important to him, this book he thinks I'm writing about him. It's why he's following me around South East Asia. He thinks I'm going to make him famous, like the Dozy Dalai Lama, or Simon Cowell. I should never have told him I'm a published author. People are always confiding in me they have wonderful ideas for stories they'd write themselves if they could do the "writing bit", but they're *ideas people*, see, so maybe if I wrote up their wonderful story ideas we could both make a lot of money. So maybe Old Guy thinks we have a working relationship, me as his ghost, sees himself on a lecture tour. Starting his own cult. It's kind of pathetic. I feel really very bullish about my thriller, it's a dynamite story, with great characters and settings, a major work, and the last thing I need is a side project typing up the rambling mystical musings of some freeloading old Burmese bum. No offence.

"The self is all about possession."

Wait a goddamn minute. I have to set the scene, so the reader feels he's here with us.

In the dying light, the bus weaves down from the hills in a fusillade of gearchanges, passing stilted shacks and grazing Brahman cows, red peppers drying on roadside mats, thick forests swarming up the hills like battling armies, and occasional vistas over smoking jungle lost in a purple haze.

There. How's that?

"Very poetic."

Cut me some slack, it's from memory.

"Okay. Possession. We *own* things, and this is very strange and mysterious, if you think about it. It's the strongest magic spell we conjure – an invisible bond which attaches us to an exterior object. Ownership of any sort, of a chocolate muffin, a duck, or a million dollars, is a magical act. A real voodoo spell. This bond has no basis in reality. You've heard of Steven Wright?"

No.

"Very wise man. He said he owned the world's largest

collection of sea shells. He kept it scattered over the beaches of the world."

I'm like, huh?

"Ownership actually works the other way round. What you think you own, owns you. It gets its hooks into you, deep. The house you think you own, and which will be standing for a lot longer than you, makes you live in it. Drags you back. You fill it full of stuff, and all this stuff tells you what to do. The garage says, park your car here. The television says, watch me. And you do. The chair says, sit in me."

The wife says, get a job.

"Owning looks like a verb, and behaves like one, but there's no action. You can't isolate owning from the owner and the owned, it's not an act, it's a marriage contract, a *spell*. Possession is nine-tenths of the law, and the law is an ass. When we own something, part of us goes out and occupies the thing owned, and we incorporate the thing owned into ourselves, it occupies us. The devilish connotation of the word possession is the true one. All possession is possession by the devil, and all contracts are contracts with the devil, a parchment you mark with your blood."

I didn't think you believed in the devil.

"We conjure up a lot of things through belief, and the most dangerous is the devil, who is entirely a product of our own warped ignorance. Our belief in the devil conjures up the money spell and the possession spell and the law spell and the whole insanely satanic so-called real world with all its troubles and strife. The selfish self gathers stuff to it to prop it up, make it convincing. The more stuff you can stick to your self, the more important and powerful your self becomes. We judge people by what they own. The millionaire – often interestingly referred to as a *self-made man* – is revered and envied, and the beggar in the street is nobody's friend. They're both just humans, sharing the same attributes, the same thoughts and feelings, they both eat and shit and sleep, the only difference between them is what they own, *that which is not shared*. You have heard the story of the Emperor's new clothes, yes?"

Yes, I have heard that story.

"The clothes are possessions. That's what the story's about. We all admire the emperor's new clothes, the palace on the hill, the collection of Porsches, the succession of blonde wives, the gold watches. It takes a Buddha, or a child, to see that spell for what it is."

You say there's no such thing as ownership, but when you lose stuff, it hurts. That's real.

"You're hooked. It's stuck to you. Separation causes real physical pain, because you've made it part of you. It goes deeper, this magic of possession, if you want to dig a little. The primal possession is the self. We believe we *own* our bodies, our personalities, our thoughts, our feelings, everything that comprises the self. The act of proclaiming and maintaining the self is the first act of selfish possession. There is nothing to own, no owner to own it, just the spell of owning. It's a massively powerful magic, ownership. Madness."

He's quiet for a while, and I use the time to catch up on my note-taking, but it's a hassle, the bus bouncing around.

He says, "You lost a lot, didn't you?"

I nod. *I was mugged.*

"You're very fortunate."

You're crazy.

"It's nearly impossible to stop owning, to de-possess yourself, to exorcise yourself. When you lose like you did, it's a real opportunity to let go."

Oh, like I had the choice.

"You have the choice, right now. You can let go right now. Let go of what you lost, and the pain of it. Don't hold on to it. Stop looking for something to replace it."

How can I hold on to what was taken from me?

"You pride yourself on traveling light. One bag, nothing unnecessary. But you're staggering under the weight of everything you owned in your past life. You're holding on to it by hurting, by not letting go, by playing scenes over and over. By being a victim. By resenting. All that holding on is a great burden to you."

It's dark outside now, all I can see in the black window is the pale blur of my reflection. That's me out there, floating in the dark and grasping at nothing.

His voice is as natural as summer rain on the roof, bamboo leaves moved by the breeze.

"It's gone. Let it go. It's a handful of dust. It's not yours. Nothing is."

I touch the *Rudraksha* at my neck, my tiny pitted moon. Rahu did me a favor. The great spitting severed head, shrieking obscenities at me from a chariot drawn by fiery dragons, is my greatest friend.

BUDDHA UNDER THE BOARDWALK

The little town where I live isn't on the way to anywhere. It's on the Mekhong, but there's no bridge, and none of the trade and tourism a border crossing would bring. It's the first place I've stayed where the urge to move on isn't troubling me. I look across at Lao PDR, the featureless low jungle, without wanting to be there. It's like I've reached the edge. The river's wide here, changes color every day, rust-red, copper-sulphate blue, green-gold, gray as a lizard's back. The sun sets behind, over the temple, sometimes creating blue rays over the river, a kind of mirror sunset in the east.

I'm up early, and Djini leads me down to the riverbank to watch the sun lift through the mist. The river's flat as silk, just one fisherman out there, crouched motionless on the prow of his narrow boat, his coolie hat tilted as he watches the dawn. Djini's down in the sand at the water's edge, nosing around, disinclined to sit with me when there's stuff hopping down there.

There are a few people about, scattered along the riverbank, all watching the sun rise. I recognise the man from the old pharmacy on my street, doing some stretching exercises. His store is like a museum, all the old ceiling-height display cases full of dusty potions. He sits there watching the television all day, I've never seen him sell a single pill. I hug my knees, it's chill. The sun shimmers, bulges, tinting the mist blossom-pink, igniting the wingtips of a flock of birds following the river south. The fisherman's drifted closer. From this distance, I can't see his face, but he's turned his head to look at me. Him and his boat, soft indigo on the nickel-colored water, bisecting the rippled fuse from the rising sun.

Djini barks, tail wagging, looking over the water. She recognised him before I did.

I go to help him tie the boat up, but he waves me away. He doesn't look me in the eye, and his face is more lined, thinner than I remember. As he climbs the steep path up the bank, he falters, and I catch his arm. He leans his sparrow weight on me as I help him to his hammock under the boardwalk. He sits in it, giving me an apologetic smile.

I missed you. Where you been?

He takes his hat off, sets it in the hammock next to him, and rubs his big, rooty hand back over the silver furze on his head.

"Nowhere," he says. "Waiting." The word turns into a cough.

What's up? You okay?

He chuckles. The sun, above the mist now, colors his face, puts a light in his eye.

"I'd like a drink. Do you have any yogurt?"

Yogurt? I haven't had any since Siem Reap. Two years ago. More. And you had that. How about some cold milk?

He nods.

You wait here while I get it, okay?

"I'm not going anywhere."

I trot back up to the store, back through to the dim kitchen, get a bottle of milk from the refrigerator, trot back to the river, all the time thinking, he'll be gone, I imagined all of it, all of him, everything.

But he's there, waiting, and lifts the cold plastic bottle to his lips with both hands. His Adam's apple bobs in the loose skin of his throat, and I hear every gulp. He smacks his lips, wipes his mouth with the back of his hand, then looks at me. "Thank you. Sit down, please."

I sit on the ground, Djini lies on my feet.

"This is the last time I'll speak to you. So you better remember."

Are you going home?

"I'm dying."

Fuck.

"You don't need me any more, and your book is nearly finished."

Of course I need you. Who's going to flatten the boxes? Sweep the floor?

"You always used to say, words is your business."

I did, it's true, they was.

"Words is all I am."

He looks for somewhere to put the empty bottle, and I take it from him. He swings his bony legs up into the hammock, and gets comfortable with his hat on his chest, his fingers folded over it.

"It's probably been something of a waste of time, all this talking."

No, no. I've learned a lot.

"There's so much more I wanted to say, I feel like I've only just started, and you've finished with me too soon."

I haven't finished with you. Maybe you've finished with me.

"Try to feel like everything is just starting, right now, always. That's the best way to feel. Always the beginning, the dawn, the sun coming up through the mist." He waggles his fingers, as if he's smiling at the memory, but it's happening right now, the sun is coming up through the mist.

What did you want to say?

"Oh . . . that was it, I think."

I don't know what to say. Mr. Glib, Mr. Wise-ass, he has nothing to say at this point. I'd expected the next of Old Guy's thorny discourses into the nature of being, of magic, of self, of time and numbers and language, all that good stuff. I was always waiting for him to wrap the whole thing up, a kind of summary, maybe, or give me something to work on next. But this is it. The old man shuts his eyes, and the space behind him, under the boardwalk, is suddenly illuminated like a shrine by the sun.

I stand and go to him, touch his hand. He holds mine, his grip barely there, his fingers cool and papery. It's like the sunlight passes right through him.

Don't go.

His thin lips twitch, and I hear the last breath lift from him, a sigh. And this hollow husk is no longer the man.

Baddha

I fold his hands over his hat, his plastic weave hat. After a while I turn to the river, and words come to me. Buddha's words, Old Guy's words, my words . . . nobody's words.

I close my eyes, breathe in, breathe out . . .

FOOTPRINTS

I'm walking on the beach, a mile or so upriver. The sand is vacation website white and I'm the only person leaving footprints in it. The dogs, suddenly three of them,, clearly not bookish, contemplative types, tumble over each other in miniature sandstorms and hurtle in and out of the water just to mess it up. A row of narrow fishing boats moored to slanting bamboo poles is the only evidence that anybody ever comes here. I paddle in the shallows, looking at the motes of gold dust in the sand. A snail shell big as a tennis ball reminds me of what Old Guy said to me, a long time ago now, about a huge private collection of shells kept on all the beaches in the world. I visualise the first time we met – at least the first time we met that I remember – in a karaoke restaurant in southern Thailand. I can see his parchment face, his clouded eye. I can hear him saying "if you want to learn about Buddha, be a Buddhist. If you're interested in what he says, you're on your own." I'm on my own now. I don't look into my Buddha Soundbite book maybe as often as I should, and there are times I'm fraying at the edges, but I'm still working through stuff in my own way, attentive to the moment. And I'm not singing from anybody's hymn sheet. But I miss the old guy. Mainly because I have to do all the menial tasks at the shop myself now, flattening the boxes, putting the stock out, putting it back again. I miss his Buddha raps, his dumb-ass parables that helped to bulk out a very thin book and get it a deal. I know that you, my constant reader, have skipped over his speechifying to get to the good bits, but that's okay, so did I.

The dogs are far off now, and there's just me and the river, that timeless tide stretching like a sapphire – I dry up – I've seen a parallel set of footprints next to mine in the sand.

"Oh, please," he says, "spare us another luminous description of the river." He's squinting out across the water, his face shaded by the coolie hat.

There's a moment when time stands as still as we do. I clear my throat, trying to not be visibly freaked out.

So, I say, in a voice higher than I'd like, *what do you think about your book?*

He turns his head so he can see me with his good eye, which pierces me, blue as the wide sky.

"My death is very sensitively handled."

I shrug modestly. *Words is my business.*

"You resisted the temptation to be glib, for once. The description of the sun rising, the *breathe in, breathe out* motif, the circularity . . . "

Yeah. Starting with a dead cat, finishing with a dead old guy. It's inspiring.

"One question."

We walk together along the wet sand at the river's edge. *Shoot.*

"Why Elson Quick? Where did that come from?"

When I was maybe five or six years old, a very little guy indeed, my sister asked me what I was going to be when I grew up, and I said, a writer. She said, because she couldn't imagine anyone being a writer with my name, obviously, she asked what I was going to be called, and I said, Elson Quick. I just made the name up, on the spot.

"True story?"

It's all true, I said. *My publisher is calling it Git Lit. I'm proud to be laying the cornerstone of a new literary genre.*

"Will it make us rich?"

Sure! I don't tell him my publisher's understanding of fine writing is deeper than his pockets. *You'll be able to get that gap in your teeth fixed. And buy a handkerchief.*

He flicks his pinkie at me.

And there's the movie rights . . .

"A movie? About me?"

You better start thinking who you want to play you, Old Guy.

"I can choose anyone I like?"

They'll be lining up for this one.

He stops, his eyes closed in thought.

"Brad Pitt."

NOTES AND THANKS

To support what Buddha says about impermanence, a lot of things have changed since this was written. Steve Jobs has moved on, taking the plastic MacBook with him. The Burmese Junta hung up their uniforms and bought brand-manager suits, ensuring a rosy future for their people. And the eternal Chai Von Hotel is no more.

I thank all the people who may recognise themselves in these pages, especially Frog, my great friend. *To all the shaking, lonely souls in the city of starless night, be still, be still.*